Bird at My Window

Bird at My Window
ROSA GUY

FOREWORD BY SANDRA ADELL

COFFEE HOUSE PRESS is an independent nonprofit literary publisher
supported in part by a grant provided by the Minnesota State Arts
Board, through an appropriation by the Minnesota State Legislature,
and in part by a grant from the National Endowment for the Arts.
Significant support has also been provided by Athwin Foundation;
the Bush Foundation; Elmer L. & Eleanor J. Andersen Foundation;
Honeywell Foundation; the Givens Foundation for African
American Literature; James R. Thorpe Foundation; Lila Wallace-
Reader's Digest Fund; McKnight Foundation; The Medtronic
Foundation; Laura Jane Musser Fund; Patrick and Aimee Butler
Family Foundation; Pentair, Inc.; The St. Paul Companies
Foundation, Inc.; the law firm of Schwegman, Lundberg, Woessner
& Kluth, P.A.; Star Tribune Foundation; the Target Foundation; West
Group; and many individual donors. To you and our many readers
across the country, we send our thanks for your continuing support.

COFFEE HOUSE PRESS books are available to the trade through our
primary distributor, Consortium Book Sales & Distribution, 1045
Westgate Drive, Saint Paul, MN 55114. For personal orders, catalogs, or
other information, write to: Coffee House Press, 27 North Fourth
Street, Suite 400, Minneapolis, MN 55401.

LIBRARY OF CONGRESS CIP INFORMATION

Guy, Rosa.
    Bird at my window / by Rosa Guy.
      p. cm.
    ISBN 1-56689-111-6 (alk. paper)
    1. African American men—Fiction. 2. Harlem (New York,
N.Y.)—Fiction. 3. Psychiatric hospital patients—Fiction.   I.
Title.
    PS3557.U93 B57 2001
    813'.54--DC21
                                                    2001028061

10 9 8 7 6 5 4 3 2 1

In Memory of Malcolm

The pure gold salvaged from the gutter of the ghetto
in which we live . . .
To All the Wades that were not . . .
And to my son Warner

THE COFFEE HOUSE PRESS
BLACK ARTS MOVEMENT SERIES

The postwar 1920s was the decade of the "New Negro" and the Jazz Age "Harlem Renaissance," or first Black Renaissance of literary, visual, and performing arts. In the 1960s and 70s Vietnam War era, counterpointing the white backlash against the civil rights movement and rising Black Power insurgencies of SNCC, CORE, and the Black Panthers, a self-proclaimed "New Breed" generation of black artists and intellectuals orchestrated what they called the Black Arts Movement.

This energetic and highly self-conscious Black Arts Movement accompanied and helped foster an explosion of urban black popular culture analogous in many ways to the cultural renaissance of the earlier era: Broadway shows and off-Broadway independent black theater; African inspired painting and sculpture and postmodern graphics; music-minded performance poetry and streetcorner "rapping"; avant-garde "free jazz" with consciously cultivated Afro-Asian references and mystical spirituality; independent and Hollywood-based black cinema riveted on street life and the politics of the urban ghettos; politico-religious sects and charismatic orators like Malcolm X and Stokely Carmichael; "soul music" performers such as Ray Charles, James Brown, Aretha Franklin—and a host of writers—who celebrated and critiqued it all from the vantage point of a newly articulated Third World conscious "Black Aesthetic."

Although most of the literary commentary on the movement emphasizes Black Arts poetry and drama, African American novelists too walked the walk. The transformations of black consciousness produced corollary changes in the forms, styles, techniques, and ethos of all the African American literary modes. The Coffee House Press Black Arts Movement Series is devoted to reprinting unavailable works of the period. In selecting the titles, the editorial panel of African American authors and scholars has employed no fixed guidelines. We have looked for works with distinctive voices, with historical value as windows on the literary and social world of the time, and with that subjective and impressionistic quality of "aliveness" that crosses boundaries of audience, era, and topicality. We have tried to choose work that is masterful, that deserves another chance and other audiences, and that will help us keep the windows to the future open.

Rosa Guy once remarked that "[t]he 1960's for all its traumas, was one of the most beautiful periods in American history." She attributed that beauty in part to the young people who believed strongly in the possibility of change. "They marched, sang, professed unity and dedication to justice and to human dignity. Black and white students understanding the dehumanizing effects of prejudice and poverty shouted the slogans 'Black Power,' 'Black is Beautiful' into black communities to arouse the black youth of their potential."[1] That potential was made manifest in the arts as well. Not since the Harlem Renaissance of the 1920s had the contributions of black artists and writers gained such widespread attention, particularly from the mainstream media. Their voices were loud, their energy and determination boundless as they shouted their slogans from the stages and performance spaces, soon-to-be-muraled walls, canvases, and pages of the books they used as platforms to fight against racism and to present their vision of what came to be called "the black experience"

Despite the singularity of the phrase "the black experience" and the tremendous pressure placed upon African American artists and writers during the 1960s to conform to the ideology of the Black Aesthetic, that experience was presented from many perspectives. What black artists and writers of this period held most in common was an opposition to the prevailing mainstream ideas of "art for art's sake" and a deliberate effort to speak directly to black people in familiar forms of expression. Poet-activists like LeRoi Jones (Amiri Baraka), Larry Neal, Don Lee (Haki Madhubuti), Sonia Sanchez, Carolyn Rodgers, Nikki Giovanni, and Jane Cortez, among others, regularly galvanized their audiences with their jazz and blues inflected poems that spoke to black people in the urban black vernacular. Likewise, black novelists in the 1960s, many of whom honed their writing skills in workshops sponsored by the Harlem Writers Guild, explored with renewed energy and intensity the lives of ordinary black people struggling to survive in a hostile urban environment. It is against the background of such an environment—of Harlem, to be precise—that Rosa Guy sets most of her novels for adults and young adult readers.

Born in Trinidad in the mid-1920s to Henry and Audrey Cuthbert,

Rosa was seven years old when she and her sister Ameze came to the United States to join their parents, who had emigrated earlier.[2] Orphaned at an early age, she grew up on the streets of New York where everyday living was a series of unfolding dramas: "dramas which out-Dickensed Dickens, and equaled if not rivaled the Brontë sisters in passion. Dramas to raise the consciousness of the truly committed: patterns of pride and prejudice, legends of the innocent and the damned, the intense struggles for human dignity—and survival . . . " (Gallo 85). As a young outsider looking in on black culture as it was lived in New York City, Guy developed a sensitivity to the struggles of isolated adolescents who, like herself, could never quite fit in. More importantly, from the time she was seven, when she read her first novel, until her mother died, Guy studied literature under the close tutelage of her ailing mother, whom she credits with having taught her "to look beyond the obvious, beyond mere words, to see the soul of man" (Cudjoe 129).

In an autobiographical sketch titled "The Human Spirit," Guy describes her relationship with her mother and how it helped to prepare her for a life of writing.

> She never played with me. She had no time. We read, walked through the parks, and talked, talked, talked. I have often wondered if the anguish of the characters in the books we read actually affected me or whether their suffering was an extension of my own in my orphaned state, an anguish that magnified as time went by. Certainly the link that bound my mother and me went beyond the average parent-child relationship, beyond the economics of our situation, beyond pain, the suffering of impending death, and death. We had unlocked doors in our minds, opening them wide, allowing the pain and the suffering of others to infringe on us. Such suffering touched beyond the periphery of our minds, forcing us to plow beneath the surface of eyes, to stretch our imaginations beyond our limits in gauging the plight of others. (Cudjoe 130)

By age fourteen Guy had quit school to work in a brassiere factory in the garment district and by sixteen she had married Warner Guy. Given these circumstances, it is astonishing that she could find the time and the energy to further this intensely intellectual parent-child relationship and become a prolific and well-respected writer. According to Jerrie Norris, who interviewed her in the mid-1980s, Guy sustained herself intellectually by associating with black artists. "I sort of went out of my way to meet them."[3] At the American Negro Theater and the Committee for the Negro in the Arts, she soon was sharing her ideas about writing with novelist John O. Killens and others who envisioned a black writers' workshop. She told Norris, "What we wanted to do was to have a group that really projected the life, the style, the dialogue, the type of writing, [the] expression that could only come from the black experience in the United States, and in my situation, of course, the u.s. and the West Indies. So together with these people we formed a workshop—a workshop called the Harlem Writers Guild" (Norris 12).

The Harlem Writers Guild was founded in 1951. With John Killens as its motivating force, it nurtured the young writers who helped pave the way for today's literary successes. Killens was particularly encouraging to Guy, who, despite her lack of formal education, demonstrated considerable talent. He encouraged her to stick with her writing, and she did. In 1966, after years of experimenting with fiction, of writing and rewriting and developing her talent, Rosa Guy finally mastered her form and published her first novel, *Bird at My Window*.

Written "In Memory of Malcolm" and dedicated to "All the Wades that were not . . . " and to Guy's son Warner, *Bird at My Window* is the tragic tale of a man whose bond with his family, and especially with his mother, is so strong that it warps all of his relationships. The novel opens with Wade Williams in a mental hospital. As he drifts in and out of consciousness he struggles to remember how he got there. What was it that precipitated this most recent blackout? What provoked him to break "one of the few spoken laws he obeyed in this world—no drinking in Mumma's house," and go on a rampage so violent that he had to be hospitalized and put in a straitjacket? Through the use of flashbacks and dream imagery, Guy, in her opening chapter, takes us deep into the psyche of a very troubled man. The familiar phantoms that confront him one after the other as he lies in his hospital bed hallucinating symbolize the extent to which Wade's interior landscape is ravaged by his great emotional dependence on his family and his need to be free. The figure of his long lost friend Rocky appears before him, positing a theme that runs through much of Guy's fiction—responsibility.

Guy's structuring of the relationship between Wade and Rocky is indicative of the creative and intellectual risks she is willing to take in order to show what happens when "the human will to live, the will to overcome—the human spirit" gives up, defeated, and turns in on itself (Cudjoe 132). Rocky is the only person with whom Wade develops a healthy relationship. His "discovery" of Rocky coincided with one of the few discoveries Wade made about himself as an adolescent—that he is exceptionally intelligent. With the help of a little man known in the neighborhood as Professor Jones, and with the encouragement of Rocky, whom most people regarded as a "little wizard," Wade began to grow. "Wade found out that he was smarter than ordinary and suddenly the world opened up for him like a flower and he drew from it like a bee. It was sweet. That's why he figured it should have been for the better—Professor Jones coming into his life, nosing around. But things are never what they seem" (122). Professor Jones helped Wade explore the world that had suddenly opened up to him. He arranged for Wade to take piano lessons when he noticed that his young student had an ear for music; he introduced Wade to an arts-and-crafts meeting where he learned to sculpt little animals out of soap. More importantly, he encouraged Wade to believe in his genius, leading him to develop an insatiable desire to learn, a desire he shared with his friend Rocky. The language Guy uses to describe the relationship between Wade and Rocky subtly suggests a homoeroticism that was rarely dealt with by African American novelists during the 1960s.

> Wade was happy. There was something about Rocky
> that touched him more deeply than the sharpness of
> his mind. Perhaps it was his smallness, his delicacy,
> that made Wade feel clumsy and overgrown and at the
> same time protective. Sometimes in the middle of a
> discussion Rocky might pause and gaze earnestly into

Wade's eyes, then suddenly lower his long lashes, making Wade stifle the desire to take him and crush him to his chest. (126)

Years later, as he lies in his hospital bed hallucinating from the drugs being administered to him, Wade imagines that Rocky is lying "gently" next to him, listening to Wade share his secret of having "only lived from time to time on the periphery of a dream" after Rocky went away.

Other phantoms, each representing fragments of his lost self, follow Rocky into the room and loom heavily above Wade's bed. The most frightening is Professor Jones, whose elongated head slips through the bars of the window and threatens to engulf him. In Wade's mind, the Professor is responsible for two things that have caused him great pain: the discovery of his genius and Rocky's parents' decision to send Rocky away after the Professor tried but failed to enroll him, Wade, and several other "Negro children of exceptional ability and exceptional talent" in a segregated high school. As the imaginary head approaches his bed, leaving the Professor's body trapped against the window bars, Wade pleads with his doctor,

> "Get him. Get him, Doctor," Wade urged. "It's easier to get him now. He can't run."
>
> "But how?"
>
> "Kill him. Get your scalpel and kill him. Make it one clean cut so it doesn't mess up the room."
>
> "Tell me why you want him to die."
>
> "I told you. He took Rocky from me. He messed up my life."
>
> "And for that he must die?"
>
> "Yes, yes," Wade sobbed. "Why must a man show you what he cannot give? Fight for what he cannot have? Preach a gospel that he cannot defend? That's him. He twists everything upside down. He shakes everybody up so there's no peace." (27)

The Professor showed Wade hope and the possibility of transcending, by developing his mind, the racism that had long confined him and others like him to Harlem and the lower rungs of the social and economic ladder. He preached education and responsibility. The problem is that Wade is never able to overcome his deep insecurity and negative self-image to benefit from the direction the Professor tries to give. By the time he graduates with honors from high school, at age fourteen, Wade has grown to resent the little man so much that when the Professor tries to talk to him about college during his graduation party, Wade chases him away with an iron pipe while his mother and the rest of the family laughs at his quick departure. The intensity of this reaction foreshadows the pain and uncontrollable rage Wade would experience for most of his adult life over the choice he felt he had to make: to side with his mother against the Professor. It also foreshadows the hatred for his mother that had begun to fester and boil from deep within the recesses of his soul.

In one of his more lucid moments during his hospitalization Wade remembers being in his mother's house laughing and joking and drinking with his brother Willie Earl and his sister Faith. "They laughed and laughed, but between that laughter and now—what?" (13). He learns from the nurse attending him that "between that laughter and now" he beat Faith up so badly that she had to be hospitalized. His disbelief about what he did to his sister is matched by his fear that his mother will shut him out of her house—and her life—as she had done when he beat his friend Buddy to death "because he made a crack at Faith" (39). "And Mumma? Mumma. His heart slowed almost to a stop. He remembered the months of standing outside her door, forbidden to enter, while Faith inside begged for him—because of what he had done to Buddy. Mumma hardly knew Buddy. What would she do about Faith?" (15). What she wants to do is have him sent "somewhere to see if anything can be done for him" but Faith, with whom Wade shares a particularly strong bond, refuses to press charges against him (31). Wade is released after several weeks because, as Professor Jones later explains to him, "they don't care." They know that he is very sick. Wade Williams is a killer. The doctor who treated him knows that, but lets him go anyway. Over the course of the thirty-one hours following his release from the hospital, Wade Williams wanders the streets of Harlem retracing in his mind the life he has lived for the past thirty-eight years. When he finally makes his way back home he wreaks havoc on the two people he claims to love the most.

The last chapter of *Bird at My Window* presents one of the most psychologically tense scenes between a son and his mother to have been written by an African American woman novelist during the 1960s. Here again, Rosa Guy took a great risk by creating a scene in which the mother is treated as the cause of all that has gone wrong in her son's life. While such a portrayal of the mother as a domineering Matriarch might rankle the nerves of contemporary feminist scholars and literary critics, those who reviewed the book in 1966 responded favorably. Keith E. Baird wrote in *Freedomways*, "This is a timely book, the first in recent years and perhaps the only to date in Afro-American literature to treat with such stark power and intelligent sympathy, the shattering of hopes, the frustration of effort and the systematic, destructive demoralization of Afro-American manhood in the Harlems of America." In the January 9, 1966 edition of *The Sunday Denver Post* Barbara Sudler described Wade Williams as being "propelled by forces almost Greek in their inevitability toward self-destruction. These tenebrific choices are emotional as well as intellectual, and herein lies the power of this novelist. . . . The interaction in the mother-son relationship is superbly done here. . . . " Writing for *Negro Digest*, Brooks Johnson praised *Bird at My Window,* calling it "a very sensitive, engaging, challenging novel." Reviews in British newspapers were equally enthusiastic. A review that appeared in the November 7, 1966 edition of the *Grimsby Evening Telegraph* described Guy's portrayal of Wade Williams as "an intimate and complete character study." A critic for the *Worcester Sunday Telegram* wrote, "There is no shirking of the dramatic moments in Williams' saga; his struggles in a world he hates, [sic] are intensely real, the inner and outward conflicts laid bare. For a first novel, all its parts fit together with extraordinary skill, indeed with distinction. . . . At once a social document and a provocative novel, this is a tremendous book. It bears ironic implications, is written with facility and a thorough knowledge of setting and actors, standing solidly on a foundation of contemporary reality." A critic for the November 13, 1966 edition of the *Stirling*

Journal had this to say: "With no wasted words and no special pleas, the author makes us see, hear, smell, feel the world that Wade Williams grew up in and to which he always returns."[4]

Jerrie Norris writes in *Presenting Rosa Guy* that Wade Williams "exemplified for Guy the tragically shortened lives of her husband and her childhood friend" both of whom had been murdered. What Guy hoped to convey through this profoundly psychological novel was the devastating effects of racism and poverty on the growth and development of an exceptionally intelligent and gifted black man living in Harlem, when opportunities for black people, and particularly black men, were scarce to say the least.

As the many favorable reviews of the novel suggest, with the publication of *Bird at My Window*, Rosa Guy was well on her way to making her mark in American fiction. But fate and literary history would have it otherwise. Although she has published two other novels for adults, *A Measure of Time* (1983) and *The Sun, The Sea, A Touch of The Wind* (1995), it is as a novelist for young adult readers that Guy is best known.

Neither *A Measure of Time* nor *The Sun, The Sea, A Touch of The Wind* received the attention and positive critical response that greeted *Bird at My Window*. Susan Isaacs, writing for the October 9, 1983 edition of *The New York Times*, gave a fair assessment of *A Measure of Time*, which she described as "offer[ing] an evocative tour of twentieth-century black America from the rural South to the streets of New York City."[5] The "tour" guide is Dorine Davis. Shrewd and tough-talking, Dorine leads us on an entertaining journey from her early years as a young and often sexually abused domestic for a white family in Montgomery, Alabama to Harlem, New York City where she uses her keen intelligence, wit, and street smarts to live a life of luxury on her own terms. From Dorine's first-person perspective we get a panoramic view of urban African American life, from 1926 when she arrives in New York up to the Civil Rights and Black Power movements of the 1960s. An absolute nonconformist, Dorine remains committed to a system of values that conflict with those held by middle-class African American society. To put it bluntly, she is a crook, dedicated to the good life as it is defined by the urban underclass with which she identifies. As Isaacs astutely points out, "Dorine wants the good life and if it means convincing a sucker that he is securing rights to the land the Brooklyn Bridge stands on, she'll do it, and do it with panache." This "panache" is one of the novel's strengths. We want her to succeed in her schemes to pull one over on the people who would try to turn her into a victim of their own criminality. And she does. The only person who beats her at her game is Sonny, her sleazy pimp of a lover. Sonny is the weak link in this otherwise entertaining novel. Readers may find it hard to believe that a character as street-savvy as Dorine would allow herself to be dominated and duped by someone like Sonny. Likewise, considering that Dorine Davis, throughout her peregrinations, is a shrewd commentator on the social, cultural, and political conditions affecting African Americans in cities like New York, Chicago, and Cleveland, it is confusing that she seems as ignorant about the events unfolding in Montgomery as Guy makes her out to be. Her response to her son's news about events in Montgomery seem uncharacteristic of a smart black woman. She is about to steer her new Lincoln Continental into the busy Seventh Avenue traffic when her son gives her the latest news from home:

> "Brother just phoned from Montgomery . . . " Big eyes bright, staring only at tomorrow's promises, he put his head up to the window as I got set to turn the wheels into the traffic. ". . . Told me to tell you he's thrown caution to the wind. . . . Says he's joining up with Reverend Martin Luther King."
> "Martin Luther King?" I snapped. "Who in the fuck is Martin Luther King?" Then pushing my foot down on the gas, I roared up the avenue—Seventh Avenue—once the grandest, damndest avenue in all of New York City." *(A Measure of Time, 364-5)*

If Dorine Davis seems surprisingly uninformed about the revolutionary changes going on around her, Jonnie Dash, the heroine of *The Sun, the Sea, a Touch of the Wind,* is her exact opposite. She and the group of decadent Americans and English women and men who have come to Haiti to escape the monotony of their lives engage in 1960s rhetoric about racism, imperialism, and colonialism to the point of tedium. An intellectual and artist, Jonnie Dash is obsessed with images of large penises which she paints over and over again. She becomes wealthy when one of her paintings sells for over $400,000, allowing her the leisure of doing nothing in Haiti, where she has come to renew her relationship with her former lover and mentor Gerard, now only a shadow of the fiery and exotic revolutionary she first met some thirty years earlier in New York City. Over the course of her stay, she and a host of other easily forgotten characters engage in much debate, drink, and debauchery against a background of fuzzy intrigues that leaves far too many threads untied for the novel to be much more than an exercise in frustrated reading. As Opal Moore and Jordana Hart suggest in their respective reviews, *The Sun, the Sea, a Touch of the Wind* tries to do too much. Moore writes, "In light of the urgency and potency of Haitian history and current events, the novel attempts both too much and too little. Though its allegorical aspects are complex enough, they seem to confine the action and flatten the characters, denying the reader the richness and depth of character for which Guy has been celebrated."[6]

Most current readers of Rosa Guy came to her by way of her young adult fiction for which she is indeed celebrated and very highly respected. In terms of her adult novels, *Bird at My Window* is a literary achievement. But it quickly slipped into obscurity, overshadowed perhaps by the more "woman-centered" works of Maya Angelou, Toni Morrison, Toni Cade Bambara, and other black women novelists who came to the fore in the wake of the Black Arts Movement and the beginning of the modern black feminist movement. Another factor that might have contributed to *Bird at My Window* receiving much critical praise only to disappear from mainstream booklists was the era in which it was first published. It was not uncommon for novels written by black writers prior to the 1980s to suffer from lack of promotion and distribution. In the mid-1980s, with the rise of a highly literate black middle-class, came a demand for interesting and well-crafted books by black writers. *Bird at My Window* meets that demand. It is a gripping novel whose themes of mental illness, alcohol and drug abuse and the devastating effects they have on families are even more relevant today than they were when it was first published. More importantly, although Guy established her career as a novelist for young readers, she helped to lay the foundation for what, by most accounts, is a boom in books being published by and about black people. It is our hope that this edition will prompt a reevaluation of this chilling novel by Rosa Guy and the important role she played, as a founder of the Harlem Writers Guild, in the development of some of this country's best-known African American writers.

[1] Rosa Guy, "The Human Spirit" in *Caribbean Women Writers: Essays from the First International Conference,* Selwyn R. Cudjoe, ed. (Wellesley, Mass: Calaloux Publications, 1990), 128-33.

[2] From most accounts, Guy is very reticent about providing information about her date of birth and early childhood. She gives seven as her age when she arrived in the United States in *Speaking for Ourselves: Autobiographical Sketches by Notable Authors of Books for Young Adults,* Donald R. Gallo, ed. (Urbana, Illinois: National Council of Teachers of English, 1990), 85-86.

3 Jean Norris, *Presenting Rosa Guy* (Boston: Twayne Publishers, 1988),

4 I am grateful to Rosa Guy for providing me with copies of the reviews for *Bird at My Window* from 1966.

5 Susan Isaacs, "From Montgomery to Harlem." *The New York Times* 9 October, 1995, Sunday Late City Edition: Section 7; Pg. 14, C1. *The New York Times Online.* Online. Nexis. 15 March 2001.

6 Opal Moore, "An Allegorical Hodgepodge of Haiti." *The Washington Post* 9 October, 1995, Monday final edition.: Style; Pg. C10. *The Washington Post Online.* Online. Nexis. 15 March 2001. See also Jordana Hart, "An Artist's Struggles in Black and White." *The Boston Globe* 24 November, 1995, Friday City Edition.: Living; Pg.A10. *The Boston Globe Online.* Online. Nexis. 15 March 2001.

He snatched the sun in his arms, squeezing it and squeezing it until it fell into tiny sputtering pieces, and he knew his job was done, even though he still felt the burning rays fanning his face and neck and rushing in little heat waves about his arms and around his shoulders. Yet they held him, wanting him to smash another sun, another world, but he was finished! Finished. Breaking the bonds that held him, he tested his freedom by dashing up the lonely dark street. Then they were upon him, dragging him backward, forcing his arms closed, making him reach for the sun again.

Wade Williams opened his eyes slowly—no, they had been open. It was the red mist from the sun that lifted, letting him see the intent, expectant faces shoving through the mist above him. He lowered his lashes quickly, glancing from the corners of his eyes to the side of the bed: white-clad legs; to the other side, more white-clad legs. What had they seen in his mist-soaked eyes?

Shook him up worse than anything to find himself in here again. Didn't make sense—no—no kind of sense. He played his fingers, tried his shoulders. Caught tighter than a sewer rat in a mouse trap. He closed his eyes; pulled thoughts from all of the dark corners of his mind. Mumma's—that's where he had been—at Mumma's—more reason for it not to make sense. Never blacked out around Mumma's. Matter of fact, that was one of the few spoken laws he obeyed in this world—no drinking in Mumma's house, ever since that thing with Buddy. He never crossed her on that. Sure, he teased her sometimes—might take a drink outside somewhere, then come around the house and blow his breath in her face, set her back a little. But no matter how stoned he was, he never went over the border around her place. What had happened this time?

Wade lay still, listening to the movements, the whispers, the almost silent footfall about him. He wanted to pretend sleep, but lay stiff as a turkey in the strait jacket, not able to relax a muscle. Rough hands pushed him over and a needle was injected into his backside. Too tense to react. They let him fall to his back, stood waiting over him. Never opened his eyes. The eyes are the mirror of the soul, Wade chuckled inwardly.

Damned if he'd let them see into his soul before he wanted. Not that it mattered with these punk nurses. They didn't fit into his class of thinking. It was the doctor he had to get his mind ready to meet. If only he could figure what happened.

He had been sitting at Mumma's talking to Faith, when in walked Willie Earl. The moment Willie Earl saw that Mumma wasn't in, he decided to go out and buy a bottle. Willie Earl was like that, the sneaky kind; smiled, nodded and said "that's right" in front of Mumma; and when she was not around, lushed like a clown. Said it was respect, and Mumma went for that. To Mumma, Willie Earl was God's answer to her praying—she deserved more from all that praying.

The muscles of Wade's back began to soften and spread out, a warm sense of comfort spread through him. Must have been the crap they stuck him with. He couldn't afford to sleep; had to figure out what to say to the doctor. Some of them never listened anyway, just looked at your record and tried to look inside your head as though they had x-ray eyes. Others talked nice and joked, making you slip out with something supposed to be the sum total of you. Some, the so-called smart turkeys, used the couch, got you spilling your guts, then they fixed you up by injecting the Freud routine and that was that. But a hell of a lot of them just looked at your records, read the notes some simple ass of a social worker took down, and diagnosed you, pulling you apart according to their particular formula.

Wade had a pat solution for all of them. Keep your eyes clear, look as deeply into their souls as they tried to look into yours. Don't answer questions too fast or too slow, and above all, don't be too intelligent. A colored man was not supposed to be intelligent. That was a sure sign of insanity, especially coming from the part of the City where he lived. Understandability, but not intelligence. He held his lips firm against a chuckle.

It was only a matter of time. They picked studs up on a routine binge, held some for seven days, others ten; but with him, it might go harder on account of that Buddy trouble. A month would be easy. He had done six months at one time and if necessary, he could cool it a year. He knew the score. Things were bad. Overcrowded, understaffed hospitals, doctors on rush schedules. Negroes and Puerto Ricans had it made if they were even a little smart. As it was, they were overrunning both the city hospital wards and Mattawan, and probably all of the other insane asylums in the country. Yes, if it was routine, he had it made.

If it was routine. Wade shook his head to throw off the sleep creeping over his mind. He wanted to give in to it. It was the best feeling he remembered ever having, but he had to think—think—think. . . .

There they had been, laughing and joking on account of Willie Earl had brought this bottle. Willie Earl, who never went in for buying bottles or anything else, was such a chinch that Wade and Faith—and oh God, what was Faith thinking now?—got a kick out of teasing him and bringing him right down front. "What? As I live and breathe," Faith cried when she saw the bottle. "Willie Earl, I swear I never thought I'd live to see the day. Even *I* have to have a sip on that."

"Don't let me change your ways of living," Willie said, sarcastic as anything. "You ain't the drinking kind." But sitting there on the couch, both hands in his pockets, he looked whipped. Willie hated like anything for Wade and Faith to gang up on him, so he had to be pretty low in spirit to just come and hand himself over to them.

"But the way you changing yours, you driving me to it," Faith teased.

"What happened to you?" Wade asked. "Your old lady put you out?" He simply asked to be asking but when Willie didn't answer, he and Faith exchanged those sly knowing looks and took him on.

"Don't tell me that Margie got hold of some sense after all these years," Faith said. "Good for her. I'm going to send her a card of congratulations."

"Ain't nothing funny, fool." Willie Earl glared at Faith. "You think it's right that Gloria should be without her father?"

"Well now, I suppose Margie will let you come to look in on Gloria from three in the morning to five minutes after three, the way you been doing all her seventeen years."

"Sure," Wade said. "Then you don't have to have those long absences from Sadie—or is it Jeanie—or Thelma—and come on, Willie Earl, help me out. Which chick will you be shacking up with?"

"Shacking up? I ain't shacking up. I'm moving in with Uncle Dan."

"Oh no, you're not!" Faith's humor turned quick as anything to anger. Nothing could get Faith hotter than someone messing with Uncle

Dan. "How come you can't make it on your own instead of bleeding poor Uncle Dan?"

But Wade never let up. "You mean all of that love dribbling out of you over what's-her-name, and you get a chance to live with her and you go to Uncle Dan's?"

"A man's got to look out for his family, don't he?"

"Yeah, your family pride sure comes down when you can figure out how to save a dollar," Faith said.

"You mean a penny, don't you?" Wade put in. "One lousy penny."

They cracked up then. They laughed and laughed, but between that laughter and now—what?

Sleep had killed the hell out of thinking, so he had to shake his mind up before he opened his eyes to the light of the sun. He let his gaze rest on the male nurse holding onto a pill bottle. "Hey, feller, how you doing, man?" The man's broad black face wrinkled into a pro-smile and his habit of walking put a tilt to his hips.

"Ain't much to me, man. Got a cigarette?"

"Why sho, if you can manage."

"Can if you take this damn thing off. Oh, my head, man. Really had a big one last night."

"Sho did." He sounded kind of noncommittal.

"All that rot-gut whiskey, mixes up with a lot of shit and then some stud comes around blowing gage, man, and that's all she wrote."

"Yeah, that stuff will mess with you a while. Guess you all right to come out of that thing?" And to Wade's nod, "But don't try no mess, man. I'd have to put you down."

Wade lowered his lashes to hide the anger that fueled his eyes. A punk like that to put him down. He forced a pleasant smile. He was the one in the strait jacket. "Be a hell of a thing if I tried, huh?"

"Sho would."

He waited patiently until the strait jacket was off, then inhaling the best cigarette he'd ever tasted, studied the cat, making his eyes wide and honest looking. "You never know what will happen from one minute to the next. There I was gassing around with some cats, and the next thing I know, here I am. I must have taken off on one of them, huh?"

"Don't know anything about that, man. Seems as though I heard it was your sister's head you went up side of."

Oh no. *Not Faith*. No, goddamn, not Faith. He never hurt his sister in his life. Someone must have lied to this turkey. Faith was as close to him as the skin of his body. *No,* closer, she was *him*. Through him. It had always been that way. They never even had a hard word to say, one to the other, so what the hell was this stud talking about?

Wade stared intently at the burning end of his cigarette. "Yeah, well, she deserved it. She a pretty lil' thing but she always got to have something going. You'll see what I mean. She'll be around today."

"Uh-uh, don't think so, man. Seems to me I hear she in some hospital."

Wade's stomach did the shakes. He inhaled hard on the cigarette. Why didn't this young punk get the hell out of here so he could decide if he wanted to cry or stifle himself with the pillow or put his fists through the wall?

"She ain't bad off," he said quietly. "I never hurt my sister."

"Dunno, I hear it took quite a few to get you off her."

Wade's arms stiffened and again he held the world in the crook of his elbow. He squeezed and squeezed, then let go—it was his head—all over again it was his head—his head. He put the cigarette out slowly in the paper container at the side of the bed, and batting his eyelids several times trying to hold the candor there, smiled. "Maybe I roughed her up a bit, but she's tough. She one of Big Willie's breed so she don't hurt easy."

"Can't prove it by me, man."

"Look," Wade reached out and grabbed the punk's arm, but seeing the face go cautious, loosened his hold. "My old man got shot through the heart in a crap game and didn't die until one year after. That's the kind we are."

"Sho, sho," the nurse put his hands on his hips and the tilt of them became more pronounced.

"Listen fool, if I was to stick you in your ass, you'd squeal like a happy pig, but I'm giving you a lesson in medical history and you crap out. G'wan, get outa here. You disgust me."

The nurse went out and Wade staggered out of bed, still drunk from the stuff they had pumped into him. He tried the door, locked.

Went to the window. No way out. He chuckled, standing there looking down at the City. Chuckled because he wanted to cry and he didn't know how. Faith—Faith—Faith. Somehow, the pieces didn't fit. They just didn't fit.

And Mumma? Mumma. His heart slowed almost to a stop. He remembered the months of standing outside her door, forbidden to enter, while Faith inside begged for him—because of what he had done to Buddy. Mumma hardly knew Buddy. What would she do about Faith?

Breakfast, lunch and the doctor. He knew the routine well. Had to get his mind in shape to greet the Doc. Then visiting. Visiting? Even if Mumma should show to give him hell, it would be like music in his ears today. Well, anyway, Uncle Dan would be here. Uncle Dan always showed; even if he didn't approve, he understood—pretended to anyway. Wade grinned wryly but let it fade as a bird came and perched on the window sill.

"Oochie koochie coo." He tapped the window lightly with his fingernails, smiling. The bird turned, twisted its head curiously to the side. "Oochie koochie coo." He tapped again. The bird spread its wings and took off for the distance. It became a speck.

A surge of impatience pushed Wade around the room. He beat his hands together, bit down on his lips. Trapped. Trapped. How in the hell to get out of here? They couldn't keep him locked up in a goddamn room without knowing. He had to get out. Had to find out what happened. But where? Lenox Avenue? A picture of the Avenue with its crowded streets rose in his mind and he walked back to the window trying to make out the speck in the distance. He smiled sadly. "Never was a bird."

Thirty-eight and never married yet never free. Maybe he'd never wanted to be. Always had Faith and Mumma and Uncle Dan, and to a lesser degree Willie Earl and Aunt Julie. Never wanted to be free of them. All tied up with them and Lenox Avenue. Never lived out of Harlem except for the time he spent in the Army. Even when his frame was working somewhere else, his mind was making it on Lenox Avenue, wondering what cats like Buddy and Tony were doing—not that he gave a living damn for anyone except his family—he was a family man—or if Uncle Dan was stoned somewhere waiting for him to show—his

　　　　　　　　　　　　　　　　　　　　　　　　ROSA GUY

shoulders had grown broad supporting Uncle Dan's weight—or if Willie Earl had stopped around at Mumma's on his way from work. No, never was a bird.

Yet there had been a couple of times. . . . The screen of his memory shifted and a crowd of thoughts tried to push in; he blanked them, and stared fixedly out of the window trying to find the bird again.

This doctor had something going for him. He was antiseptic looking like all of the others until it came to his eyes. They were a clear look-right-through-you green, that had a way of expressing the idea that they liked folks.

"I'm Dr. Forest. I have been assigned to your case."

Something in Wade responded. Not that he liked the man. The time had long gone since he got to liking people.

Maybe it was his eyes, or something about his manner reflecting in his smile. Or maybe he just needed someone to help him clear this fog out of his mind—needed to know how he came about hurting someone he could not have hurt—doing something impossible for him to do. Dr. Forest must have been around his age, too, maybe a little older. That made him Army age. Wade tensed, studying him. Doctors usually made lieutenant. If they were bright as he supposed this one was, they got promoted. Too young to be top brass. . . . Wade took a guess. Putting out his hand he said, "Glad to meet you, Captain Forest."

Doc caught the ball as he threw it. "You seem to have something against the Army." He said it casually, but shades went down in his green see-right-through-you eyes. Wade looked into the eyes that were trying to look through him and matched the casualness.

"Figure of speech, Doc. If I ain't calling folks 'Mister Charlie,' I call 'em 'Captain.'" Wade wanted to kick himself the moment he said it, because the eyes lit up with that sympathy and understanding bit that went through him like salts. His lips turned up into a sneer and he bit down hard on his teeth to stop himself from shouting, "Yeah, it's just about a bitch, ain't it? We both in this shit together, now what can you do for us?"

He never cracked his lips but Doc read the message because shades of red colored his face way up to the roots of his blond hair, and he went to examining the chart in his hands as though his life depended on it. When he looked up again, his eyes had gone professional. He glanced at his watch, smiling one of those polite smiles. "We'll be getting to know each other better, Wade. I'll be looking in on you."

Anger against himself rose like a wave driving Wade to the door as it closed behind the doctor. He lifted his hand to beat against it, call Doc back, but checked himself and backed away, feeling the sweat sticking his shirt to his back like skin. God, they'd throw away the key if he kept up crap like that.

Fight the war all over again? It had been over fifteen years. Fifteen goddamn years and nothing about it could be done or undone. And yet, here it had come sneaking into the room, standing between them, a monster, breathing its own brand of fire on them.

He sat on the edge of the bed, digging his head down into his fists. Acting smart, and he had not even found out about Faith. What good was all this waltzing around if he had done her in? He needed help. He'd never in his life felt so bad that he needed help, yet here he had gone putting up walls between himself and Doc. Or had *he* put them up?

The next few days he spent walking around his little cage, rehearsing his lines for the Doc's next visit. "On this Army thing," he intended to say, "we might as well just have it out." No, that wouldn't do. He might just simply say, "Now look, Doctor Forest, the Army was a bitch of a life and people did some shitty things. . . ." No, no, he didn't think he could ever say that. He might start off, "A man must always reserve the right to fight for his dignity." Yes, that was the way, professionals always went in for that human dignity bit. Then he had to ease in with the Army thing and they could take off from there.

But days passed and the doctor did not come again. Days when Wade only got some pills for his nerves, and a handful of books that he could not read. But the pills stopped him from walking up the sides of the walls or waltzing out of the window, bars be damned. Pills that shortened the hours from one day to the next, but didn't give him a clue to what was happening to his sister. Neither did the case workers and psychiatric aides who came in to question him. It was as if they had written him off.

It got to him one night, when he lay, arms folded under his head, digging the male nurse switching around his room, after he had taken his pill. He wanted like anything to ask the cat to sit awhile, chew the rag, pass a session of bull, find out all he knew about what was going on outside. But then he realized the cat was doing a lot of unnecessary things around the room, little things that made Wade wonder if he might be angling for a quick lay. So Wade settled for lying there, counting how many things a stud could find to do in one hospital room. And it turned out he could find a hell of a lot to do. But then he was gone, leaving a silence in the room that made Wade want to kick himself for not hanging onto him no matter what the cost.

"What the hell they think they're doing to me?" he said out loud, just to have the sound of talking in the room. "If I did something so bad, they should have me in jail, or else give me some of their time. Some of their goddamn time."

But no matter how harsh he tried to make his words sound, when they were said the silence settled again. He decided to cry out, roar like a lion, make someone come in and talk to him. He opened his mouth and cried out, "God help me. Help me. Oh God, help me."

He lay still, frightened by the sound of his voice. His words. He never called out to God. Never prayed. Never believed in Him. So the cry didn't come from habit. Weakness? He'd never been weak in his life. Not Wade Williams.

But as he lay there heavy in his sweat, he knew something was happening around him—something queer: He heard the opening of a door, where he had not known there was a door, near the head of his bed. He knew someone had entered the room, approached. He did not raise his head, afraid he might have really called out a miracle. Afraid that if he looked up and saw God—the God Mumma and all the other folks prayed to, all surrounded by a halo—then his life would be even less significant than he thought it to be, and that was insignificant enough. His eyes felt like pinballs trying to probe the dark but he didn't move and he refused to talk. Then the figure at the bed bent over him.

"Wade, Wade, what is it, Wade?" The sound of the voice made Wade sit up. He didn't believe it. Yet there was about the room an eeriness that said anything might happen, and he allowed a surge of happiness to fill the giant cavities of his loneliness.

"Rocky? Rocky, that's not you?"

"Yes, it is Rocky, Wade." It was the same voice. Not quite so youthful but the same modulation. The same preciseness. "It is I." The room was suddenly encased in a soft glow, but the figure at the bed remained in shadow. "Come." Wade probed the body of the man with his hands, then finally pulled him down beside him on the bed. "Lie next to me." But as Rocky stretched gently down on the bed, Wade grew suddenly shy. The heaviness of his tongue made him fumble for words. "Yes, it is you, isn't it?" He kept feeling the body with his hands, testing the slimness, the clean long graceful lines. "Yes, it is you. This is how I figgered you to be."

"I was passing in the hall when I heard you call. I recognized your voice right away."

"Did you?" Wade smiled, not thinking it strange that Rocky should be in the same hospital. "Don't seem right that you should."

"But you sounded so strange. So strange that I had to come in. What is the matter?"

"You have heard about Faith?"

"Yes."

"I didn't do it. I have to get out to find who is responsible."

"Who do you think is?"

"I don't know, but whoever it is I'm going to kill them."

"You sound so hard, Wade."

"Hard? Life makes us that way."

"But not you, Wade. You had so much to offer."

"I didn't have you. I was lonely." It sounded so natural the way he said it, like it was everyday talk, yet he had never said this to anyone. Not even Faith, and she knew everything there was to him. Hardly admitted it to himself.

"Lonely? Since I left? But that has been a terribly long time, Wade."

"My lifetime."

"But how ridiculous! You should not have gone on like that."

"Haven't you ever been lonely?"

"I have worked too hard."

"Not even for me? You never thought of me?"

"Of course I thought of you. You belonged to that part of my life that was most painful, but I had to go ahead."

"How can you talk like that?" Wade cried, hurt beyond words. He had lived and relived every moment that they had met and talked, every act that had stamped them as friends. "I done nothing but remember the times that we had together."

"That was wrong for you to do. You had to go on from there."

"I never got off the ground. Seems like when you left, the soul was gone."

"But you never believed in souls, Wade. Only in life and spirit."

"The spirit then."

"But you were so young."

"I never been young." They lay silently for a while, Wade relaxed and happy, glad to be free to talk. Free to be able to share a secret that he'd never known he wanted to share. Happy to be with the only one in life with whom he had ever been truly able to share any secrets. "No, I've never been young, or satisfied, or happy. I have only lived from time to time on the periphery of a dream."

"But you have Gladys."

"Gladys?" Wade jerked his head around, and there she was, standing at the foot of his bed, her beady eyes shining, her twisted face mocking him. Yet he knew she was not really there for he saw the door right through her body, and when her hands reached out to touch him, though his body tensed, he felt nothing. He closed his eyes to get her out of his sight and when he opened them again she had moved. But he knew she was standing behind him because he could feel the heat of her breath on his neck, and the animal quality of her breathing made the skin crawl along his spine.

"Why did you bring her in here?" he whispered hoarsely.

"I didn't bring her. She was here all the time."

"You brought her in here when you talked about her."

"It seems to me you ought to want her with you."

"Can you say that after seeing her?"

Rocky seemed to be studying Gladys where she stood behind Wade. Finally he said, "She is ugly, isn't she? Exquisitely ugly."

Wade closed his eyes, afraid that he might turn to look at her, but her face pushed through his lids and hovered like a spectre in the foreground of his mind. "Yeah," he cried vindictively, needing to stamp out the image. "She took it so many different ways on that puss of hers that you have to twist your head fifteen different ways to make sure you're looking at a face." But the face did not disappear and he opened his eyes now to tear her away from his mind, to still the broad smile, the triumphant gloating.

"Then why do you stay with her? You're still young and virile and good-looking."

Wade's hand went automatically to his face. It had been a long time since he'd looked in the mirror for anything but a shave. Yet he supposed he still went for good-looking, like all of Big Willie's breed with their light-tan skins and round brown eyes.

"Yeah, like I'm Beauty and she's The Beast."

"But I know, Wade," Rocky said sympathetically. "We all need someone to push away loneliness."

"Gladys is my loneliness, Rocky," Wade said in despair. "I look at her and see how empty my life is. If I could destroy her, I could save myself."

"But how can you destroy a woman like Gladys, Wade? Look at her." They studied the heavy form that hovered near the bed, only now it seemed made of rubber and was swelling up like some huge balloon. "Her life has been so full of abuse that she is immune to abuse. You can't destroy her, you can only destroy people like Faith. . . ."

"Shut up," Wade cried, pierced by the hurt that Rocky, of all people, could say this. "You know that Faith is the only link I have to life. I'd kill any son-of-a-bitch who would hurt her," he shouted.

"But you hurt her, Wade. As you would try to hurt me. . . ."

"No, no never—never. How can you say that? I would not be what I am if you had not gone away. I would be different, believe me. . . ."

"You say that because you live so much in the past. If you saw me now, you would want to destroy me too."

"No!"

"Life isn't that kind to any of us, Wade. Look at me. You haven't seen me in so long. Look at my face."

Wade suddenly saw Rocky's face clearly: The lines that, when Rocky was a boy, had been lines of sensitivity, had now folded into deep grooves of hurt and disappointment, of pain. The lips were puckered as though from the habit of crying. And Rocky's hair and even the long lashes that fanned his face had prematurely whitened.

Wade's first impulse was to draw away, jump out of the bed and out of reach. But in that instant the body that had been swelling until it filled the room pressed him back onto the bed, rolled over him, smothered him. Wade managed to free his hand, searching for his friend, crying out in the small bit of air that was left to him, "Rocky, Rocky! It don't matter. It don't matter. Better to have you like this than not at all. Don't leave me. Don't leave me!"

He screamed, as the balloon completely covered his face.

"What is it, Wade? What's the matter?"

Wade looked up to see several faces peering at him—grinning faces, serious faces, leering faces. He wanted to shout, but the emptiness in him was greater than his fear, making words meaningless.

"Come, Wade, tell me," one voice in particular insisted, and Wade thought it must be Doctor Forest. "I am here to help you."

Wade caught the doctor's arm, clinging to it in desperation, searching for the face to go with it in the group around the bed; but he couldn't find it. "Doctor," he whispered secretively, and with the word everything faded from the room except the arm he clung to. "I need your help. You have to help me."

"I'll do everything I can, Wade. Tell me . . ."

"You must help me find the one responsible."

"Responsible for what, Wade?"

"For my sister, that's who. For Rocky. For everything."

"You don't think that you are responsible?"

"I know I'm not. It's the man, I tell you. He's responsible. I wouldn't be here talking to you if I wasn't sure, would I?"

"Who is Rocky?"

Wade looked up at him, bewildered.

"You wouldn't understand but I'll tell you after you help me get him."

"And you say this man is responsible."

"Yes, yes, he is. He is."

"Who is he?"

"That little guy right out there climbing up to the window sill." Wade pointed and Dr. Forest turned to look out of the window. "You see him?"

"No, I don't. I don't see anyone."

Wade wiped the dryness of his lips with his tongue and stared hard at the window. Was Doc blind or was he batty? The little man had laid his portfolio down in order to get a firm foothold on the window sill. Now he had picked it up again, sticking it under his arm, and was examining the bars outside trying to find a way to get through. "He's out there," Wade insisted. "He's trying to get through those bars and he will, too. Watch him, he gets into everything. Every goddamn thing. He's the one that discovered my genius."

"Then why should you want to hurt him?"

"You didn't know I was a genius, did you?"

"I knew you were very smart. . . ."

"Not smart. Brilliant. Me and Rocky, we were brilliant. That Rocky was a walking encyclopedia and I came right next to him in thinking. We would have been together still, doing all kinds of big things if it wasn't for that nosey son-of-a-bitch."

"What did he do?"

"He was the reason that Rocky went away."

"And he also caused you to hurt your sister?"

"Who said I hurt my sister?" Wade's scalp tightened.

"You said he was responsible." Wade wiped his face with his hands, confused. He didn't remember saying that.

"I'm going to kill him."

"Is that what you want to do, Wade? To kill and kill and kill? Do you want to be a killer?"

Wade shook his head. The doctor didn't understand anything. But before he could form any reply he heard a crash at the window and looking up saw that the little man had smashed the window and was sticking his head in.

"Didn't I tell you he'd get in?" Wade whispered. "He always gets into things."

"Who is he?"

"Professor Jones, that's who. Promise me you'll help me get him." They waited to see what the little man would do next.

"Help me, that's what. Help me." But it was only the head of Professor Jones that came into the room. Wade, noticing the Professor's frame jammed up against the bars, knew he would not get the rest of his body through because of the portfolio clutched against his chest. But the head came in, kept coming in, pushed by the neck that kept stretching and stretching until it resembled the head of a puppet suspended on a snakelike body, manipulated by strings.

"Get him. Get him, Doctor," Wade urged. "It's easier to get him now. He can't run."

"But how?"

"Kill him. Get your scalpel and kill him. Make it one clean cut so it doesn't mess up the room."

"Tell me why you want him to die."

"I told you. He took Rocky from me. He messed up my life."

"And for that he must die?"

"Yes, yes," Wade sobbed. "Why must a man show you what he cannot give? Fight for what he cannot have? Preach a gospel that he cannot defend? That's him. He twists everything upside down. He shakes everybody up so there's no peace."

"He sounds like a prophet."

"He's a goddamn fool."

By this time the head had spanned the space of the room and was approaching the bed. Wade, realizing the doctor had no intention of helping, grabbed up the bedclothes in both of his hands, waiting. He felt the push of his breath shaking his body and even the bed, as the head eased on to the bed, turning first one way and then the other, as though in search of something, yet not seeing Wade raise the covers silently, slowly, hardly breathing. Then as the head rested in the middle of the bed, Wade lunged forward, wrapping the bedclothes tightly about the face, which suddenly became a struggling ball that moved under the pressure of his assault like greased iron with more strength than Wade was prepared to handle. He looked into Dr. Forest's eyes wanting to ask his help, but he grew aware of the movement in the room—whispered conversation, footsteps. He caught words from whispered phrases: "extremely agitated . . . needs the . . . give him . . ." He eased back on the bed still holding the ball wrapped tightly in the bedclothes. It had been causing a terrible pain in his chest.

As he lay back, Wade realized he might have been dreaming and tried to struggle to full wakefulness, but he could not free himself from the dream unless he released the ball in his arms and this he did not want to do, for fear he might not have been dreaming. Someone was approaching the bed. He put one hand out to ward him off. Too late. He was being pushed over on his stomach, felt an almost comforting feeling of being smothered—smothered. . . .

Time melted like grease, days slipping and sliding one into the other, and he knew just about as much as he had known on the first day he opened his eyes in this place. No one had been to see him, and to make matters worse, he didn't know where he stood with the doctor.

Even though he had calmed down and they had taken him off most of the drugs, he still had a hard time telling where dreams ended and reality began. It was because of the loneliness. It made him not want to get up from his dreams. And he might not have wanted to except that he knew that Faith was not dead. He kept enough reality about him to tell himself that if he had killed her, they would have been here to pick him up—take him to the courts—get an indictment. That was the one thing that kept him from cracking up—the sure knowledge that Faith was not dead. He tapped the window. "Kootchie, kootchie, coo." But the bird wasn't there.

The door opened and the Doc walked in as though he were reading Wade's mind. "Company for you." He stepped aside, his warm smile reaching to the very inner part of his eyes, seeming to say: "Now I'm making it up to you for the time I haven't spent with you."

Mumma and Faith walked in. A warm glow burst through him, and for the first time in weeks, Wade felt like a person again. He opened his arms for Faith to rush in, the relief in him making him wish he could cry. He held her close, wanting really to crush her, but her smallness and her softness got to him, making him remember that he might have hurt her. He held her gently. Then he searched her face, so much like his and Willie Earl's and all of Big Willie's breed, with wide, soft brown eyes and pretty, full mouth.

A blue-brown mark that said it was there for life discolored the clearness of her skin under one eye and an almost invisible scar pulled back ever so slightly the top of her lip. He wanted to pull her close again, tell her he was sorry; but he knew the doctor was digging them, so he eased his hold. He didn't want to throw out any false cues. He knew these doctors. Give them an inch, and they would take off on Freud like it was a Bible. Wade had cut his teeth on Freud thinking it was a dirty book, and he sure didn't want breast envy to mess up the already muddy issues. He tried giving his voice a light turn.

"Looks as though some cat did you in."

"Do I look done in to you? Nothing in me but some life." She smiled, returning his open-faced stare, giving him back a little of himself.

"Hey, Mumma." He stood quietly for Mumma to search through to his soul the way she used to do, but she simply nodded her head and turned away. Since he had done Buddy in, Mumma had begun to realize that she saw only as far into him as he let her. Now she didn't even bother to try.

He searched her face, letting his eyes rest on a new line that had set in near her mouth, and held back a smile. Mumma's face touched him like that. Black and soulful beneath its graying hair, the lines of worry and disappointment drawn hard on it. He knew the history of each line. It was as if he were the artist who aided the brush of time on every little valley in his constant battle with God. She would throw herself on her knees, praying over something he had done; and when she looked up again, there would be the new line. His satisfaction came from knowing that he alone could have carved it so well.

Doc's attention turned to Mumma, so Wade went up to her, kissed her cheek and playfully squeezed her nose, trying to force her stare to meet his. But Mumma wasn't having any. "How you like my family, Doc?"

"Nice-looking family," Doc answered, giving Mumma that honest, warm smile and Mumma brought her eyes around to sort of pray into his. "Are they twins?"

"No sir. They exactly one year apart to the day. He's the baby. But neither one of them got much sense."

Wade chuckled. "See why I like my family? They all got a sense of humor."

"Your sister wants to sign you out today, but I told her I thought you might want to stay in a few more days." He searched through Wade's eyes and Wade thought of his dream.

"What? What do I want to stay in here for?"

"There might be something we might do . . .".

"Why you gon' let him out, Doctor?" Mumma cried unexpectedly. "Why don't you keep him in here or send him somewhere to see if anything can be done for him? Why you want to let him out? He done tried to kill my baby."

"No, Ma, I didn't," Wade pleaded. "I . . ."

"I'm only the doctor, not the law," Dr. Forest broke in. "If your daughter is not pressing charges and wants to sign him out, there's nothing I can do. It's up to your son if he wants to stay and see if we might be able to get to the root of his disorders."

"I came out of the hospital yesterday," Faith cried stubbornly, "and I don't see why he can't come out too."

"This isn't exactly the same kind of hospital." Dr. Forest laughed. But Wade didn't see anything funny. Yesterday? One month, just about. . . .

"You got done in pretty bad." He wanted to hear her reproach.

"Oh, I don't know, guess it was my fault. I had no business coming in between you and Willie Earl."

Willie Earl! A roaring filled his head, rushing past his ears and he stood frozen.

He realized Mumma was talking and strained to hear her. "Why you got to put Willie Earl in you-all's foolishness? It ain't Willie Earl that done nothing to you, it was him."

Wade found his voice, forced it out, listened to it drop like a stone in the quiet room. "Willie Earl? What did he have to do with it, Faith?"

Color rushed up into Faith's face as she realized he didn't know— he really didn't know. Her lashes dropped to hide her confusion and she shrugged. "It must have been some stupid little thing. I don't remember what it was myself." But doubt sounded in her voice as she turned to the doctor. "It was nothing but the whiskey, you know, Doctor. Only now Wade won't be drinking because he knows he hurt me. He would never hurt me, Doctor."

"What makes you think it was only the whiskey?"

"Don't listen to her, Doctor," Mumma cried. "Don't listen to one word she says. That boy is just mean clear through. If he gets out he won't be doing nothing but drinking. He ain't gon' work. He ain't gon' do nothin' but cause a mess of trouble."

"We can't hold him on an assault charge if the victim isn't

pressing charges. It is up to your son if he wants to stay. We might be able to help him. . . ."

"Faith, leave that boy be. I swear to you, if you sign him out and he cause any trouble—as God is my witness, I ain't going to never have nothing to do with you, nor lay sight on you as long as I live."

Faith's mouth tightened. She never paid Mumma much mind. She bought the bread in that house and no matter what was said, Mumma had no substitutes.

But it got to Wade, the way most of Mumma's one-sided arguments always did. She had heard Faith say he had really gone after Willie Earl, but she never stopped to question it. She threw it out of her mind before it even got a chance to settle. Figured *he* was wrong, always wrong, and there was nothing he could do about it. He had been wrong before.

Yet he had tried. God, how he had tried to keep walking that thin line that divided her rights from his wrongs. He had tried because the one thing that mattered to him was to be able to visit them, Mumma and Faith. It was like death to be shut out of their one-room kitchenette, not to be able to sit just looking at her, looking deep inside her soul; not to be able to wait for Faith to come home from work, after he had spent a giant part of an endless day throwing the bull with his one and only friend, Tony; not to be able to talk and joke with Faith, and maybe end up eating dinner there, forcing a pleasant evening to a burdensome day before leaving and making his slow, reluctant way home to Gladys The Beast.

Looking at her set mouth, the wrathful eyes turned full force upon Faith, he knew that there was nothing to say against the fact that Faith had spent a month in the hospital. She would never listen to him. But he could make her listen to Willie.

Faith mistook his brooding. "Don't feel guilty on my account, Wade. Do what you think is best. If you think you should stay, go ahead. You can always have someone call me if you change your mind." The shadow in her eyes begged him to say yes. "Anyhow," she laughed, "I didn't do so bad. The detective that took you in was cute as anything. He came to see me every day I was in the hospital."

"A cop? Lousiest thing in the whole of New York City. How did I bring you to that?" He tried to joke back.

"Oh, he's real cute, you ought to meet him."

Wade allowed himself a chuckle. Faith was thirty-nine years old and as yet had never allowed a man to put his hands on her, that he knew; but anyhow he laughed. "See Doc, like Mumma says, she ain't got good sense. She put faith in anybody. She better be careful that faith don't kill her as dead as she's gonna die."

"Let us hope that it doesn't." Dr. Forest gave a tight smile.

They all seemed to be waiting, the doctor giving his got-to-be-going look at his watch. Mumma would see that he was still trying if he gave in, so he said, "OK, guess I'll hang around here for a couple of days."

It was like sticking a pin in a balloon the way the tension exploded. Everyone talking at the same time. Mumma giving advice. "Doctor, it might be because he gone too far from praying. People can't live good if they go too far from praying. That was the fault with his daddy too."

The doctor turned in time to see the anger flare and then die in Wade's eyes. Wade tried to catch his eyes again to show him that they were clear and calm looking—but Doc was busy showing Mumma and Faith out.

That night he dreamed he was raised out of bed by a giant hand that suspended him, kicking and scratching, high in the air. Though he fought with all of his strength, he knew that he was no match for this monster. He had already given up when he looked at the other hand of the giant and saw Doctor Forest fighting as hard as he. That gave purpose to his struggle and now with renewed energy they tried to bring the enemy to his knees. But every time they thought he was almost subdued, the arms regained strength and there was a great struggle again. At one time when they were sure he was overcome and they stopped to breathe, the arms reached around, entrapping them in huge snakelike coils that flung them around like toys, holding them a great distance apart and then suddenly crashing them together.

Wade could not see himself, but he saw the doctor, noticed the bruises, the new swellings that appeared every time they were crashed together, until the whole of Doc's face was a mask of bruises and blood, his eyes almost closed, and Wade knew that his own face looked the same. Yet they kept on struggling, fighting and scratching, feeling the sliminess of the giant's blood mixed in with theirs, slipping and sliding together and apart, until again they held the monster prisoner. Exhausted and breathing heavily, they pulled him to his feet and found they had in their hands a uniform. A dirty Army uniform.

Now they stared at each other, hate and distrust bloating their beaten faces, wanting to rush at each other, tear at each other as though each had betrayed the other. And while they stood thus, Wade found that he was moving away swiftly, even though his legs were like stone cementing him where he stood. "Don't go, Wade," Dr. Forest called, his face still filled with hate. "Don't go. How can I help you if you go away?"

"I'm not going anywhere, Doc. I'm standing right here." Yet as he spoke the distance between them widened and a rush of water roared between them. A body of water that in a short time resembled an ocean making it all but impossible to hear the doctor's cry, "Come back, Wade. I want to help you. I want to help you."

And he began searching around frantically, even though he knew the doctor was on the other side filled with hate and distrust, searching about the long stretch of beach where he found himself—a beach remarkable for its desolation, bordered by a formation of the smoothest stones rising like mountains, coming together at the top to form spearlike peaks that glittered their warnings of inaccessibility. And though Wade knew that on the other side of the mountains lay all the familiar things that he had ever known, it was to the doctor on the other side of the water that he yearned to return. So he searched this bare stretch of land where there was nowhere to search, looking for a hiding place where there was nowhere to hide, digging into the sand, turning it over in his hands, beating his hands against the smoothness of the rocks that bordered it.

"Watcha looking for, boy?" Wade spun around, recognizing the voice but not seeing anyone. "I say, watcha looking for?"

Wade looked up. Perched on the very tip of one of the spearlike points, Uncle Dan sat, looking first to one side of the mountain then to the other, crossing and uncrossing his legs, as though he had been long used to this position and found it the most comfortable in the world.

"Uncle Dan, Uncle Dan." Wade rushed to the rock and stood looking up. "Can you help me? I'm looking for a way back."

"Way back to where, boy? You mean the other side of this here mountain?"

"No, over there, back to the Doc. I was standing right there next to him, when all of a sudden I find myself over here. I got to get back, Uncle Dan."

"Well, that's the easiest thing in the world, Son. All you got to do is find the bridge."

"I been looking and looking and I can't find it nowhere."

"Well now, maybe it's got to be that other feller to find it. He the doctor."

"But suppose he don't, Uncle Dan. Suppose he don't?" The stirring of fear twisted his stomach as Uncle Dan crossed and uncrossed his legs, looking up and down the long span of empty beach, his eyes squinting so that the lines marking the corners deepened.

"I reckon it ain't gonna be so easy at that. That man ain't got no understanding of Big Willie."

"What's that got to do with it, Uncle Dan?" Fear mounted. An overwhelming helplessness claimed Wade.

"How you sound, Wade boy? You ought to know that a man can't find the bridge if he ain't got no understanding of Big Willie!"

"That ain't got nothing to do with it." Wade shouted his desperation.

"That's got everything to do with it, Son. A man got to have understanding in order to find a bridge. How can he expect to, if he ain't got no understanding of how a big man like your Pa—who could make any man's knees buckle, who could just about make thunder roll, who could turn a town upside down, and more than likely change the course of history—come to be treated the way he was?"

"How come he don't know that if he's the doctor?"

"You got to ask him, Wade. How you going to find out if you don't ask him? Why, a man got to know how a big man like that come to leave his home town and come up North like . . ."

"Come up North?" Mumma's voice loud and clear, scornful, like it always was when she talked about Big Willie, sounded from the other side of the mountain. "You mean when he got chased out of town and shot up here like a bullet out of hell."

Wade's anxiety turned to sudden anger at the sound of Mumma's scorn, but Uncle Dan had spun around on his little pointed seat and was looking down on the other side of the mountain. "Watch your talk, woman," he called down to her. "Something gone wrong with your Bible learning. You shoulda said, like Jonas from the belly of a whale."

"You hear my Mumma, Doc?" Suddenly the ocean was not so broad. "She's got religion."

"Your mother must be a very wise woman."

"You heard how she goofed that line? She said a bullet out of hell instead of like Jonas from the belly of a whale."

"Is that why you hate her?"

"What the hell you talking about? I love Mumma. She ain't never made a fault in her life that wasn't done in God's name." Try as hard as he was able, he didn't stop the sarcasm from seeping through, so he shouted, "Do you hear? I love her."

"As you love your sister?"

"Yes, almost—as much as I love my sister."

"Is that why you tried to kill your sister—because you love her?"

"Don't say that! I told you not to ever say that. I'll kill you. I swear to God I'll kill you!" Now he was back where he started, standing before the doctor, his legs heavy as stone, only now his movements were toward the doctor, his arms reaching out trying to catch the doctor. Now it was the doctor moving away, away from his reach, so he shouted, "I'll kill you."

"The way you killed your friend, Wade? The way you killed Buddy?"

"Yes, just like I killed him. I'll take your head and put it here." He crooked his elbow. "And I'll squeeze and squeeze. Then there'll be no more bridges for you to . . ."

"Now Wade, do you want to tell me about your time in Mattawan?" Wade snapped awake. He looked around the room, then to the side of the bed where calm, antiseptic as hell, Dr. Forest sat with the chart in his hand, looking at him.

Wade wiped his face with his hands, trying to hold on to the threads of his dreams to get a clue to what he might have been saying.

His head was heavy and his tongue dry, either from overtalking or from a long silence. But every time his mind touched a cord, it would shrivel and dry up, disappear from his thoughts and he was left confounded except for the bout with the giant and meaningful words of Uncle Dan. "Ask him, Wade. How you going to find out if you don't ask him?"

"Well, do you?"

"Do I what, Doc?"

"Do you want to tell me about your time in Mattawan?"

"Nothing to tell. I stayed there six months. They said I wasn't crazy."

"You agreed with them, of course." Dr. Forest laughed.

"I'd be a fool if I said different."

"Tell me about it, Wade."

"About what?"

"The man you killed."

"It was self-defense. I got tried when I came out."

"But the violence had something to do with your family?"

"Yeah, I was down to his house, and he made a nasty crack about my sister. I socked him. Then I got ready to leave and he comes behind me with a knife. I grabbed his head with my arm here." Wade crooked his elbow, staring hard at the doctor. Dr. Forest glanced down at the chart in his hands.

"The report said he died of a fractured skull."

Wade let out a long sigh of relief. He hadn't been running out at the mouth then.

"Yeah, I grabbed his head here and sort of flipped him. He fell and hit his head on the concrete. See, he had one of them basement apartments with a concrete floor." Dr. Forest looked down studying the chart without speaking for a few minutes, and Wade tensed. "My friend Tony was there—he testified for me."

The doctor got to his feet, looking at his watch, and Wade put out his hand to stop him. "Look, Doc. There's something me and you got to talk about. You know it and I know it. It's been here since the first day you walked into this room. Why don't we just get to it and be finished?" The doctor sat back down in his chair, his brow knitted in bewilderment. "It's about the Army, Doc."

"Yes?" But from the blank look in his eyes, Wade knew he hadn't reached him. It didn't seem right somehow that that first day hadn't made as deep a dent in the Doc as it had in him.

"Don't you want to talk about it?"

"I'm here to help you, Wade." He leaned forward giving Wade the full benefit of the honesty shining through his eyes. "If you feel it's important that we discuss something, then by all means we must."

Wade looked at him for a long minute, feeling the hopelessness of continuing, but then decided he had to take the plunge. "You must have had a hell of an experience in the Army, huh, Doctor?"

"I? Oh—yes, I did." Then realizing Wade was waiting, he smiled. "I was a captain in an all-Negro company. That's where I first became interested in psychiatry." He examined his pure-looking finger nails. Then, noticing Wade was still waiting, he laughed in a buddy-to-buddy fashion, leaning toward Wade. "You know, you people can make things difficult for a guy sometimes."

Wade sat still. A tingle started in his toes. It's nothing, he told himself. It's nothing. I must let this slide. But he felt the words hit, deep inside of him.

You people.

2

The heat rained down upon the sewers, stirring up a stench that embraced the air like a shroud and Wade stepped out of the subway and into the hot arms of Harlem, breathed deeply, wrinkled his nose, fanned his upper lip to cover his nostrils, then chuckled. He was home.

Habit had forced him out on the wrong side of the station, so he had to cross back on 116th Street to make it down to Uncle Dan's. As if his feet had an itch and the only way to get it scratched was to lay them flat kissing Uncle Dan's floor. He walked fast, not looking to the right of him or to the left, not wanting to see a living soul, that was, except Lil' Willie Earl Williams this morning.

Lil' Willie with his laughing on two sides of his face, as if his face had joints, all of them double. A sweet-talking cat who could spit in your face and tell you it was raining outside and make you believe it. Only there would be no grinning or sweet talking this morning, not until he had snatched him and set him down in front of Mumma and made him spill his guts. Set the record straight.

Wade closed out of his mind a doubt that kept pushing in: What if, after Willie talked, what came out didn't deserve a pat on the cheek, much less the beating that Faith had gotten? After all, being stingy was the only thing anyone had ever been able to put against Willie Earl. *That* was no secret. It was only something to laugh about; as Uncle Dan said, from the day Willie Earl was born, he got to sucking on one of Mumma's titties while holding like hell to the other to make sure no one would get it. It was their lifetime joke on him. Still, if it was so simple, why didn't Faith tell Mumma? No, he wasn't buying that doubt.

He had almost reached the corner where Uncle Dan lived when he saw Rudy, one of Willie Earl's oldest friends, standing with his hands in his pockets, making the hot morning look cool with his light-gray suit and light-gray fedora.

"Hey, Daddy-o." Wade flicked his eyes in appreciation as he spoke.

Rudy always looked sharp and smelled as if Yardley's was his body odor. He was as black as a man could get with skin so smooth it never needed a shave, and features that made you want to call him "pretty boy," but somehow you never did. He went for bad and though Wade had never seen him busy at it, he never had a doubt. As a matter of fact they had that kind of respect for each other that kept each politely casual, so when Rudy said, "Do I look like Daddy to you?" Wade tensed, staring hard into the eyes that were red where the white should be. He realized the cat was ready, but although he didn't feel like pushing him right then, he had no intention of backing down.

"I ain't passing out compliments. I'm looking for Lil' Willie."

"You look like you in a hurry."

"I am. You know where he is?"

"Yeah." Wade waited a while but Rudy just stood looking at him, twisting a toothpick around in his mouth with his tongue.

"Where is he?"

"Somewhere you never heard of."

"I ain't up on the puzzles this morning. Where's that?"

"At work."

Rudy faded out of his vision along with his animosity. At work! Funny he hadn't thought about that. Yet where else would Willie be? He dashed up the stairs to Uncle Dan's apartment and gave vent to his annoyance on the door. He banged and rang the bell, listened, thought he heard some sounds, banged and rang again. No one answered. He made it back to the street, disappointment zigzagging like a saw in his gut.

Eleven o'clock—a whole day to wait. Willie Earl never came home before six in the evening. Even Uncle Dan and Aunt Julie never came home from their part-time jobs until about three. That meant he had to wait until night to see Mumma. Why hadn't he asked Faith to sign him out after she came from work instead of before? He was always in a hurry to get somewhere only to find he had nothing but time. Time.

He walked slowly up Lenox Avenue, letting the sounds of Harlem invade him.

"It's a downright rotten, low-down dirty shame."

Music static on the air just as the day he left. It was coming from the Best-Bar-B-Q-in-Harlem joint. Wade walked up to it thinking Willie Earl might be around the joint if he had decided to skip work. No Willie.

"The way you treating poor me
When I know I'm not to blame. . . ."

Wade looked around the street for one familiar face. A lot of
them. The no-talking kind. Some never had been friendly, others had
stopped talking years ago. Those who had stopped talking in the past two
years, still self-consciously pretending they were too deep in thought to
see him. He finally caught the stare of a nodding acquaintance but before
he could get his nod working, the stare had slipped away.

Wade thought of Rudy and got a buzz. He had lost another
round to the good Harlem citizenry. He chuckled bitterly, then let the
sneer that was trying to claim his face harden there.

"Jelly, jelly, jelly
Jelly stays on my mind."

He walked up to the Best-Bar-B-Q-in-Harlem joint and stood,
letting the music beat against his ears. He exchanged meaningless nods
with Old Nat, the proprietor, then searched the jostling crowd for a
chance look of Willie, and barring that, his one remaining friend, Tony.

"Jelly roll killed my pappy.
Turned my Mamma stone blind."

Not even a goddamn brass band. Guess he had to make it
home. Home. Funny, when he thought of getting out he hadn't
thought of the broad, yet his feet led him as straight as though they
had nothing to them but some plans. He walked absently toward the
antique fixture of Miss Clara sitting crouched over her West Indian
sugar-cake stand, thought dimly of the days when she used to break
off pieces from the penny cakes and slip them to him. Now she looked
through him as if he were cellophane. Behind her at the curb some old
newcomer was shaving ice for ices, too slow for the group of shouting
children around him.

He crossed the street to the smell of sauerkraut from the hot-dog
stand cluttering up the other corner; heard through a haze the shout of
the vegetable man leading his cart horse up the street.

"Hey, Wade. Wade man. I been looking all over for you." Charlie
the wino and his buddies next to the curb peered at him through their
blur. "Let me have two bits, man. I'll pay you tomorrow." Charlie wove an
unsteady path to grab his arm.

ROSA GUY

"Naw, ain't got a dime." He shook the drunk off. "Ain't that a bitch, gone a whole month and I get that to greet me." His gaze followed the back as it staggered away. "Dead already but just forgot to stop breathing."

He stood at the next corner looking around vaguely, thinking that he really did have to make it home; but no sooner than the thought came into his mind, he walked into Skinny Stevens—walked into him because Skinny had his head down. When he looked up and saw Wade, he froze, did a dancing step to get out of the way, turned to run but ended up saying with a feeble laugh that did not want his face, "Oh, Wade—when did you get out?"

"Just did."

"But Willie Earl said . . ." Skinny's voice trailed off.

"What did Willie Earl say?" Sweat jumped to Wade's face. He let his top lip take the side of his face up into its nastiest sneer, pushing it into the open door of the punk's fear.

"He ain't said nothing. Well man—good to see you—damn good to see you. . . ."

Wade studied him a moment, shrugged. "You seen anything of Willie today?"

"No, no, ain't seen him. Ain't seen him in a while. Well—I—I got to run now."

Wade reached out and caught him by his shoulders, kind of pulled him to feel him give. "What's your rush? Let me buy you a drink."

"Wish I could, Wade, but I got a lil' job down the way. Can't stop now."

Wade debated whether to let him go or shake him up. He was a goddamn liar. Skinny Stevens never let an off job stop him from chiseling a drink. He drank before he worked, he drank while he worked, he drank after he worked and then stopped for a few relaxing moments to drink some more. Ought to drag him into a bar, make him drink. Make him tell why a low-down cheap punk like him acted like a shy sixteen-year-old trying to protect her cherry. The lower a punk, the harder he was to frighten and Skinny was pretty low. He released the thin shoulders, giving Skinny a push to make sure he stumbled. "G'wan, get out of here." Skinny made it on the double.

Wade stood in the middle of his anger gazing at the slippery back trying to become small in the crowd and thoughts raced to his mind—of men, frightened, running before a barrage of bullets and he had shown no mercy. Then he remembered one on whose fear he waited as a price, but now he knew—he knew—it would have happened anyhow. He could not stand the fear; he could never stand fear.

He knew he was clenching his fists in a desperate effort to keep from following the stud. He started forward, but just then a little figure came out of the houses between him and the disappearing back. A figure of a man with a portfolio stuck under his arm. Wade about-faced and made it to his corner. Second time today an attitude got to him and he sure didn't have the temper to hold out for another. That would be all Mumma needed—not out one good hour and already trying for time. He had better make it to the broad.

Wade stood on the stoop, not wanting to enter, waiting for his excuse in the form of Lil' Willie, or even maybe Tony, but he strained his eyes searching the Avenue and no excuse showed. Yet he stood, gazing about absently at the parade of people going in and out of the liquor store across the street, pulling a match out of a book of matches to clean his teeth. Different grades of drunks, he knew them all: the skinny housewife who hid from everyone, including herself, that she had to have a taste. Fooled herself up to the minute she was in front of the store, even pretended she was going by, giving a swift look around before she darted in, coming out moments later, a bottle well hidden in her overlarge pock-etbook, her craving eyes glittering, her hop-skip-and-run as she made it to her loneliness. The big social drinker, loud, expansive. He would make a few more trips to the store before it got dark, never staggering but louder and louder with each trip. The sneaky drinker, one pint at a time, afraid someone might see him to put on the beg. The wino, with his half pints, social on a lower scale.

Wade's eyes followed a fat woman, burdened down with shopping bags, waddling through the mass of hot, shouting, loud-talking, eagerly whispering humanity, being trailed by about five children who didn't seriously try to keep up with her, glaring at the crowds she pushed through as though they were responsible for her burdens, every last one of them. He let his gaze climb to the old familiar buildings, where heads pushed out, eyes stared downward at the mass of busy nothingness scrambling around on the sidewalks and in the streets, escaping from the heat of the house into the arms of the hotter streets; fire escapes, playground for little children and lines for airing clothes.

The janitor came out of the basement, rolling an ash can. He looked up, saw Wade, stood and stared an empty moment, grunted, then made his way back to his underworld. Never said a decent word to a living soul. Called himself minding his own business. Guess he did at that.

The five-dollar bill Faith had given Wade earlier lay heavy in his pocket. If Faith had come up with him that would have been home-coming. But no, she had to go to work. True, she might look a lot like him but in most ways she was a total stranger. He didn't go for that working every day trying to make it into the upper class. It was a lie. Work every day and he'd still do what he was doing now. Live. Still, he wished like anything she were with him. He searched the street. "Oochie koochie—naw—no birds in Harlem. Isn't even a goddamn sky in Harlem."

Wade turned to stare into the darkened hallway, up the straight stairway, behind which the stink from urine hit out like a fist. A picture of Mumma's one-room kitchenette, clean as a pin and inviting, jumped into his head. He bit hard on his teeth. That Willie Earl! That goddamn Willie Earl.

Every step felt like a hundred-year sentence on a chain gang but he made it. He stood an unpleasant moment outside of the door, then kicked hard. It opened, and there she was at the end of the long hall, that insipid smile on her face. He walked up to her. She did not move.

"Get out of my way, woman. I got to wash. Get this hospital stink off. Put on some decent clothes." Up to that moment he thought he was going to stay in. Wait out the hours for Willie Earl right here. Or at least until Uncle Dan came home. But now everything inside him quickened. The house seemed to fold in around him and he knew only that he had to run. Never stop running.

"I was looking out of the window." He tried to get a picture of the window without her looking out. He couldn't.

"So?" He remembered her the first time he saw her, like an answer to his every need, sitting at a bar, lushed, beaten, ugly, abandoned. She looked up and saw him standing over her and thought that she was in a dream. She was still dreaming. Only now she thought that she was superior.

"What took you so long to get up here?"

"My intentions."

"Oh, thinking of going someplace else?"

"Maybe."

"Where?" She laughed a high mocking laugh, and sweat jumped out on his face and around his neck.

He walked to the window and stood staring out. Then, for no apparent reason he thought of Dr. Forest. "That punk doctor," he muttered. "He ought to be a goddamn diaper changer."

The room was the way he had left it. Half broken down, half clean. Everything about the place in half except her. She was wholly disfigured, with that dull, simple grin; her eyes, beady like a teddy bear's, glinting at him as though just his being there was her triumph.

An old picture that she insisted on keeping on the dresser stared out at him while he undressed. Pretty as hell before her buxomness had turned to slop, her teeth white and even before they had been replaced by an ugly gold plate that made her smile ten-carat insipidness. Her hair, thick and bushed out like an African queen, now thinned to the point of baldness by daily trips with hot irons to the stove. He never knew why she bothered. She never used lipstick anymore. She stuffed herself with calories to prove how far the human skin could stretch. Yet it was as necessary for her to straighten her hair as it was to open her eyes in the morning.

"It ain't a day that I ain't missed you."

"Well, I'm back."

"Sho is a long time for a woman to be without her man." Her man. She knew that went through him. That's why she pushed the knife.

"Well, here I am, so pull your pants down."

"Why sho, Baby."

"I didn't say undress. I said pull your pants down." It didn't make any difference, she would undress anyway. Damn. He was sick of her and mad as hell with himself for feeling a need. Yet here he was, heavy, throbbing, demanding.

She pressed herself to his back. "Get away, you disgust me." He shoved her across the bed and she laughed.

It got all of him, this disgust, because his need was so ordinary. Yet he couldn't walk away. Not even from her laughter. In his anger he threw himself savagely upon her, not letting her move to get into bed and try to pull that gentle crap.

That was what she wanted, to get him into bed and claim him with her nothingness. Own him completely if only for a brief moment. But he'd be damned if he'd let her. Wasn't that why he stayed with her? Because at least in this he could stay above her, not having to pity her. Because he was filled with the awareness of her abuse by everything walking around with a hard on and some without even that for an excuse. Because he could always feel he was doing her a favor even though she tried to mock him with her laughter.

He looked down at her face. "You're an ugly son-of-a-bitch, you know that?" Her face twisted in a grimace that started to be laughter but changed to a scream as he entered her, hard. He glowed in satisfaction. That was the way he wanted her, screaming in pain, not clawing over him in passion. Screaming and holding tightly to the bed clothes because she was too frightened to beat his chest, to push him away. In too much agony to call herself making love. He looked down at her. "Go on and laugh, you ugly bitch. Laugh and laugh and laugh."

Passion spent, he moved away quickly. "Wade, Wade, Baby."

"Got to take my bath. Got to see what's happening in the streets."

He listened for her movements while in the bathroom. Heard nothing. Probably in bed now, thinking or praying or hoping I'll get a new hard on. Well, wait, bitch.

Dressed to go out, he stood looking down at her curled figure on the bed. "You got any money?"

"You going to leave me like this?" Hate flared like a torch in her eyes.

"How else?"

"Baby, you been gone a long time."

"Yeah, that's why I got to see what's shaking outside."

"It ain't gonna take you that long."

"Longer than I got time. You got any money?"

Sullen-faced now, shifty-eyed. "Naw."

He reached quickly behind the bed and drew out a pouch. Opening it he looked at her.

"That's rent. If you take it what we gon' do?"

He counted out the rent. Five dollars left over. He pocketed the five, threw the rest to her. Sure enough, if she didn't use her home-relief check for rent there would be no other. A broad who couldn't turn any kind of trick to make a buck. And the home-relief people were not hard on her. Looking at her they knew how hard it was for her to find work. Yet she felt that she was better than he.

Starting out through the door, he couldn't help looking back and giving her one for good measure. "Patience, Baby, don't go getting off none on your finger."

Mockery flooded back into her eyes. "Don't have to, you'll be back. You ain't got no wings."

Wade walked quickly away from the house to get away from the emptiness that she left him with. Emptiness, not even a thought, nor did he have to think about her until time to go back. Still, the emptiness had to be filled. He peered at a clock through the open door of a pharmacy. One o'clock. A couple of hours before Uncle Dan. Where the hell was Tony? He usually held the buildings up at this corner.

Frantically he searched through the crowds, milling around in intense discussion or languishing under the blistering assault of the midday sun, closing himself away from the side glances, the sudden breath-intakes, the slight drawing away of people he had never bothered much with anyway, wishing he could conjure up Willie Earl instead of making do with his last speaking acquaintance.

There was nothing to Tony. Just a guy to booze with, and sometimes when Tony had taken a fix—Wade hated guys who needed a fix—a guy to chat with. A guy who generally talked away about all of the great things he could have been and all of the great things he might still be; and as if he knew he was saying nothing, never expected an answer, which he never got because Wade never listened. Yet he needed Tony sometimes because a day could be a heavy thing on your shoulders if you didn't have someone to support it with you. Even a couple of hours could be a killing thing.

Dashing into dives where Tony might have stopped, and others where there was no chance, making a hurried search, evading hostile stares, he felt a surge of desperation, even of fear that he might not find him. He turned down the street and into a big apartment building where the apartments had been cut into holes that rented for rooms, and without hope, pounded for two solid minutes on the one that Tony called "home." No one answered.

Quickly now he turned his footsteps to the park where he and Tony often shared a bottle on a hot day. Anxiety mounting, he searched through the people on the grass, in the shadow of trees, in the bush, on the benches, and even gave a few quick glances under some of the benches. He rushed out of the park at the north side and into the office of the old refugee doctor who gave cheap shots to cats that got burned, examined each face. . . . No Tony.

Racing down the steps of the brownstone house, he almost crossed the path of the little man with his portfolio stuck under his arm, shouting aloud that he was important. But Wade had seen him in time and flattened himself in the shadow of a tree, waiting for the little man in his gray wool suit, hat, coat and tie, as if he'd never heard about the heat, to pass.

Anger pushed up like a wave through Wade, feeding the open mouth of his emptiness, his loneliness. Anger at himself for hiding from the nosey little punk, anger at the little man for being around. The little punk had been around for almost as long as Wade remembered and here he was without even a wrinkle to prove that time had passed. Only way to get rid of him was to kill him and no one seemed to have the guts to do that. Not yet anyway. . . . Professor Jones. Suddenly Wade's anger widened to include the whole population of Lenox Avenue, who seemed now to be responsible for forcing him into the path of the little punk bastard.

He knew that he had better make it off the streets. Make it to Uncle Dan, even if he had to stand outside his door for the whole night waiting for Willie Earl. His mouth was tired of the silence it was forced to keep. The quick glances, slipping and sliding off his face, of people who a month before had either nodded to him or ignored him, really got to him. He had to make it off the streets.

Yet when Wade turned back onto the Avenue he stood waiting, expecting any minute to feel a familiar pat on his back, wanting to use that stagnant phrase, "Hey, man, what's happening?" And to get the same electrifying reply, "Not a thing, man. Not a thing." His lip turned up, pulling his face into a sneer. Here he was black man's rich, ten hard dollars weighing down his pocket and not a soul to help him spend it.

Glaring around at the sweaty, shiny faces, ambling at each side, he had an almost uncontrollable desire to herd them together and stand before them shouting, "Hey, this is me, Wade Williams. You ain't going to think me out of existence or wish me off Lenox Avenue. I belong here. More than you. More than any goddamn one of you." That was the way it was, too.

Folks came and went in Harlem, those from the South pushing out those who had lived here for years. People from the South thinking Harlem was a hell of a place, the last stronghold of freedom. New Yorkers, saying it was the end of slum life, ran from it, cutting their roots, always cutting their roots. But not them. Big Willie had brought them here from the South when they were little bits of things and set them down. They had taken roots and never run away from it. From 116th to 125th exclusively, except that Uncle Dan and Aunt Julie had moved to 115th Street a few years ago. None of them had ever left except the way Big Willie did. And Wade Williams wasn't about ready, they could believe that.

The way folks were acting, you would have thought that he had killed Faith. He hadn't killed her. She was working or she would be right out here with him. Did they think that they cared more for her than he did? Where in the hell did they get their thinking? He and Faith had grown up right under some of their very noses. In this neighborhood. Wade looked around him. Matter of fact, on this very street. They had played together, cried together, laughed together, shared every joy, every grief. They had even learned the meaning of sex together, right here in this very street. So where the hell did these sons-of-bitches get their thinking?

Grim-faced and sweaty, his shirt sticking like skin to his back, he crossed the street and turned into his barbershop. "Sam, you seen anything of Willie Earl today?"

Sam spun around and stared. "No—no, I ain't seen him in a couple of days." A tiny pulse beat somewhere in Wade's temple and he wanted to reach up and touch it, but to touch it might mean to lose balance. He stiffened the muscles of his face in an effort to stop them from jumping to pieces, and forced his eyes to blankness.

"What's the matter? You look scared."

"No, no, it's just that I didn't expect to see you around."

"Why? Willie Earl been telling you I'd be gone for good?"

"Well—no—no, not exactly. I mean. . . . You know how it is, man. I ain't seen you for a spell—and you come popping up so sudden-like."

"Yeah, yeah, I know." A rush of sweat poured out at the back of Wade's neck and ran out of his armpits. He held himself rigid, not daring to move, but with a superhuman effort managed to look with detachment from the razor in the barber's hand to his eyes.

"You ain't sick or something, are you, Sam?"

"No—no—why you ask?"

"On account of the way your hand is shaking. You best be looking for a next profession."

"What—ho-how you sound—ha-ha, ha."

Wade found himself outside leaning against the building, fighting down the mist claming his eyes, silencing the roar trying to claim his mind, clutching his fists, in an effort to stand, then trying to move away. But it was impossible to move and he grabbed hold of the iron rail outside the building, feeling the prongs at the top digging into his hands.

"Not Sam. No. No, not Sam."

Sam had given him his first haircut in New York. Big Willie had brought him in to Sam's, sat him on a piece of board in the barber chair. . . . Sam stuck a lollipop in his hand, laughed and joked with him so that he never realized his hair was being cut. . . .

Wade felt blood gushing, even though he did not feel the pain from the prongs pushing into his hands. He could not let go. He could not see. He could not hear, and in one last effort to push back the mist, he cried out, "But Sam was Big Willie's friend!"

3

This was the street that Big Willie had brought them to when he blew into Harlem in all his fury, and Big Willie was mad when he hit into town. There was no getting away from that. He knew because he had grown up in the white heat of Big Willie's anger, had been nurtured by it, up to the day Big Willie dropped dead and even long after. It was a way of life with him, something he never bothered to question.

The way Wade had it figured, without anyone ever explaining, was that Big Willie never wanted to run. Big Willie wanted to stay down there and take on those peck-o-woods, but it was on account of his family that he didn't. He didn't care about dying. He could just as soon go as long as he was taking some of those crackers along with him. Big Willie didn't, and it caused a big hate in him until his dying day. That hate was a part of Wade's smell and taste and sight, as long as he could remember.

It always seemed to Wade that that was the reason why Big Willie didn't ever pay them much attention as he went about his way of doing things. As if they were the barrier between him and his self-respect. . . . As if he was ashamed of loving them, hated it, because it was that love that stopped him from acting like the man he wanted to be. Wade never knew how that feeling came about. It was nothing that he thought out, but it was there, a part of his knowledge just as his nose was part of his face.

Just as he could never figure out how he came about remembering Mumma's face, all through that long ride from the South, first by car and then by train and then by car again, all funny and strained-looking, her eyes never blinking or closing as though sleep was a far distant thing and the only way she could catch up to it was for them to get where they were going. They all slept and got up and went to sleep again, but Mumma sat stiff and unbending as a board, looking out of the window with her staring eyes, until they came into Harlem and into the little kitchenette that a friend of Big Willie had rented for them. Then they all realized that she had been afraid, because she crumbled to her knees and cried:

"Thank you, Lord, for delivering us from your just wrath, and leading us into safety. Oh, Lord, I will ever be grateful."

　　　　　　　　　　　　　　　　　　　　　　　　　　　　　　　　　　　　ROSA GUY

Big Willie stood over her and said in a voice so terrible that it touched fear to the center of each of their hearts, "Get up from your knees, Evelyn. Get up from your goddamn knees."

Mumma looked stricken. "Willie Earl, as God is my witness, I must have laid with the devil the day I laid with you."

"If you laid with the devil, Evelyn, then all your children are misbegotten. I am a man. There are them that would forget that, but don't you never. I am a man."

It had been the beginning of a strange conflict for Wade because Mumma never really got off her knees and Big Willie never got finished with his anger. Little as Wade was, he understood them both. Never once did he doubt their feelings for him, even though they had a hard time understanding each other.

Wade remembered Mumma taking off on Big Willie one day, calling him all kinds of names because he didn't come home nights, didn't do a thing in the house, and in general acted as though he didn't give a damn.

"You got three children in this house, and you don't do nothing for them. You don't as much as take them around the corner. What kind of man are you, anyhow? You don't care one bit about them. I declare, you don't care one bit."

She said it loud enough for Wade to hear because she wanted to set him against Pappa. It was like a regular game with her, trying to set them against Pappa because he stayed out so many nights gambling and sometimes went for days and nights without sleeping. Mumma even tried to make out at times that Pappa had a girl friend, although she never came right out with it. But Wade would have dug his eyes and tongue out before he believed it. Yet she tried to turn them against Pappa and Pappa knew it.

"Come here, boy," he called Wade roughly after Mumma said that. Wade went up to him and Big Willie looked him hard in the eye. "Go get my slippers." Wade went and got his slippers and that was all that was said. But Wade knew that man loved him—loved him as he would his foot or even his heart. And since he wasn't the kind of man who would forgive his foot or his hand if they had to be cut off, making him less of a man, he had never forgiven that love that had started him running and making him less a man.

Sure, they had made up jokes about it through the years—belly-busting jokes; even Big Willie used to laugh, loud, long bitter belly laughs, laughs that didn't change anything, not even a man's opinion of himself. But Wade had whittled his laughter down through the years. Somehow the sense of Big Willie's hurt had got bigger after Big Willie's death and had grown as his memory had dimmed.

Yes, this was the street, with Sam's Barbershop at the corner, the oversized barbershop pole with its red and white peppermint stripes spiraling up; the Father Devine shoe-shine parlor that operated year after year even though the "Father" had faded into the past; the rooming house where Mabel used to live with her whore of a mother, the room-to-let sign forever hanging by one ring, always seeming about to but never falling; the long row of brownstone private houses that the West Indians had bought from the Jewish people, giving a semblance of decent living in the midst of squalor.

That was the reason Mumma remained in the neighborhood, even though they had always lived squeezed together in one or one-and-a-half rooms with kitchen. Here you did not have to worry about the heat or hot water. True, sharing the bathroom could sometimes be dangerous, but they were kept reasonably clean because the Barbadian or Trinidadian woman, and it usually was a woman, lived in the building. Their kitchenette was usually furnished, making it easy to buy only a few things to call it "home."

This was the street. And right in the middle of those brownstones was the house that Big Willie had fallen over in. Dead.

The men had all been crowded into the front part of the room near the kitchenette playing blackjack; and the children were crowded into the bed behind the curtain, with Mumma. It never bothered the children. They usually fell asleep trying to stay awake, listening to what was happening on the other side of the curtain. But Mumma usually lay praying and damning Big Willie, never understanding that there was nothing else Big Willie wanted, nothing he could do to make a living except gambling.

The men usually played until late in the morning or sometimes to midday. Not that they always played at Big Willie's. There were six of them playing regularly and they all got the chance to disturb their families. But although there were six regulars, every game had at least twenty players, coming and going, standing around, whispering, going broke and going home.

It was at one of the big games that it happened. They had been sleeping to the quiet laughter and cussing, when suddenly Wade found himself wide awake. Not so much because of the noise as for the lack of it.

Mumma, who had been sitting bolt upright, slipped out of bed, quietly moving toward the curtain, and Wade wiggled past the sleeping form of Willie Earl and hit the floor as he heard Big Willie say, "I ain't never cheated a man in my life but I killed a-many."

"But I ain't cheated," a voice answered, quivering the way the man himself must have been quivering. "I swear to God, I ain't known how that card got there."

Wade peeped into the room and saw the men sitting around the table, silent, watchful, grim, made unreal, like a ten-cent mystery or weird tale, by the thick smoke drifting over and around the players.

Big Willie had pushed his chair back so that it had fallen, and he moved toward a skinny little fellow who was shaking as if he had caught a real bad chill or something. Uncle Dan, who never played cards, sat near the wall all boozed up, trying to fight through the haze over his mind to what was happening.

The little fellow really wanted to run, but he was too scared. He was hemmed in by sitting near the wall instead of the door and all he could do was sit and look as Big Willie approached, but when Big Willie was almost upon him, the stud stuck his hand in his pocket and came out with a gun. He fired right at Big Willie's chest.

Big Willie never stopped walking toward the man. Big Willie grabbed him and he let the gun drop to the floor as he covered his face with his hands and cried. It didn't do a bit of good. By the time Big Willie was finished, the man's jaw was broken in three places and they carried him out, more dead than alive.

Uncle Dan struggled to his feet. "Willie boy, Willie boy, looks as though that son-of-a-bitch shot you. Let me see. Let me see." They opened his shirt, and sure enough, there was a bullet hole clean as anything right through his chest.

Uncle Dan and a couple of the other men took him to the hospital while Mumma sat in a chair waiting. By that time Faith had got up and sat beside Wade. They silently watched Mumma rubbing her hands together, rocking back and forth, but never saying a word, just waiting. Willie Earl never even turned over in bed.

They came in about noon, Uncle Dan and Pappa. Uncle Dan's face was ashen with worry. "That man is dead, Evelyn. Big Willie is dead. That bullet took him right in the heart. Doc couldn't take it out so he just closed the hole up, but Big Willie is just about dead."

They all looked at Big Willie, towering over the room, a cigarette stuck in the corner of his mouth, the smoke drifting up over his face so that his eyes narrowed, and they did not know if they were narrowed from the smoke, or from the pain they thought he must be feeling. He didn't crack a smile over what Uncle Dan said, but went to answering that stunned question in Mumma's eyes.

"I got unfinished business, Evelyn. Ain't no man got a right to die if he ain't finished up his business."

Wade and Faith nodded in agreement. And Uncle Dan, catching a look at them, nodded too, only he was kind of bewildered. But Mumma sat rubbing her hands together for a long time before she came out with what was on her mind.

"It's the devil's doing, that's what it is. Ain't no man got no call to live with a bullet in his heart, if it ain't the devil's doings."

Faith and Wade stared at each other in downright surprise. Mumma knew better than that. It was no secret that Big Willie was sworn to go back South and have his revenge on those crackers. They never spoke about it but everybody knew it, so it was sort of natural to him and Faith that Pappa just couldn't die until he had got them all back home.

Mumma went to church every day now, taking them and trying to force them to pray for the deliverance of Pappa's soul into the hands of God. Little as he was, Wade refused to pray. He didn't want Big Willie delivered into anybody's hands. Still she kept after him wanting him to pray so hard that one day he stood up in church and shouted, "I don't want God to have Pappa's soul. I hate God. I hate Him, I hate Him, I hate Him." He raised so much fuss and shamed Mumma so badly that she took him home telling him that he was Big Willie's son in the soul, as he was in the flesh, and she would never take him to church again.

Wade never knew what Big Willie did toward finishing his business. Pappa kept right on with that hard gambling, sitting around a table full of people playing cards, while Uncle Dan sat behind him boozing. Later, Wade had it figured that Pappa had been trying to make enough money gambling to do what he wanted.

One day, almost a year to the day he was shot, a game started in the house. It was an early game. Willie Earl was still in the streets playing and Faith had not come home from Aunt Julie's. Wade sat in the big chair in the front part of the room, glad to be around Pappa and Uncle Dan and their rough-talking friends, who rubbed his hair or pushed his head, or made boxing jabs at him. This was something he liked doing, sitting in a hot, crowded room, surrounded by rough voices, until he nodded, and then Mumma picked him up and put him to bed.

It was just about the time he got to nodding that he heard Pappa say in a funny voice, "Evelyn—get me the . . ." Pappa never finished the sentence, just doubled over and died.

Mumma rushed to get all of the brothers and sisters from her church to come over to the house to pray all of that night and into the next day and the next night. Pray and sing . . .

> "It's me, it's me, it's me, Oh Lord
> Standing in the need of prayer.
> It's me, it's me, it's me, Oh Lord
> Standing in the need of prayer. . . ."

Mumma might not have been happy, but she looked right contented. Wade heard her say to one of the sisters in a grave but satisfied voice, "He said he wouldn't die unless he finished his business, but he died before he could even finish his last sentence." It suited Mumma that way. Things fitting into place. She was happy, not so much that Pappa died, as that nobody dictated to God. He took you when He wanted to and you hadn't one earthly thing to say about it. It relieved her that, after all, she had been living with a mortal, and that made her thankful.

But it shook Wade to his very soul and when Mama and Faith and Willie Earl stood up singing with the rest of the brothers and sisters, he sat in Uncle Dan's lap and cried, rubbing his thick fat fists into his eyes until they were red and swollen. Uncle Dan cried too, but for different reasons. He had lost his brother and only pal, and he didn't know who would take care of him when he got boozed up. Wade cried, running from the house and from the pious, religious sisters, beating his fists against the stoop until they were bruised and bloody. When Uncle Dan pulled him away, he flung his arms around his uncle's neck and cried harder than ever. Folks thought it was strange that one so young—that lil' bit of a thing—would take on so over anybody's death. But it was not Big Willie's death so much as it was that he had no right dying if he hadn't finished his business.

Maybe the reason Mumma turned, from the very beginning, to Willie Earl instead of to him was because of the way he took on over Pappa. That, and of course the fact that Willie Earl was much older. Older and more able to get around her prayers, tears and fears. Mumma's praying doubled instead of lessening after Big Willie died. It seemed to her even more the work of the devil, that she had to be crucified in the bowels of a city like New York with three children as her cross.

Mumma was afraid about everything, not only for herself but for them. She refused to let them go out of the neighborhood, setting their limits between 116th Street and 125th Street. She wouldn't go downtown shopping, afraid to tangle with the white folks, buying instead at the higher-priced stores of 125th Street, saying that what she put out in money, she made up in peace of mind.

Willie Earl listened to everything she said, nodded his head and went about his own way of doing things. But once when someone saw him go past 116th Street and Mumma got after him, he pleaded and cried, argued and got excited, angry and then repentant, saying that he was not a baby to be confined to a ten-block limit. He carried on in such a way that Mumma, tired and worn, unable to endure such persistence, gave in, extending his boundaries to most of Harlem.

Faith and Wade listened to everything Mumma had to say, never questioned her, never went past the limits she set for them, except for that one time when Wade went with Willie Earl. That one time was enough and he never did it again.

After Big Willie died, Willie Earl had taken to hustling shoe shines to help Mumma out. And one morning, after months of listening and ignoring Wade's pleas, Willie agreed to make Wade a shoe-shine box and take him along.

Mumma helped them dress, kissed them, sending them on their way. He was proud as anything to be going out with his big brother. Willie was six years older and tall for his age. Folks said he was just like Pappa. But Wade, ever since he could remember, clung to the idea that he was the one like his father, and the idea of bringing home money and throwing it in Mumma's lap casually the way Pappa used to, saying, "Here, Evelyn, see what you can do with this," pleased him.

Willie walked him right past 116th Street to 110th. It was the first time he had been that far from home, but before he could get used to the excitement, Willie Earl had grabbed his arm and was pulling him into the subway. "Listen, Wade," he whispered as though Mumma might have been right behind them. "I'm going to take you where we can make a lot of money, but if you tell, I'm going to knock the hell outa you and I ain't never going to take you with me again." That was always Willie Earl. Nothing but a bag of secrets.

Willie Earl waited until the train rushed into the station and had almost closed its doors before pushing Wade under the turnstile, dragging him across the platform, shoving him through the closing door, and wiggling in after him. They were off, making it to "Willie's" corner in a place that Willie called "wop-town," and all the while they were riding, Willie Earl kept giving instructions: "Keep your eyes peeled for the kids on the block. Never set up when you see a kid around. If he ain't seen you, hide until he passes. If he catches one glimpse of you, we can just call it a day, understand? Cause if you see one, you'll see a dozen."

Wade nodded to every instruction. He didn't understand anything, but he was puzzled more than a little at Willie's running battle with Mumma for a 110th Street limit, when the whole city was already his stomping ground. That was the way with Willie Earl, he had a natural knack of fighting over a little bone to hide a whole *side* of meat he had stored up somewhere.

Willie's corner was near a broken-down tenement on the Lower East Side, where people came and went as if it was a train station. Fine cars stopped here and well-dressed men flashing big diamond rings jumped out to disappear into the interior of the broken-down house, coming out in a very few minutes to drive away. But many, seeing a shoe-shine box, decided on a shine. The boys started making money right away. These men didn't mind paying twenty-five cents or fifty cents, and sometimes as much as a dollar for a five-cent shine. Of course, Willie made the big tips because he knew how to shine. He could have made even more, except that he had to stop every few minutes to give Wade pointers, and even to finish some of the shoes Wade started. But he still made money, and Wade did too.

It was because of Wade taking so long to finish one pair of shoes that they got caught. Willie looked up in the middle of a shine, saw one of the neighborhood kids and said under his breath, "Psst, chicky Wade, let's cut." He gave the shoe he had been working on a lick and a promise, then he was ready. Wade, stuck with too much of the thick liquid over his customer's shoe, was afraid to stop, and by the time Willie Earl had run to the corner, to look around, come back and grabbed his arm, pulling him away from the unfinished shoe, they were surrounded.

"Hey," one big boy, the leader, called. "Don't you know we don't let no spooks around here? How you get out of nigger town?" That was the first instant when Wade realized that he had not seen one black face since they started. The very thought made him shake inside.

Slick Willie Earl wasted no words, he just kept looking around for a way out, holding on to Wade's arm, because he knew he could talk his way out of anything with Mumma, except leaving his little brother in another part of town. Willie Earl tried to inch toward the corner, but they were locked in. The leader was a boy much older than Willie Earl; and the youngest, much older than Wade, who was hardly rid of his baby fat.

The kids called them black sons-of-bitches and dirty niggers and coons. Told them that they would show them what they did to dirty bastards when they caught them where they didn't belong. Willie Earl never wasted a breath, he just kept looking around and thinking.

Wade later heard Willie Earl often say, "When you know all you can do is talk, start working your mouth so that nobody gets in a word. But when talking ain't gon' do it, save your breath and use your head." That was what he was doing then, because when the leader of the group took a long switchblade knife and started playing with it, touching the blade as though he saw it already disappearing into their guts, Willie's hand left Wade's arm and before anyone knew what was happening, he had brought the shoe-shine box down on the boy's head. The crack of bones sounded in the air and at the same time, Wade felt himself flying, his feet not even touching the ground.

The surprise attack upset the white boys, giving Willie and Wade a good head start. They had almost reached the subway when two of the bigger ones caught up with them—and the fight was on.

A policeman broke it up and took them down the steps into the station, paid their fares and said, "Look, this part of town ain't no place for you little niggers. Stay uptown where you belong because the next time I catch you guys around here, I'll run you in myself."

Wade remembered looking at this giant of a man with his big pistol bulging at his hip, and promised himself and Mumma that he would never go around where white folks were again. He had never been so afraid, not before, not since.

All the way uptown on the train he was terrified and he thought Willie Earl must be too, that is, until Willie started talking. "How many pairs did you do, Wade?"

"What?"

"Shoes, Wade. How many pairs did you do?"

"I dunno." Shoes were the farthest thing from his mind. He had left his shoe-shine box along with the unfinished pair of shoes and had not given it another thought.

"Count how much money you got." Wade dug into his pocket and came out with four quarters. "Good. Now you give Mumma fifty cents and keep the rest."

Willie Earl dug into his pockets and counted his money aloud. Wade, self-conscious, looked around noticing the people looking at them with their noses pulled down, their eyes pointed and accusing, those sitting next to them pulling their clothes away not wanting to touch the two dirty, badly beaten-up boys.

He and Willie might as well have been stink from a garbage can placed into the subway for the prime purpose of disturbing the gentle noses of the fine white people there. Wade caught a glimpse of a couple of well-dressed colored men. Unlike the white folks, they pulled their gaze away and were busy looking out the windows, pretending those two dirty colored boys did not exist. For Willie, it was the people around who didn't exist. He talked loud, counting his money, never noticing them.

"I got seven dollars and fifty cents," he said. "Now I'll give her two dollars. I'll keep the fifty cents on account of I don't want to have to break into the five. . . ."

"You can't do that to Mumma," Wade whispered, horrified.

"Do what to Mumma?" Surprised, Willie raised his voice even louder. Wade's face burned because he knew that all of the white folks in this silent car were looking and listening, and he knew he couldn't shut Willie's mouth.

"We ain't doing nothing to Mumma. You better wake up, boy, and get some skin on your simple head. Number one, if we give her all the money, she's going to want to know how we made so much. Number two, if we tell her we been downtown, she going to cry and carry on and turn us every way but loose. Number three, if we had stayed where she wanted us to stay, let me see—you did about four pairs—you would have got one nickel a pair and *no* tip cause you slow. I did about ten and I would have got one nickel a pair, and maybe a nickel tip from some studs trying to play big. That would have been twenty cents from you and less than a dollar from me. Now, you tell me, what we doing wrong to Mumma?"

Wade pulled his mouth together and didn't care what kind of figuring Willie Earl did. They had gone out to work to help Mumma and all the money rightly belonged to her and he was going to tell.

And sure enough the minute Mumma opened the door and gave one look at their faces, she got to crying. "Lord, where in the world you-all been?"

"Oh, we just been in a scramble with some guys around . . ." Willie Earl began, but Wade wouldn't have it.

"No, Mumma, we been downtown and them white boys jumped on us and . . ."

He didn't go any further because Mumma grabbed Willie Earl just the way Willie said she would and started to beat him as if she had taken leave of her senses.

Willie Earl got to yelling and screaming as though he was being killed, and people from upstairs came down and people passing in the streets crowded around the window, but Mumma didn't let up her beating or Willie Earl his hollering.

"You fool. You fool. They could have killed you-all. They could have killed you-all." And every time she repeated this she would start on him again as though she intended to do just that, and Willie Earl would go into his hell-raising scene.

Wade sat in a chair quietly waiting his turn but she never touched him. She didn't have the strength. After she had finished, she sat down and cried. "You don't know white folks, Willie Earl. You don't know them. They ain't no different up here than they are down home. They'll kill you and leave you in the streets and ain't nobody know where you come from. They could string you up on one of them lamp posts and set fire to you and leave you in the street and don't nobody know what you even look like. And we all the way up here not even knowing where you been. Ain't you got no sense at all?"

Her love for Willie Earl, her fear, all came out in that cry. But it passed right over Willie's hard head and fastened into Wade. He knew it had no effect on Willie because later that night, when everything was quiet, Willie said he was sorry and he wouldn't do it again, and gave Mumma just what he said he would, not one penny more. Anybody who knew Willie knew he'd sooner die than leave that money downtown.

But to Wade sitting there quietly, filled with shame at what they had done, the terror in her voice and in her face as she cried got right to him, the very center of him, and he remembered the first night in the city, when she fell to her knees and prayed; then he had not known whether to go to her or stay away, and he sat very much as he was doing now, hurt and sorry, only now he bore the guilt of her fear. What the policeman standing with his big red face, his gun bulging at his hip, had started, she had sealed with her fears. His limits, his boundaries, forever.

4

It was in that house in this street, where he and Faith had spent their early and most intimate childhood. Where he used to look out of their basement window, past the iron grill that offered supposed protection against thieves, to examine the legs of passers-by, and where the legs of little boys and men, the legs of little girls and women, changed in significance in a very short time to male legs and female legs. Here he and Faith and Lil' Willie Earl Williams, packed into the same bed like sardines, talked and laughed, telling dirty jokes, never thinking of what went on on the other side of the curtains, where Mumma and Pappa lay on the couch turned bed, listening perhaps half consciously to Mumma's prayers or Pappa coming in, getting into bed, to Pappa's big laugh—he never heard Mumma laugh—perhaps wondering why the bedsprings of their bed creaked so hard so long after Pappa had come in.

But then Pappa died and Mumma took Faith into the bed with her. Somehow that change in the house started the change in Wade's thinking.

At first it hadn't made much difference. He had been happy. He had been relieved of being squeezed into the middle. He spread out in his new freedom, getting into fights with Willie Earl over an inch of space, if even by accident Willie happened to move over into his "half."

But as he grew older, it kept aggravating him, a little pin-prick of annoyance—the reason Mumma had chosen Faith to sleep with her, "because she was a girl." Then to add to his annoyance, they had suddenly begun to act strange and even downright comical about the curtains being closed. Now, curiosity forced him to lie awake for hours after he had gone to bed, peeping through the curtains waiting until Mumma or Faith walked by the slit of an opening or stood there undressing, unconscious of his eager staring eyes.

This was how he learned of the differences between boys and girls, men and women. It surprised him that Faith, long and skinny, was so different from him at the lower part of her body, but it was Mumma with her full breasts protected by her burdened shoulders, her smooth black skin interrupted by the bushy growth of hair, that excited Wade's interest, causing him to gaze panting, until the drop of a nightgown, or the pulling up of a pair of panties, closed him out of their secrets.

He wanted to discuss with Willie Earl the new things he saw, but even then Willie had become a breed apart, acting grown, or as Uncle Dan said, "as if he was smelling his pee." Willie had been keeping late hours, coming home just to fall into bed, stinking of cigarettes and of another smell, which Wade looking back later knew to be the fresh smell of sex. But Willie Earl was a natural-born slickster, willing to spend time polishing up his art in order to keep Mumma off his back; he had a new way with him which he used to tell Wade was "charm." Uncle Dan said he probably read about it in some dirty magazine, but that the true meaning of the word was really "two-faced."

At any rate, it worked on Mumma. Willie learned how to laugh at everything she said, snitched on everything Wade and Faith did, went to prayer meeting with Mumma once in a long while, and even shouted louder against the word "sin" than Mumma did herself. He sometimes brought in one flower to her, or maybe a piece of candy, and somehow Mumma never smelled the cigarettes on his breath, and trusted him so that she was dead asleep most nights when Willie came in.

Wade decided to find out by himself, starting off by touching Mumma's bosom, poking around at the fullness that child-bearing had not flattened. Standing at her knees, fondling her, he slipped his hands into her bosom. He did not fully understand why she snatched him around, getting his probing hands away. But he did not miss the point a few days later, when he let his hands slide up her dress and into the bushy section of her thighs while she was giving him a bath, when she spun the soapy wet washrag into a rope and let him have it across his backside. He screamed, looked up into her fire-and-brimstone eyes, and knew he had done wrong.

It was not long after this that Mumma pushed Faith into bed with him to make room for one of her prayer meetings. It was the chance he had been waiting for. "I know why Mumma let you sleep with her and not me," he told her.

"I do too," Faith answered. "It's because I am a girl and you're a boy."

"Yeah, but do you know why I'm a boy and you're a girl?"

"Because it's so silly."

"But what makes it so?"

"I don't know. It's because God wants it that way."

"It's because you don't have a peepee."

"I do too have a peepee."

He took her hand and placed it on his body. "You don't have that."

Faith was silent as she touched and held him in amazement, making a funny feeling go right through him, a feeling which deepened as he heard the preacher in the other room saying, "It is death to sinners who do not repent." He wondered if he was really sinning and if so, if he would get up the next morning, dead.

Faith giggled and taking his hand placed it on her thigh, and they played together, exploring, whispering, snickering at things they found strange. And right there while a sister shouted, "Do Jesus, I have cleansed my soul of all sin. I have turned my eyes to the path of righteousness. Thank you, Father," and another rang out, "Thank you, Lord, for showing me the way of everlasting peace," they rubbed their bellies together and discovered sexual sensation.

From that day the terror and magic of their first feeling kept them seeking each other out. Every time they were alone—and now they even planned ways of being alone—their hands found each other, forever searching, holding, playing, ending with the same rubbing of their bodies, the remembered sting of Mumma's lash across his back adding a sense of excitement, a sense of danger.

It might have gone on forever, except that Mumma caught them one day. He never knew how she came upon them without them hearing, but suddenly the covers of the bed were pulled back and there was Mumma, screaming as though she had gone clean out of her mind. "Sinners," she shouted in a voice to wake the dead. "What are you doing in that bed? You bringing the devil back into my house with your lusting sinful bodies."

She rushed around getting Big Willie's old belt, made them strip naked, kneel at the side of the bed. Then she beat them until she was weak from exhaustion, forcing them to pray all night and into the next morning, digging the strap into their backs if they fell off to sleep, not caring that they shivered from the cold.

"What greater sin than brother and sister to be lusting after one another?" she cried to Willie Earl when he came in. "What greater cross can a woman have to bear?" Glancing through his sniffles, Wade thought he saw a cross, weighing her down, causing her face to grey and be lined.

Willie Earl walked to the far side of the bed so that Mumma did not smell the whiskey and cigarettes on his breath, but Wade did not see how she could miss the red in his eyes when he opened them wide to show how shocked he was. When Mumma went to her side of the curtain, Willie Earl grinned and making a circle with one hand, worked the index finger of his other hand through it suggestively. Sadness for Mumma filled Wade. He knew for sure that Mumma's cross must have become bigger and heavier because of what Willie Earl was doing and he wished he knew of one prayer to help lighten it for her. Even back then, he never knew how to pray. Faith just looked at Willie. She looked at him a long time without ever saying one word, just kneeling there all naked and pitiful.

With Wade, his first taste of sex released him, and there wasn't one little girl, starting with Mabel who really taught him, that he didn't go after at least once.

It made a change in Faith. Before that, she had been considered smart in school, helping him with his school work, playing teacher, hitting him over his fists with a ruler if he grew inattentive. Afterward, she became cold, withdrawn, hating anyone to touch her, even Mumma, unfriendly to anyone except Wade, and after the orphanage, Uncle Dan.

Maybe Faith might have eventually overcome her withdrawal, except that something happened a few years later that tore her to pieces and shook her confidence in Mumma for the rest of her life.

It was in this house, too, that Wade had been first called on to give protection to his family. He and Mumma had been sitting around after dinner listening to Faith's footsteps as she climbed the stairs to the bathroom. The bathroom was one flight up, which meant two flights from their basement apartment. Mumma usually left the door open as a precaution against danger. Wade and Faith had developed the habit of timing each other, counting the other's steps as they went up and came back, making it into a game.

Now as he waited, sitting on the big chair, picking his teeth, listening intently to catch her footfall as she sneaked down trying to frighten him, he heard instead of footsteps a terrible scream.

Wade jumped out of the chair, instinctively grabbing a heavy piece of wood that they kept in the corner for just such emergencies, raced up the stairs two at a time, reaching the landing to find the door of the bathroom closed and silence hanging over the entire floor. Wade never stopped running. He rammed the door with his shoulder, ripping off the tiny hook-lock, bursting the door wide open. Seeing in a crazy instant a giant of a man, standing as though he had not heard the bursting of the door, as though he had no eyes or ears for anything or anyone but Faith, as though indeed he was almost transfixed by the sight of Faith standing, shivering naked except for her little panties, before him. Scratches ran down the valley between her small pointed breasts where the man had brutally torn away her dress, moving like a deaf-mute toward her, holding his sex rigid in his hands.

Raising the stick high in the air, Wade came down on the man's shoulder, putting all his weight behind the blow. The man did not seem to notice. Wade raised the stick and came down again and this time Faith, realizing he was there with her, gathered courage and opened her mouth, screaming in such a terrible voice that, shocked into sudden awareness, the man bolted, running out of the bathroom. He was down the stairs and out the door by the time Mumma had reached the top of the basement stair, panting and wanting to find out what had happened to her little girl.

Faith brushed her aside, crying hysterically. Later, when Wade came to her expecting some kind of praise for protecting her, she only looked at him, saying, "Who's going to pray all night for this, Wade? Who's going to pray all night for this?"

It peeved him that she didn't feel much more indebted to her little brother. He never figured out how she came to put any blame on Mumma. Not then, anyway. It wasn't until years later that he became critical about the way they lived, and by that time, Faith's words had been long forgotten.

Not that he would have blamed Mumma. He never blamed Mumma for anything. From his earliest childhood, he realized what a rough time she had. He always felt sorry for her. He loved her. The earliest pain he remembered was seeing her poor hands and knees swollen and stiff from arthritis. He knew that it was because of the way she had had to work in the cotton fields from sunup to sundown when she was a child. She had walked on her knees from one patch of cotton to another, until, as she said, she never really knew a time, even in her earliest years, when she wasn't ailing from stiffness in her joints.

Yet as much as she suffered and as little as they had, Mumma always kept a clean house. That one-and-a-half-room kitchenette always sparkled with the bright colors Mumma used for her bedspreads and curtains. Artificial flowers were always around the house, in jars or empty cans.

She made the flowers from wire and crêpe paper and sometimes sold them in order to stretch the home-relief checks that they had been getting since Big Willie died. All in all, it seemed to Wade that they were getting on fairly well. But then the swelling in her joints grew worse and Mumma had to take to the rocking chair for such a long time that Willie Earl, who had never cared about school anyway, decided to drop out to help with the bills.

Willie Earl had always been tall for his age, tall like Uncle Dan and Big Willie, so it was not hard for him to get a job. But somehow the home-relief woman, a woman called Miss O'Neil, who was the only white person he had ever seen Mumma talking to, found out about the job. She carried on as if the home-relief money actually came from her own pocket, and she stopped them from getting their checks. It didn't make any difference that Willie Earl was too young to be out of school and had to stay one jump ahead of the truant officer. Their relief was cut off anyway.

Mumma tried to make it on what Willie Earl made, or anyway, on what Willie Earl gave her every week, which was five dollars. Five dollars in those days was considered quite a bit of money but Wade heard from a friend of Willie's that he was making much more. There were two things that Willie Earl locked up tighter than any oyster when it came to his money—his fists and his jaw. When Wade approached him about it, Willie threatened to tell Mumma about Wade's trip to the roof with Mabel. There was nothing for Wade to do but be quiet.

It never made any difference to Willie Earl either, that the family ate greens boiled with one piece of fat back every day in the week with Mumma explaining to Faith how to mix together corn meal and water to pan-roast on top of the stove, making corn bread. Willie ate it right along with them, sopping his corn bread in the last little bit of potlicker, and was happy.

In the morning, Wade and Faith killed their first pangs of hunger with a cup of tea; hurried to school and waited anxiously for lunch time and their free lunch of soup, brown bread and jam or peanut butter, a cup of milk with fruit for dessert; then in the evenings, back to their greens and corn bread.

To children, life never seems bad. Wade and Faith never complained but Mumma did. One day Wade heard her saying to Uncle Dan, "Life is too hard, Dan. I just can't make it if you don't help me out with these children."

"Why, Evelyn," Uncle Dan answered, "why ain't you never told me about it before?" It certainly wasn't that Mumma hadn't told Uncle Dan about it. It was just that Uncle Dan forgot about most things that had to do with money. Not that he had a stingy bone in his body, he just never thought about it. Now when Mumma spoke to him, Uncle Dan simply took Wade by the arm and brought him home to explain to Aunt Julie. Uncle Dan didn't trust himself when it came to money and neither did Aunt Julie trust him. She tied the money in a handkerchief, pinned it into Wade's pocket and told him not to stop on his way home; but she forgot to keep Uncle Dan in the house.

Uncle Dan caught up with Wade a block after he had left the house, and about another block later, they met with some down-home buddies. One thing led to another and Wade found himself in someone's house listening to the usual loud talking and laughing, feeling the handkerchief being eased out of his pocket, untied, tied, replaced, until in time there was nothing left to replace. Wade tried protesting, only to be answered by a gentle rubbing of his head and a promise: "This is the last now. This is the last."

It finally ended with Wade having to take Uncle Dan home, supporting his heavy weight with his young, strong shoulders, weaving from one side of the sidewalk to the other, helping him up the stairs and helping Aunt Julie put him to bed. Of course Uncle Dan was sorry—Uncle Dan was always sorry—he promised to do better the next week, but that week went into the next and then the next.

One morning Mumma got up early, told them that instead of going to school they were going with her. She took them downtown. It was a long train ride, longer than they had ever taken. Of course he had gone that far once with Willie Earl, but he still knew nothing about trains and Mumma had never been out of Harlem. However, it turned out she knew exactly where she was going.

It was the children's court.

Mumma cried that morning and told the judge how sick she was, how there was nobody to help her and how much she loved them, that she couldn't take care of them anymore, she just couldn't.

He never realized what was happening. All he knew was that Mumma was crying and he resented it. She always used to complain against white people. She hated them. Yet she cried every time she had anything to do with them. She cried to the teacher when she went to school for Faith. She cried when the policeman brought Willie Earl home because he caught him shooting crap. She cried to the home-relief woman, Miss O'Neil, and now she was crying to a judge.

The judge was kind and kept them.

This was the first time in his life that he had ever been separated from his family. This was the first time he had ever been separated from Faith, because this too they did.

Waiting in the little back room after their case had been decided did not seem too bad. They sat clinging to each other, bewildered, not knowing what might become of them, but satisfied that they had each other. But as the buses pulled up they saw that there were two buses, and as the names were called out they realized that one bus was for girls and the other for boys.

Now they clung together, refusing to be parted; but the matron for the girls and the instructor for the boys pried them apart, picking them up bodily and putting them in their respective buses, holding them while the other children filed in obediently, and the door was shut and locked.

Released, they ran to the doors of their buses, lacing their fingers through the iron workings and screaming to each other.

"Wade, Wade, Wade," Faith cried, and he answered in the only words he could think of: "Faith, Faith, don't leave me. Don't leave me."

Even as he screamed, her bus was moving away and her fingers stretching out toward him.

Her bus turned a corner and he no longer saw her but he continued to hear her screams and the echo of her screams: "Wade, Wade, Wade." He rattled the door and when it refused to give, banged his head against it until he sank to the floor, weak from exhaustion, listening indifferently to the sniffles of the other children, affected by his crying.

What a world he came into, this place for unwanted and delinquent children! They had been beaten for going into it, cautioned against it as part of a prayer, and here Mumma had brought them and set them right in the middle of it: the white world.

Of course there were many black children. Black children and brown children and light-tan children, with a Chinese child thrown in for good measure. But it remained authoritatively, structurally and in every other way, a white world.

The supervisors were not so cruel as he had been led to believe from looking at movies, or hearing about homes, reform schools and other institutions from threats by teachers and parents. But there is the cruelty of indifference, which—if it is to be judged by feelings—is five times more cruel than anything a parent can do to you physically: your mother's backhand slap that fattens your lip, your father's growl, your brother's spiteful pinch, all single you out for special treatment. Cruel it may be, but special.

But to be a part of a group, toes touching, fingers interwinding, wide eyes searching, begging for some show of attention, of affection— and to be almost invisible. To be pulled out of a line, your head rubbed, then, "Ugh, that grease, wash it off, every bit of it," a piece of strong soap, probably containing lye, pushed into your hand to do the job, not because you are Wade or Harry or John but because you are a colored child and they know that colored children usually have vaseline on their hair and they refuse to have any.

It might not have been so bad if every one of the children had been treated with the same dose of indifference. But some of them were singled out for special treatment because of their looks. "Look at those pretty blue eyes, and that wonderful head of blond hair. How could his mother bear to part with him?" "What beautiful white skin. Such a pretty child, his parents must be monsters to put him in a place like this."

Maybe it was Big Willie's anger hard inside him, because the other children never seemed resentful. But *he* got every message as it was being sent and he could pin-point *that* time in his life as the time when the flame was lit, which he later recognized as hate. Hate not only against the authorities, or against blonde hair, blue eyes, white-skinned children, but even the little black children who, in the batting of an eye, had become beggars. Beggars, begging with widened eyes, their too-quick smiles at any little kindness that was thrown to them. Accepting, as it were, that *their* parents were not monsters for throwing them in there, for after all, they had black skins and kinky hair.

From that time too, he developed the heaviness of tongue that made it difficult to express himself except to his family, and the way he had it figured, this was the place where his laugh began whittling down from his family's big belly laugh to his own chuckle.

Faith had a pretty rough time of it too, as she told him later. The authorities had, from the very first, disregarded the fact that she had been sent as a charity case, and had submitted her to a physical examination usually given to delinquents to verify their virginity, then had placed her with the delinquent girls, girls hardened from the streets around Harlem and the Lower East Side. She spent the entire time while she was there protesting that she had never been "touched." And she had not. The only sexual experience Faith had ever had was with him and rubbing their bodies together could never, by any stretch of the imagination, be termed intercourse. That night-long beating with its endless prayers and the terrible experience she had undergone afterward had made Faith so sensitive and ashamed of her body that, to be examined by a man, have her innocence questioned, and to be placed with a group of girls to whom sex was an everyday occurrence, touched her to the tenderest part of her.

It seemed to her that the only Negro girls in the so-called virtuous group were children so young that the suggestion of sex would have been madness. Years later in talking about it, she often said, "You know, Wade, to the white world, every black girl past the tooth-ring stage is screwed," making him realize that a feeling corresponding to his hate, though not so extreme, had been injected into her at that time.

He must have had some premonition of what she was going through as he went around, half numb, in the youth house. In his mind he saw her being cruelly beaten by the matron, because she was pretty and soft, because she was not white. He cried every night.

He cried, too, for Uncle Dan, night after night, seeing him going home drunk, no one to take care of him, perhaps falling in front of a truck, being crushed to death, slowly, painfully. But worst of all he suffered for Mumma. In his mind, he followed the slow movement of a thief, step by step, as he pried open the outer door, then the inner door, tip-toeing into the room, going through the drawers of the dresser. And Mumma getting up suddenly, catching him, frightening him, making him rush to her, grabbing something and beating her to death. Or sometimes he imagined their home would catch on fire, burning almost to her bed, and she not able to get up because of her swollen knees and hands. Willie Earl was never home. Never home.

One rainy night as he lay sleeping, the sounds of fire engines mixed with the sound of thunder filtering into his dreams. He saw Mumma burning to death, and jumping out of his sleep and out of bed, he ran screaming and crying, and banged at the window. "Mumma, Mumma, Mumma, come out. Come out. My Mumma is burning. My Mumma is burning." All of the children in his section joined in and it was hard to quiet them. By the time they were put back to sleep, it was time to get up again.

It might have been a lifetime that he spent in the youth house, silent, sad, sullen, gloomy, unheard, unloved, unhappy. It might have been a lifetime but it was only a week. One week and he was called back to court, and there, in the little room where the boys and girls were emptied from their buses, waiting for their cases to be called, he saw Faith again.

One week should not have made the difference in anybody that it had made in Faith. She had grown much thinner, her skin so transparent he could see her veins. Even her fingernails had a look-through quality. She had grown quieter. It wasn't only something you could see, but somehow you could feel it, and you knew this would stay with her forever. She didn't run up to him shouting his name as he did to her; and

ROSA GUY

as they sat quietly waiting for their case to be called, she seemed satisfied just to clasp his hand silently.

"What do you think is going to happen?" She shrugged as though it made no difference. "You think they'll let us go home?" She shrugged again. It hurt him to see her so pale, so lifeless, acting as though she didn't care about anything any more. "I can hardly wait to see Mumma, can you?"

Faith said, "I don't ever want to see her again. Don't you ever talk to me about her."

That hurt him. He had missed Mumma so very much and he thought it would have been the same with Faith. "But why, Faith? What's Mumma done?"

"I just don't, that's all." Her face was set. He had never seen her like this before, but he was to see that same look in her face many other times. It's possible that if Mumma had been in court that day, Faith might have refused to go home, but as it turned out, when it was their turn, Uncle Dan was sitting there. Uncle Dan, looking a little older and a lot more unhappy than they had ever seen him.

"It's my fault," Uncle Dan pleaded to the judge. "It's all my fault, Your Honor. I ain't done right by these here children. Sure I intend to but somehow—things keep kind of getting in the way. But I swear, Your Honor, I swear before the Lord, things will change."

"They my children, you know. They my children. They all I got. God knows. . . ." At this point Uncle Dan broke down crying and had to pull his handkerchief out to blow his nose.

Nobody in the world could doubt that their Uncle Dan loved them and that he had suffered every bit as much as they had in the past week. Nobody. On the strength of this, and on the recommendation of their probation officer, they were released.

Wade and Faith held on tight to his hands as they walked out of the courtroom but the moment they got outside, he knelt on the sidewalk and grabbed them each in an arm, squeezing them so that it took away their breath. And he cried and they cried, and it was a long time before they could get themselves together to go sit in the little square near the court and finish their crying. Then Uncle Dan hailed a passing pushcart and bought them both two hot dogs and a bottle of soda apiece before they took the train uptown.

5

"Hey, Baby." She switched by, letting her strong-smelling perfume hit him full face. Wade looked up into the sudden, unnatural silence that flooded him. He loosened his hands from the rail, noticing how deeply the spikes had penetrated through to the most inner part of his palm, and reached for his handkerchief. As he roped it around his most painful hand, the right one, he realized from the air being still heavy with her perfume that she might still be there. He looked around.

Pretty lil' black gal. Nothing he liked better than pretty black women, and it didn't hurt that she was wearing an ice-blue dress that soothed his eye and somehow lifted the somberness and pushed the ticking movement of time back into this day.

"Ain't you going to say nothing, pretty boy?"

His hand went automatically to his face and right away he felt foolish so he decided to answer.

"My, but you cute." She gave him the signal with the light from her slanty mischievous eyes. "Only one thing," he added, "God made man, society made woman and you ain't going according to the rules." She switched away and he called after her skinny buttocks to soften the jibe, "Anyway, you naturally built for speed." He wished he could go with her. Pump up his sex. Make it the biggest, most important thing about him, everything that happened today into another world, another time, another history, but the truth was, sex wasn't that big. He turned his head and forgot her, quickened his feet to make it to Uncle Dan.

He had crossed 116th Street and stood eyeing the hot dogs in Teddy's Shanty when he felt a stare heavy on his back. He spun around and there was Mabel, perfumed and powdered, out early catching the strays. He was sure it was her gaze that had knifed him but she never glanced in his direction. Might have been an accident, except her eyelids sort of quivered as she walked by.

Shifty-eyed bitch, he had screwed her on the roof when he was nine years old, and again every once in a while during her climb to whoredom, and now here she was pulling a shift. Even after Buddy, she'd been eyeballing him when she got hot. But now. . . .

He stopped to glance at the menu in the Japanese Fugiyama's Chinese restaurant, walked into the liquor store next door, coming out with a pint of Four Roses that he stuffed into his back pocket. Buy Uncle Dan a bottle and he could sit with him until their pockets ran dry. That was the trouble, they usually did. Then they had to go face Aunt Julie.

Funny about Aunt Julie—she'd get hotter than the sun if he started Uncle Dan to drinking again, but she never used to say a word back there when Uncle Dan used to pull him out. Even way back when he was little, she used to kill herself laughing when Uncle Dan dipped his finger in a glass of whiskey and let him suck it. "Ain't he a big devil," was all she used to say. You didn't bother to cross words with Aunt Julie or remind her of that time either. When Aunt Julie said something, everybody listened, or pretended they did, anyway. Now she was like Mumma. You didn't go back after a few minutes and "huh" and "aww" or anything like that. You simply bowed your head, wiped your mouth dry and shut up.

She answered right away to his ring, which surprised him, but then he figured it had to be about three o'clock and was glad he didn't have to be waiting around. "Wade, I sure am glad to see you and I know your Uncle will be tickled to death." She meant it. Aunt Julie never said anything she didn't mean.

"Well, I'll tell you, Aunt Julie, this ain't the worst place in the world to be." It was as if he had been holding his breath and now he could let it out, breathe again. He smiled broadly and they stood looking at each other. They were not given much to showing affection, this family, but there were many times Wade wished he could break down and do something silly like kissing. This was one of them. He put his arm around her shoulder and right away felt stupid and clumsy. "Where's Willie Earl and Uncle Dan?"

"Willie Earl ain't come in from work yet, but your Uncle Dan is in bed. He ain't but two feet away from the graveyard and the doctor says he'll just about make it if he drinks another drop. So don't get no ideas about drinking with your uncle. Not that I think you will after the way you did your poor sister. I hope you ain't thinkin' about drinking no more."

The bottle weighed heavier than lead in his pocket but he went on talking, to cover up his confusion. "Uncle Dan sick? But I been here earlier today and nobody was home."

"He just too weak to get out of bed, and I just got in from work myself."

"Seems to me I hear Wade's voice. Who is that, Julie? Wade? Come in here, boy. Come see what those old folks done to your poor uncle."

He wanted to rush inside and throw himself at his uncle, the way he used to as a kid, so he swaggered in casually. "Hi, unc . . ." Shook him up to see his uncle like that. One month ought not to make that kind of difference. "Hey, what you been doing to yourself?"

"Let me take a good look at you, boy. I sure am glad that my two children is back to normal."

"What? Worried about your sins catching up with us?" Wade chuckled. "You know Faith and me are Big Willie's breed. Ain't nothing about to happen to us."

"Lord," Aunt Julie stood in her familiar position at the door— one foot in the hall as if she were ready to run, leaving them to their bull session, one foot in the room, hands holding each other beneath her apron. "He carried on worst than a fool after what happened. Day after he come from seeing Faith at the hospital, Willie Earl picked him up stiff, in the middle of Lenox Avenue, cars coming every which-a-way. Don't know how he wasn't killed. Guess there's more than a speck of truth, that God looks after fools and drunks. But I sure wish they'd give Him a little time to devote to us that needs Him."

"Wade, I just didn't know." The old fingers probed the hardness of his muscles. "I got to thinking that if she had died, you would go stone out of your mind. I'd have lost the two of you."

"That's right, Wade," Aunt Julie called on her way down the hall. "Can't figger what came over you getting after that poor child like that. Lord knows ain't nobody more in your corner than she is. That's why I know you ain't about to start that drinking again."

"The bottle, the bottle. Your Aunt Julie got to blame all of the devil's doing on the damn bottle." Uncle Dan's voice was old and tired now. "But Wade, the bottle is only half of it. The other half is life. Put it together and what do you have? A whole. And that's where the crap begins."

Wade searched the affection in his uncle's eyes. If Uncle Dan had had schooling he would have been a genius.

"Come on, pull up a chair and sit by the old boy and tell what's been happening."

"Ain't nothing to tell. Same old crap."

"Same old crap, huh? I kinda hoped that you might get a doctor—to—you know—kind of . . ."

"Aw, they all the same. A bunch of antiseptic bastards."

Uncle Dan said, "Too bad—too bad." His old voice shook and a tear ran back into the curly hair that even sickness refused to whiten. But his face had taken a beating. It had sunk into so many tired lines that it sort of sucked in all of his handsomeness. That got to Willie—deep. Big Willie's children were all the family that Uncle Dan and Aunt Julie had. And sure he had done wrong by them a lot of times but it was the kind of wrong that a weak man did out of loving.

"Yeah, we a tough bunch all right. You know how long it took that bullet to get Big Willie—still—I kind of hoped a doctor . . ." His voice trailed off again.

A picture of Doctor Forest with his clear green look-right-through-you eyes, jumped into Wade's mind but he blinked it away. "Naw, a doctor couldn't help but I'll bet Lil' Willie Earl Williams can."

"Willie Earl, how so?"

"Cause it was him I was going after when Faith got in the way and I want to know why." Wade said this kind of quick, his gaze fastened to Uncle Dan's. But Uncle Dan's held steady.

"You don't say? Well now . . . Nope, all Lil' Willie said is that you got drunk and then you took off. Yes, that's all he said."

"You know Faith don't be making up things to say."

"Nope. That's for sure. But then you know Willie Earl. He ain't one to go shooting off his mouth if he figger he to blame for something."

Their agreement kept them silent a moment, then Uncle Dan's old voice picked up again. "Yeah, I been telling Aunt Julie, we a tough old bunch all right. Ain't no use her thinking she going to collect no insurance as long as one drop's left in me. But no, she got me in here drier than a milked-out tit. Tell you, Wade, ain't no sense in it. Stuff kept me alive all these years—how it goin' kill me now?"

"That's right, Uncle Dan, ain't never thought of you going any other way but stoned." Wade chuckled. "If you got to go, might as well go happy."

He meant it. Seeing Uncle Dan lying there all dried out twisted him worse than anything. But people didn't go around playing with Aunt Julie. He listened for the sounds of her cleaning in the house, and heard her in the kitchen. Good old strong Aunt Julie, one of those top-heavy, slim-hipped women that work seemed to make stronger and tougher. She had been cleaning white folks' homes and coming home to keep hers spotless as long as he could remember, and she appeared tougher and more formidable now than ever.

He pulled the bottle out of his pocket and they got hammer-tongued silent. Then realizing how quiet they were, they both hurried to break the silence, scared that Aunt Julie might hear it too. "Well, I sure am glad to see you, Wade." He had said that already but it served the purpose. Uncle Dan's eyes glittered like a brand-new ten-cent piece as he watched Wade unscrew the bottle.

"Yeah, well, maybe you will do a lot better if you do what Aunt Julie says and lay off the bottle."

"I been off for over a month and I'm nearer to death than ever before."

One long pull and the old face was already becoming younger, more relaxed. "You always was my boy, Wade," Uncle Dan said appreciatively. "You know that."

Wade closed the bottle and moved it away from Uncle Dan's anxious fingers.

"Yeah," Uncle Dan went on, "you ain't never been like Lil' Willie Earl Williams, always pussyfooting around the womenfolk when he knows he's hell to pay when they not around. Honest, Wade, you should see how he big-manning it around here, trying to put on for your Aunt Julie now that I'm laid up. I tell you, boy, women will buy anything, providing it's wrapped in pretty-looking paper."

It was a chummy silence they fell into now, and Wade, digging the Jekyll and Hyde change his uncle was going through, knew that if he had any added information on Willie Earl he'd give it without more pushing.

But the silence lengthened and Uncle Dan just got more quiet and comfortable looking, the shadows that had haunted his eyes passing, leaving them childlike, undisturbed. "Tell me, Uncle Dan, what started you to boozing?"

"I don't rightly remember." Uncle Dan smiled that young smile that had the habit of going through Wade, making him feel like the grown family man. "But I reckon it started when I was chasing after Big Willie. Son, when a stud tells you that a black man is the evilest man, don't you believe him. Ain't nothing in the world eviler than a red Negro. Especially when he comes from a white father and a black mother and his pa ain't fixing to let him go, nor willing to own him outright. He almost got the world but he ain't got a damn thing and he knows it. He spends his life trying to stop folks from knowing he ain't got nothing but they been knowing it and he knows they know it. Still, they can't tell him they know it because he done gone for bad so long that every living soul is scared to tell him they know. Kind of confusing, ain't it, Son?"

"Naw." Wade smiled. He had helped Uncle Dan unravel that one before he was nine.

"Well, that was your Pa, mean as anything. I used to follow after him everywhere he had to go proving himself. Course, I wasn't near as ornery nor as wild as him, but then I wasn't so big nor so bright as him, coming so far down the line that the old man sort of got over the kicks of having us kids. But I did love Big Bru. Why, if he told me to shit, I'd try to put out enough to fertilize an entire field. That's what I thought of him. If he gambled, he had to win. If he went stealing, he'd better not get caught. If he wanted trim, man, the bitches had better say nothing. Tell you he was as mean and harder than clear crystal on a zero morning. Naw, when they call you mean, they don't know what they talking about. You don't light a candle next to your Pa."

Wade grinned. He had spent a lifetime trying to live up to Uncle Dan's concept of his Pa's meanness but as far as Uncle Dan was concerned he'd never make the grade.

"Why, it was nothing for Big Willie to kill up some studs on a weekend, steal a mess of chickens to sell or go into a house to stick some chick he'd seen. And I'd be right behind him, hoping to get some booty. Killing went against me. Stealing, I just went along with, but man, I went for that booty." Uncle Dan let out a wicked laugh and winked out of his whiskey-livened eyes. Wade cocked his ear to listen for Aunt Julie.

"Yeah, I guess that's what started me to boozing. After a killing I'd get one on. Swim in the stuff. Take me the whole week to clear my head good, but by week end, I'd be after Big Willie again. And he—he never touched a drop." The bitterness in his voice surprised Wade, and he looked up quickly to catch it in his eyes, but Uncle Dan was tapping Wade's leg, begging for the bottle. Wade took it out of his pocket and gave Uncle Dan another swallow.

"But one thing." He settled himself on the pillows, the years just slipping away, leaving him his Uncle Dan-looking self again. "He'd look after me. Ain't never let a thing happen to me. Think nothing of carrying me on his back when I got so stoned I couldn't move and he'd stay with me, too, until I was straight again. Yes sir, Big Bru sure took care of me.

"Never had to worry about the sheriff. He was related to our Pa so we got away with everything. They ain't never given to worrying who we killed or stealed from as long as it was just niggers. They never cared if we kill each other, long as we ain't touched no white folks, and your Pa, mean as he was, went along with that line. Funny, huh?"

Wade searched his uncle's face again. Still no sign of the mockery he heard in his voice. Yet it seemed somehow that it had always been there, that mockery, that undertow of bitterness. Maybe he just heard it better now when Uncle Dan's voice sounded whiney because he was sick. Uncle Dan probably couldn't muster that voice, that loud hearty laughter, to carry it off as he could before.

"Course, you'd have liked him better if he'd have tangled with them white folks, huh, Uncle Dan? You'd have had more respect for him." It must have been the slur in his voice that brought Uncle Dan's eyes, startled, to meet his.

"I ain't never had nothing but respect for my big brother." He said it and meant it. Uncle Dan was like him: a close family man.

"But I tell you, Big Willie had one weakness." Uncle Dan shifted away from the subject. "Black women. Yeller as he was, he'd never so much look at a light-tan, much less a yeller woman. That's how he come about marrying your Ma with all that hog-wash law-and-order routine of hers. Black and pretty as she was, she was working every day the good Lord sent in Old Man Blackwell's cotton fields. You ever see anyone work in a cotton field, Son? Let me tell you they don't walk on their feet, they walk on their knees. So when your Ma tells you that Big Willie made her a hard life, don't you believe it. She'd been working on her knees out in them cotton patches since she was no bigger than a toadstool. If you ask me, that's why she married your Pa, to get off her goddamn knees. Way she talk, like Big Bru added to her burdens. He did her a damn favor by taking her out of them cotton fields, that's what he did."

Wade chuckled. This was perennial between Uncle Dan and Mumma. Both of them got cussing mad when they talked about it.

"Guess he figgered if he married her he would shake her up a bit. But at first she the one that did all the shaking. Yes sir, when you-all started coming, Big Willie had gone to settling. Evelyn had even gotten him to take his seat on the sinners bench. So I picked our Julie and went to settling too. Funny thing though, that's when everything started catching up with us.

"You see, Julie had been working for a white hag called Miss Suzie. Ain't never gonna forget her as long as I live. Guess your Pa didn't either. You see, she had one good eye and one bad eye. Well sir, that one good eye done gone over Big Willie and marked him for her. Now, I told you how Willie liked a black piece, but I ain't never told you how he hated white women. I ain't never been able to understand that, on account of to me a piece is a piece, that is, so long as it's good." Uncle Dan let healthy mischief take over his eyes for a while. "But your Pa ain't never been able to stand for no foolishness from no white woman.

"One day, she got to pulling and finagling with your Pa after he had gone in the kitchen to see Julie about one thing or another. The bitch was so hot she didn't let him go even when Willie got all red and warns her. I tell you she had one good eye and one bad eye? Well, Willie let go with a jaw full of tobacco juice right in her good eye. She let go all right but she was hollering 'rape' so loud that your Pa, big and bad as he was, had sense enough to pull up stakes and clear out. Every living one of us went with him. Went so fast and gathered so much dust that the sheriff didn't know it wasn't a wind storm until we were long gone.

"It undid all the good that your Ma thought she was doing with your Pa. He ain't never got over his mad till the day he died. Big son-of-a-bitch like him and ain't even worth the spit in a white whore's eye."

Uncle Dan got to laughing loud and there it was again—the feeling that something had happened to that joke which had been their big joke on Big Willie all of Wade's life. It sounded as if Uncle Dan were somehow lying there indicting. "That joke ain't funny worth a damn," Wade said.

"Sure ain't, when you get to thinking about it." Uncle Dan wiped eyes that were watered up from laughing.

Wade didn't understand what was happening to him. He never in his life found fault with Uncle Dan. Sure, he had added up through the years that much as Uncle Dan loved Big Willie, he was kind of jealous of not being so big or so brave as he. But that was one of the reasons he used to take care of him when Uncle Dan got stinko in the streets; he knew Uncle Dan could never be what he or his Pa was. Uncle Dan was weak. Natural-weak, with the kind of weakness that got to you. He never lied about it. Most of that joking and loud laughing he directed as much to himself as to Big Willie. That was standard procedure. The laughing and doings of Big Willie and Uncle Dan. Yet somehow Wade felt himself getting tight around the head, so that he had to lean forward to catch Uncle Dan's words.

"What bothered me, though, was that you kids had to come here to Harlem to stay. You ain't never known the things we known. What it's like to live in a place where life is pretty." The hot streets he had walked today rose fiercely in Wade's mind, grey, dreary, the sidewalks hot slabs of concrete. "Where there is a lot of green grass to play in and woods to hunt in—and shoot . . ."

"A mess of niggers?" Maybe that was it. What Uncle Dan was saying got mixed up with some of the things he had been thinking about. Things about the hospital and Doctor Forest and . . . "But if you had mixed it up a little, added maybe one white to the mess of niggers, we wouldn't have had to come and be stuck out on Lenox Avenue."

"What you talking about, Son?"

"Talking about Miss Suzie, Uncle Dan. If you had closed the other eye for good and put her some place where no one could find her, we'd have been able to know about that green grass. . . ."

"Son, you wouldn't have wanted us to do nothing like that."

"Why? You been doing it."

"But we ain't been doing it to no white folks. . . ."

"I never seen the difference in doin' it to white folks." Wade leaned ever nearer to Uncle Dan and lowered his voice. "You never let me tell you

ROSA GUY

about my time in the Army. . . ." Sweat jumped to his upper lip as he caught Uncle Dan's stare in a hard one of his own. It was as though they were wrestling. Finally, in desperation, Uncle Dan snapped the hold and fumbled around with the covers on the bed as though he had lost something.

"Sure, you told me about the Army." Uncle Dan was talking fast now, too fast. "All about how you met that lil' old French chick and thought you might stay over there. Course I knew it was nothing but talk. How you figger you could stay away from your Ma—and Faith—and—and your poor old Uncle Dan. It ain't like if Willie Earl was real close to us. You know how that brother of yours is. . . ."

Uncle Dan had deliberately changed the subject. He always did. Get it back to where they could agree—to Willie Earl and what a bastard he was. Be on safe ground. He didn't want to know, he felt safe as long as he didn't know. Perhaps he figured he might make heaven that way. He didn't want to share the guilt. Yet he shared it. Deep down inside he shared it and knew every bit of it even though he didn't want to be told. Just as Mumma shared the guilt over Buddy. Yeah, they were all tied up in the same shit—even if they didn't want to own part of it.

"Here, Uncle Dan, have another swig." He handed Uncle Dan the bottle and sat biting hard on his lip to keep the sneer from taking his face upward as he studied the anxious gulping, the busy trying to get away from things. The pulse throbbed in his temples and he blinked back the red mist that wanted to cover his eyes. Then he allowed himself a chuckle.

What the hell was the matter with him, anyway? He knew Uncle Dan never could stand responsibilities. Never used to mind getting them drunk, if Mumma put them to bed. Or making them stay out of school to keep him company, if Mumma had to explain it to the teachers. And he had the best reason in the world for it: he loved them. Nobody in the world ever doubted that. No, Uncle Dan was someone you had to feel about, you damn sure could never think him out. And as Wade sat there pushing up all of his old familiar fondness for his uncle, the front door slammed shut and heavy footsteps sounded outside the bedroom door. Willie Earl had come in.

6

Wade tensed, his mind a confusion of not knowing what face to put on for his brother: whether to put on a tough show, and rattle an apology out of him, or whether to act the nice brother, the everything-is-forgotten-and-forgiven bit, and ease an explanation out of him. Willie Earl was a cat from the streets. Once he got out of a corner it wasn't easy tracking him down. And if he so much as guessed that Wade didn't remember, it would be no-show time. But even as Wade fumbled with his thoughts trying to get them together, Willie Earl stuck his head through the doorway.

He stopped short at the sight of Wade, then eased himself into the room searching through Wade's eyes as though he expected to read his soul. And in just that tick of a second, guards went up in his own eyes as though he had dug that Wade did not remember. The hairs at the back of Wade's neck bristled. Willie had really expected Wade to go after him on sight.

Wade got up and moved toward Willie, feeling his brother shrink inside. "Hey, Willie Earl, I been waiting for you."

"Yeah, well, how you doing, man?"

"I got some talking for you."

"Yeah, what about?"

"If you come in and sit awhile maybe we can get with it, man."

The words seemed to put Willie Earl more at his ease and the pain in Wade's hands called his attention to the fact that he had balled them into fists. He looked down at the sore, aching cuts that today's anger had brought and he fought for his calm.

"Hey, Lil' Willie," Uncle Dan called. "Ain't it good to have our feller back home?"

Willie Earl stood, undecided which part he was going to act—the good-buddy part or the man-of-the-house part. Then his gaze fell on the bottle in Uncle Dan's hand, which Wade had forgotten to put away, and he decided to act the fool.

"Wade, what in the hell are you doing? What are you giving to Uncle Dan?" His voice was too loud for the little room and that meant he was playing for a point.

"I wish you'd come in so we could talk and stop playing the fool."

"You trying to kill Uncle Dan?"

"I'm saving his life."

"Ssh, boy," Uncle Dan pleaded in a low desperate voice. "You want your Aunt Julie down on us?"

"I'm going to *tell* Aunt Julie. Wade, you ain't coming in here with Uncle Dan sick and about to die to start nothing."

"I'm in here, fool." He stood squarely in front of Willie Earl looking at the face that was just like Uncle Dan's and Faith's and his own, except for the natural shifty lines that ran through like a thread. Start pulling at the thread and you unravel the whole damn face.

"You cause enough trouble for us. You ain't . . ."

"You ain't telling your part in the trouble, Lil' Willie," Uncle Dan said. Guilt jumped into Willie's eyes as he jerked his head around to study Uncle Dan. "So if you come in and sit down it'll be much better for all of us."

Willie Earl must have found what he was looking for in Uncle Dan's simple stare, because he turned back to Wade, assured and talking tough. "If you got something to say to me, Wade, say it. If not, get the hell on out of here. I don't have nothing to say to you after what you did to Faith and I'll be damn if I'm going to let you come in here and upset Uncle Dan worst than he already is. It's you the cause of him being laid up like this." Willie strained to get his voice higher.

Wade knew this bit well. Willie Earl wanted Aunt Julie in here to hide behind, while pretending he was the righteous family man. Only today he was making a big play, a lot bigger than was usual. Raising hell about the smoke to hide the dirt that was burning. Willie had something to hide real bad—dirtier than Wade had imagined. Only trouble, he didn't know how to get it out of him.

Wade studied Willie as he walked over to the bed trying to act like a loud-mouthed crusader. "Uncle Dan, you know better than to let Wade drink." Another way to get a pitch in his voice.

"Don't go upsetting your poor aunt," Uncle Dan began.

"Wade, I—Uncle Dan . . ."

"You worried about Uncle Dan or scared I might come after you like the last time?"

"What you coming after me for?" His voice got off track. He wasn't so sure of himself as he pretended. "I ain't done nothing to you."

Wade knew he had cracked Willie's calm. How to keep him rattled now so he could have him spilling his guts? "You say you didn't. Well, I say you did. Only last time you was doing the buying, this time it's me." He pulled the bottle out of Uncle Dan's hand and offered it to Willie Earl. "Let's start at the beginning." Willie shifted around as though he was caught in a trap. He kept wetting his lips, pretending he didn't see the bottle Wade had extended to him. "OK, if you like, I'll break the ice."

Uncovering the bottle, Wade put it to his lips and threw his head back, taking a sip. Willie Earl let out a scream as though he thought that one sip would send Wade off his rocker. *"Aunt Julie!"*

Wade's arm reached out even as he tried to hold it back, even as he said to himself this wasn't the way. He heard the crack of Willie's jaw under his fist. He hadn't meant to hit him, he hadn't meant to. His first impulse was to rush to Willie Earl, help him to his feet, tell him he was sorry. But as he saw his brother crawling on his hands and knees, his jaw hanging loose, probably broken, as he heard the strange gurgling sounds coming from his throat, he saw every chance of learning what had happened, every hope of getting Willie to explain, slipping out of his reach. A surge of anger drove him back to Willie Earl.

"Watch it, boy. Watch it." Uncle Dan spoke from the bed as though he were talking to a loonie or something. The cautious voice checked him and he found himself pulling back.

"What in the world? . . ." Aunt Julie stood in the doorway, staring from Willie Earl on the floor to Uncle Dan in his flushed glory struggling to hide the bottle Wade had let drop on the bed.

"Oh no," she cried, as if she couldn't believe what she was seeing. "No, no, no. You ain't fixing to start no stuff like that in here, Wade Williams." She stood strong as a bull, all top-heavy and stern, with him on one side of her and Willie Earl and Uncle Dan on the other. "What you trying to do, boy? Hurry your Uncle Dan off of this earth, much as he thinks of you? Why, I expected more from you than that." She actually meant it. "I'm going to ask you to leave this house and not come back until your Uncle is well and about, or ready for his grave."

ROSA GUY

That was Aunt Julie. She didn't care about Willie Earl and him having a fight. She expected things like that. What burned her was that he went against her word. Aunt Julie never let a body go against her word. Wade waited for Uncle Dan to come to his defense, make his usual protest, but when he looked over Aunt Julie's shoulder into the watered-up old eyes, he knew he was outvoted.

The neon lights had started making Harlem look like a tricky chick ready for play, covering the grit and grime. Even the music was no longer stagnant but flowed in the walk, the movement of the people. Nighttime on Lenox Avenue. Never impressed him. It was like an old overrun film that had started way in his past and extended all the way into his future. It's never going to change.

Locked out. He forced a laugh, and it came strained and harsh even to his ear. Who'd have thought it? He who had been the wheel of his family, didn't have a spoke to stick up for him. Life was just about a bitch, always shedding time-worn experiences for some damn newborn ones. Yet Willie Earl didn't suffer. Willie Earl was the cause of all the happenings, and he didn't suffer.

Wade thought back hard to that last scene, and funny, he saw as clear as anything that Willie Earl was scared as hell about Wade remembering. But the other things that struck him—he got the idea that Willie Earl wasn't too keen about Uncle Dan finding out either. What the hell was that dirty, smooth-talking two-faced, sneaky, mother-for-you up to this time?

"I'm glad I let him have it. He deserved it. I should have taken him apart," he muttered loud to convince himself. But a voice like a hammer kept pounding at him: "Tell Mumma it was his fault. Tell Mumma you took and broke his goddamn jaw because he didn't want to talk. Tell it to her and tell it to Faith." Faith—oh God—Faith. For a fleeting moment he wished praying would do some good. He quickened his steps. It was way past time for Faith to be home from work. She had said she would stop at the house and he had to make it there before any fast-traveling word got to her about what had happened. He had to explain to *her* at least.

"Hey, Wade, honey. How you doing, Baby?" Mabel standing pat

with a brand-new stud. Bending her elbow all afternoon, now she felt no pain. He never turned his head or parted his lips.

He made it to his street and blending himself with the shadows across from his window, looked up studying it. Gladys sat in her usual place taking up space, telling him there were no visitors. Still he kept searching around her form for Faith, in the little light that she allowed. No, no one was there. Where in the hell was she? She had probably gone home first, of course. To Mumma.

Wade tightened himself in the shadows to wait for her, unseen. He sometimes thought Gladys could see right through the dark, the way she sometimes told him what he'd been up to. He gazed longingly toward the street where the better half of his family lived. Maybe he ought to walk up to meet her. Walk up and stand on the corner waiting for her and that way if Mumma came by, he could say hello and start right in explaining to her. Explaining and begging her to believe him for a change. It didn't matter if she lost her temper and took a stick to him, beat him all the way home. Let her do that. Let her do anything except keep him locked out. She had to know how bad it was for him out here. How could she help knowing? She . . .

"Hey, Mister, what you doing standing there scaring people for?" A little boy turning the corner cut his whistle short. Wade's gaze left the window and descended to catch the boy's angry stare. Then for no reason that Wade could explain, he let his hands fall heavily to the back of the boy's thin neck and holding it between his thumb and palm, he twisted it around, thinking how fragile it seemed and realizing that with a mere twist of his wrists . . . He squeezed a little waiting for the fear to climb to the boy's eyes.

"Hey, what the hell gives? Take your goddamn hands off me, yer punk." Caught off guard, Wade laughed a little, releasing him. Spunky kid. He took a quarter out of his pocket and flipped it to him. The kid snatched it out of the air, looking him up and down, and made it without even a "thank you."

He liked a spunky kid. That's the way folks should live, like they had balls. Why in the hell be frightened? He shook his head. He wouldn't have done anything to the kid, just wanted to try him a little. Just the same, he moved out of the shadow. He didn't want to upset another mother's child this day.

ROSA GUY

What was keeping Faith? She must know that he was waiting for her. Or did she think he was sitting it out with Uncle Dan, having a ball? Entering a bar farther down the block, he went into the telephone booth and dialed her number, trying to think up some excuse in case Mumma answered, leaving the door of the booth open, listening to the nothings that everyone at the long, half-empty bar felt they had to shout to each other: "Yeah, he been good to me," one woman who might have been Gladys' twin yelled to another woman who, sprawled over the bar, was not believing a word she said. "That's why I'm good to him, Baby. He buys me anything I want. Believe me when *I* say that I don't want nooooo body who ain't good to me."

One man at the other end of the bar shouted down to someone at the other end, "Sure, Willie Mays could have stolen home. Why he didn't is because of that goddamn manager. Everybody in the world know that he could have got home. What? You a Yankee fan? You goddamn son-of-a-bitch. What in the world I'm doing talking to a damn Yankee fan?"

What did all of that talk mean? Nothing. Empty. Empty like the ringing of the telephone in that empty house and the emptiness in his head. The only thing that made sense was the pounding of his heart, because he still had a body jammed up with things to keep it doing the same things everyone's body did. He rushed out of the booth and into the streets, sure that he had missed Faith on the way and that she was headed straight to Uncle Dan's. Meaning fell away from his life. He had to go somewhere. But where? Home? To Gladys? No, seeing her now might make her the reason for his emptiness and he might forget that she was the result, not the cause.

His gaze caught the glitter of the neon of the Best-Bar-B-Q-in-Harlem joint, and remembering he hadn't eaten all day, he moved toward it. "If Buddy were alive," he thought, "I could go there and kill some time until I was sure Faith would be over. I most likely would run into Tony down there, listening to some of the guys throw the bull. Too bad I had to kill Buddy." Yeah, he half-grieved for the cat. But then you couldn't kill a stud you knew, and not kill that part of your life that he occupied. It was like letting anyone who meant a lot to you just vanish out of your life. Just as he would never stop grieving for Rocky and Gay and Michele,

Michele, Michele. . . . He clenched his fists. "Oh well, c'est la fucking vie." As if his whole goddamn life was one big grief.

He was about to enter the restaurant when Charlie grabbed his arm. "Hey, Wade, that's the way you treat a friend, huh? I knew you when . . ."

"Get away, get away, will ya?" Wade gave the drunk a shove and watched him reel backwards, then right away he was sorry. Here they were, two lockouts together with nothing to bind them but the streets. How did he come about thinking he was so much better? Wade entered the restaurant.

"Hey, Nat," he called, going up to the counter. "See Tony today?"

"Naw. What can I do you for?" Stone-faced like the ages, bald head glistening from the combination of light and grease from the bar-b-q pit, shining as if he were done in ebony.

"One bar-b-q, spaghetti."

"Eat here? Take out?"

"Eat here." Good old Nat. Can't shock him, can't scare him. Been on the same corner for forty years and seen everything that eyes could see. All kinds of men and women doing all kinds of things: he respected money.

Wade sat drowning his spare ribs in O-So-Hot to burn out the last of the hospital garbage, keeping one eye on the door for Faith, reflecting on his shrinking acquaintances in his even faster-shrinking world. People came into the joint and went out and a few more hundreds passed through the door and he still never got an excuse to use the muscles in his face or even in his neck. Funny as hell, where other families had grown, theirs had somehow stagnated. Except for the daughter Willie Earl had given them some seventeen years ago, they had all suffered from locked bowels, so he could only lose and lose and lose. "Won't hardly be no one around for the funeral."

"What will you be doing with yourself now that you are out?" It was as if the sentences going around in his brain since he stepped out of the subway this morning had formed themselves into words, only he hadn't formed them. He looked over his shoulder into the blinking eyes of Professor Jones.

He froze, his forkful of spaghetti suspended, then realizing the spaghetti was slipping and sliding off the fork back into his plate, he lowered his hands, all the while looking into the stud's blinking eyes. Then he felt it coming. Down from the bottom of his toes he felt it coming, bubbling and racing around in his stomach, pushing up through his chest and up his throat and he couldn't stop it: the laughter. It kept coming and coming in waves, and he was bending over, pushing himself away from the table, doubling over, his hands holding his stomach, feeling the straining of his muscles, his face hot and red, his eyes watering.

He wanted to stop but couldn't. Each time he looked up and saw the blinking little man, sober, unaffected by his laughter, it came pushing out again, leaving him weaker and weaker, until he barely had the strength to keep sitting in his chair. He placed his elbows on the table and hid his face in his hands. He felt the shaking of his shoulders, the stone quiet of the room, the question mark of every eye in the joint digging into him. Finally he found the strength to fumble in his back pocket for his handkerchief and applied it to his eyes.

"Hey, Prof, pull up a chair and have a beer."

"Don't mind if I do. Don't mind at all if I do."

Wade didn't know what he might have done in the morning if he had come face to face with the little cat, or whether he would even have come into the restaurant if he had seen him sitting in here; but seeing him at this particular time was just too funny. Funny as hell. As funny as one lockout pushing another lockout in the street because they didn't have the same smell on their breath. It made all life a goddamn joke. He looked across at the little man, chuckling, feeling another wave of hysteria fighting to claim him.

He had met Professor Jones right after he had come from the orphanage. Mumma had put Uncle Dan out of the house because she had caught him giving Wade something to drink, and Uncle Dan had simply disappeared off the face of the earth, and though the whole family searched and searched they couldn't find him.

Then one day coming home from school, Wade had to fight through a crowd of people in front of Sam's barbershop, to get through to his street. They were a laughing, jeering bunch of people, mostly grown-ups, supposedly attending to grown-up business. It might have been a fight between two men, or one of those street-corner speakers with the usual gab of wit and corn that grown-ups never seemed to tire of. He had gone through the crowd and was clear on his way home, when a sudden silence allowed him to hear a voice shout, "Get away, get away. Let me be."

The crowd roared with laughter, but Wade froze. That was his Uncle Dan's voice. Grabbing a stick he found in the street he fought his way back through the tangle of people, ready to beat heads, if beat heads he must. But when he finally pushed through the crowd, he only saw Sam, trying to push back the people, shouting, "Come on, come on, get a move on. Get out of here." No one moved. He looked around and at first didn't see Uncle Dan, until following the gaze of the crowd, he saw a man wrapped around the very top of the big barbershop pole. Staring open mouthed, it took Wade a few moments to realize the man was his uncle. How he got up there turned out to be a mystery never solved, but Wade wasn't thinking of that when he swung around to help Sam take on whoever had chased Uncle Dan up there.

There were no takers and he was at a loss, because no one even looked angry. Everybody just kept looking at Uncle Dan, grinning and laughing and joking as if they were at some sport. Wade eased over to the pole, looking around suspiciously until he was sure that no one was after his uncle. Then he called: "Uncle Dan, come on down, ain't nobody gonna hurt you. I'm here now."

Recognizing his voice but not even looking around, his Uncle called, "Wade, boy, look out. They gonna trample you."

"No they ain't, Uncle Dan. They ain't gonna hurt you and they ain't gonna hurt me. Me and Sam taking care of them for you. Come on down."

"It's them elephants, Wade," Uncle Dan squealed in terror. "Look out for them elephants." The crowd screamed with laughter and Wade got the feeling that all wasn't right with his uncle.

"Ain't no elephants here, Uncle Dan. It's me, Wade. Come on down and let's go home, please."

"Yeah, Dan," Sam tried to grab hold of Uncle Dan's coat tail. "The kid is here to take you home, so come on."

The more Wade pleaded and the more Sam pulled, the tighter Uncle Dan hugged, wrapping his legs around the slippery pole, and the louder the crowd roared. Once it seemed that Sam had succeeded in getting him down, but at the noise from the crowd, Uncle Dan actually slid right up the peppermint stick again.

That was the moment when the little figure, portfolio stuck under his arm, queer little pointed face accusing, eyes blinking from behind his gold-rimmed glasses, stepped out to face the crowd, calling, "Shame! It is to your everlasting shame that you should stand here, joking and laughing at the suffering of a poor sick man instead of trying to help him. I call this a crime against humanity. Suppose it was a member of your family, would you treat him so?"

The laughter diminished to a guilty grin. No one disputed the little man. "Sir," he called up to Uncle Dan. "Sir, I believe everything is all right now; you may come down."

It might have been the sudden silence, or the precise way the little man spoke, but anyway, Uncle Dan opened one eye and saw the little professor and Wade looking up at him, and allowed them to help him down. Then they took him home and helped Aunt Julie put him to bed.

The little squirt had been a welcome addition then, with his sharp features and blinking eyes. Even then, Wade had been the same height as he. Professor Jones strode into their lives, taking over, mainly because he was so upset by the lack of understanding the family showed when he tried to explain Wade's shame in facing the mob.

When they had explained what had happened, the family had cracked up. First Aunt Julie laughed so hard that tears rolled down her cheeks, and when she had enough control of herself, she asked Uncle Dan, who was shivering and feverish, "Dan, Dan, what color were them elephants, huh? What color did you say they were?" Then they had told the rest of the family and before the story had time to fall from their mouths, Willie Earl had doubled up on the floor.

Mumma started off trying to be stern, saying, "I knew that old fool would go off sometime," but then it hit her hard, and she started laughing fit to kill. Even Wade, thinking back, joined in; and Faith too, after she saw Wade laughing. Professor Jones naturally did not understand, but then Professor Jones didn't understand their family.

Everybody laughed and never stopped laughing either. "The old fool had best stay away from that bottle if he knows what's good for him," was the most that any member of the family had said. But at anytime in their lives, through sick spells or worry, all one of them had to say was, "Remember Uncle Dan on that barbershop pole," and the laughter started again. That was their lifetime joke on Uncle Dan.

Only *now* they weren't laughing. No, now they locked him out.

7

Wade wiped his eyes and stuffed his handkerchief back into his pocket, feeling the hysteria subside. He looked across at the little man, studying him, glad in a way that he was there. His activities of the day weighed like stone on his shoulders and he was more than a little tired of the circles his mind had been making. At any rate, he needed a chance to exercise his face muscles.

"Fancy seeing you, Wade."

"Yeah, a big surprise. Bet you're tickled to death."

"No, not at all. To be perfectly frank, I must say I am outraged, but at least it is interesting."

"What, my face?"

"No, your case."

"Oh, still interested in my case?"

Professor Jones leaned forward, his bright eyes blinking, his little pointed face shining under the assault of the heat and the pressure of his grey wool suit. Probably the only suit he had, the professor with his important portfolio under his arm. "Yes, yes, I'll always be. You remember how bitterly I fought to try to get you a decent education?"

Wade smiled. How could he forget?

"It is too bad that after all of my efforts on your behalf, you ended by dropping out of school."

Wade looked up. "I didn't drop out, I graduated."

"At fourteen? As far as I am concerned, *that* was dropping out. And even at that it would not have been so criminal, if you had not been such a brilliant child. You were brilliant. One of the most brilliant children I have ever known." The professor took off his eyeglasses, took his handkerchief out of his pocket, polished the lenses, put them back on and blinked at Wade. "That, my dear Wade, was when the crime against you reached its zenith."

Wade laughed. He liked to hear the professor talk that talk. Always twisting things around so that he could unravel it for people. Here were folks jumping clear out of their skins when they saw him coming and Professor Jones saying the crime was against him. But that's the way Prof was. Funny how one little man not only could start but keep things moving, once he became interested. Professor Jones, once he had become interested in Wade, became a steady visitor to their house—and Mumma was happy to have another ear to unload her troubles into, another ear to tell about her unhappy life since the work of the devil had forced her to come up North. Sometimes it seemed that Mumma thought she'd had an ideal life down South; at least she claimed to, when she wasn't going into detail about how she first came down with her arthritis. Professor Jones listened to her tales sympathetically as if it was the first time he'd heard such tales, then went right into helping them.

First he went to the home-relief bureau to demand on what basis they had cut off a poor woman's relief, because of a son who still had many years to go before he came of age. The relief people put up a fight but not a very big one, when they realized that they didn't have an ordinary colored man to deal with. The family was promptly reinstated. Things looked brighter for them. Uncle Dan got better and promised everyone including the good Lord Jesus, someone he had never shown much use for, that he would behave himself forever more. But Professor Jones did not stop there. He started going to school, digging into Wade's records past and present, and came up with a startling revelation: Wade was a genius.

He was almost eleven, almost finished with his first year high school and nobody had ever bothered to find out that he was smart and here he was a little genius. Sure, it had been generally agreed that he had a good mind, that he remembered things even about the South that the two older children, scratch their heads as much as they wanted, could never remember. Then of course there were always the report cards with high grades that Mumma signed as a matter of routine and that he took back to school. He had been skipped and had been placed in special classes and skipped again and Mumma didn't even know enough to pay that any attention. But then Mumma hadn't gone to school a day in her life, and everything seemed to her the way it should be, as long as he didn't cause the teacher any worry.

Mumma did everything she could at home for them. She washed and ironed, sent them to school clean and starched, kept house as clean as she could, and since cleanliness was next to godliness, she was doing her bit. Plus that, she made them pray every night, even though she couldn't make them behave if she took them to church, and that was an accomplishment with Big Willie's breed. She realized, of course, that Wade had whizzed past Faith in school, but that was, as she put it, because Faith was slow, and probably would drop out like Willie Earl by-and-by.

Uncle Dan was different. He pressed Wade to work hard so that he might finish. When Uncle Dan said "finish" he meant exactly that. Uncle Dan was lonely. His old buddies didn't fill the bill any more. Willie Earl, though not in school, was just too busy with *outside* people. Uncle Dan had hopes that when Wade finished, Wade would keep him company. That was one reason. The other was much simpler: Wade wanted to finish so that he could hang out with Willie Earl and his friends.

Wade never remembered the time when Willie Earl went to school regularly. Willie was in and out of school, just as he was in and out of jobs, until he got tall enough to simply quit outright.

With Wade it had been different. He started off growing slowly, with a chubby babyish look about him that could be spotted a mile away by a truant officer, and because of this, Willie Earl's friends refused to let him tag along with him. In school he used to look out of the window and see them playing stick ball in the streets, yelling and shouting so that the feeling of the game crept into the classroom. It used to get to him, this sitting in the class not being able to play with them, so he decided he had to hurry and come out of school in such a way that no one could bother him. Then suddenly to hear he was a genius!

This was when he discovered Rocky. Rocky—otherwise known as Clovis Rockford, Jr. He had really known him a long time. They had been in the same class all through junior high school, skipping and going to special classes together, saying hello and smiling at each other, but Wade had never really dug him. Now, however, with the new realization of himself he began to study the brilliant little cat.

Rocky had always known he was a genius and it was sure that his folks knew it too. The teachers certainly did. Rocky was the type of kid whom teachers usually made a lot of—that is, Wade supposed, if there were no white children with blond hair and blue eyes about. He was pretty, almost like a girl, clean; not that he was any cleaner than Wade— Mumma sent Wade to school stiff with starch. And that was it. Even without the starchy look, Rocky's clothes fitted better. He never had his hair simply combed; his was carefully combed and parted, and though his was much softer than Wade's, it remained combed and parted all day.

He didn't take lunch in school like most of the other kids, but went home afternoons, something that impressed Wade as did the book bag he carried with his name engraved in gold. Rocky was tiny with large brown eyes that provoked a person by their straight, honest stare, and by their long lashes that made him resemble a girl. His rimless glasses added a look of high intelligence.

He never used slang, for he had a facility with words that made all the other kids tongue-tied by comparison; yet he never jumped up shouting when he knew a question, as did the other kids, but stood when called, taking his time and usually starting with, "Eh, ehm, well you see," or, "you know of course . . . ?"

At home they must have schooled him in politics because he knew what was happening in a world that the other kids never heard of. Sometimes, he even went so far as to challenge the teachers on things they said, causing a good many red faces in classrooms, yet they loved him and it was no secret that Clovis Rockford would go far.

It pleased Wade no end when Professor Jones poked around and found that he was in the same league as the little wizard. It gave him all kinds of respect for himself. It got him trying to control his heavy tongue when answering questions, so that he might be heard loud and clear, instead of in his usual mumble. He enjoyed giving a correct answer in order to smile back to Rocky's superior smile. Rocky was like that, superior but not resentful of competition. But then he could afford to be superior, because no matter how smart Wade appeared in class, it was a cinch that he did not know a thing about politics.

Yet it is strange, when a person gets to know himself and to have confidence, the things he can do. Wade found out he was smarter than ordinary and suddenly the world opened up for him like a flower and he drew from it like a bee. It was sweet. That's why he figured it should have been for the better—Professor Jones coming into his life, nosing around. But things are never what they seem.

He went to a concert with Professor Jones one day and suddenly realized that he dug music. More than that, he began picking out a tune on the piano in the school, the music teacher heard, and said he had an ear for music. Professor went right away to arrange for a school where the first few lessons were free. Sure enough, he picked it up so easily and learned so fast that his music teacher held her breath when he came around, and spoke to Professor Jones about him in that awed tone reserved for the dead and the great.

Uncle Dan was mighty proud of him but Mumma just went around as if nothing revolutionary were happening. And when Wade said to her one day, "You know, Mumma, we got to get a piano now," she simply raised her eyebrows, twisted her mouth and pretended he hadn't said a word.

But the next day when Uncle Dan stopped by the house, Mumma said to him, "You know, Dan, I'm going to have to stop that professor from coming around here."

"What you talking about, woman?" Uncle Dan answered. "As much as that man done for you and Wade? You must be out of your mind."

"Did he do so much? Well now, I don't know about that. Do you know what Wade said to me yesterday?"

"What?"

"He asked *me* to buy a piano. Just as simple as though he done took leave of his senses. You know that man just about turned his head around, don't you? Where, in all your borned days, have you heard talk like that?"

"Well now—I—I . . ." Uncle Dan seemed to be searching like the devil to remember where he had heard that kind of talk. "Well now, Evelyn, you know you never can tell what will happen. I guess when you were a lil' girl working down there in them cotton fields you'd never have thought you'd find yourself up North now, did you? Ha, ha, see, anything can happen."

It hurt Wade to his heart to hear Mumma talking like that, and he decided to show her a thing or two. So that evening he did not eat his dinner.

"Don't take on so, Wade," Faith urged. "Go on and eat your food." Then she added in a spiteful voice, "Uncle Dan will think of something."

"Don't worry about him," Mumma snapped. She was always jealous of Faith's feeling for Uncle Dan. "He'll eat when he gets hungry; he ain't got nothing but belly."

That really threw Wade in a rage, the first anger he ever had against Mumma. He left the table, refusing to eat all that night, just to make her suffer. He didn't know how much good it did, because the next week was time for the first payment on his lessons and when he asked her for the money, she looked at him hard and asked, "Where we going get it from?"

Everything that happened around that time seemed to pull Faith and Wade more into one corner with Uncle Dan, and turned Mumma solid and blind toward Willie Earl. Funny, because up to that time, they had never asked Mumma for much: Ten cents to go to a movie, or sometimes she might give them a few pennies to buy candy, that was all. Poverty had set their needs to the limits of the house. His new needs upset the balance.

He was conscious as hell about it too, never wanting to push his demands, knowing that with every new need, he wrapped her sentiments more firmly around Willie Earl and the lousy couple of dollars Willie threw her way every week. He didn't want to lose her. He loved her.

The music teacher, as much as she thought of Wade, lost some of her warmth when she realized that he couldn't pay and probably never would be able to. She did not ask him to stop coming but one day Wade overheard her telling Professor Jones that she had to eat too. He decided not to take up any more of her time. He might have heard the message wrong, because she sent the professor to beg him to come back every week for months. Maybe it was Big Willie's pride hard inside him, but he refused. It did not seem right, somehow, for a stranger to do more for him than his own mother.

Professor Jones was downright sad about it. He had already pictured Wade as some great virtuoso on the world stage. Nor would Mumma allow Professor Jones to discuss it. She had already begun putting little ice blocks in his way: "You better get away from here, Professor Jones, with your talk about money, money, money. People ain't got no right to big ideas if they ain't got no money to back it up with. Dollar heads and penny pockets is what starts kids on the wrong foot."

Professor Jones might have paid the money, he was that upset. But Professor Jones never had money.

Funny. Wade never bothered to wonder until right now how Professor Jones ate, he who was always so busy fighting causes and sticking his nose into everybody else's business. Wade looked up from his plate to the Professor sitting across from him in a shield of silence, just studying him. "Have something to eat, Prof?"

"No, no, the beer will be enough, thank you."

Wade opened his mouth to tell him that he looked as though he could use some food, but changed his mind. He had once heard a big corn-fed woman saying to Professor Jones on the street, "Professor, you sure is puny, I got a good mind to take you home and fatten you up a bit."

"Madame," Professor Jones drew himself up to his full height. "If you took care of the nourishment of your head as you do of your gut, you'd be surprised at the growth of my significance in your eyes." With those words, he walked away, leaving her shaking her head, not knowing whether he had made a joke with or at her.

Wade looked back to his food, trying to keep up the pretense of eating.

He had turned to sculpture next. Professor Jones introduced him to an arts-and-crafts class meeting afternoons in a church in upper Harlem. It was free, so no one objected. They started off learning on soap. From that moment every piece of soap in his hands became an art object: A tree, a statue, an animal.

Wade never remembered what Mumma had used to wash their clothes and dishes with before his little soap animals came into the house, because suddenly she ran out of soap at the same time she ran out of her last penny and his work was so convenient. They all went, one after one, except for a few pieces that he won prizes for in an art exhibit at the church.

Yet he believed in his genius. He realized it was in him, like some giant force, pushing him toward doing something, anything, a million things at the same time. He discovered the library and began reading every book he laid his hands on, his mind, making up for lost years, soaking up all subjects like a sponge: books on flowers, trees, fish, beasts, the stars, the moon, birds. He read philosophies, psychologists—Freud, Jung, Aristotle, Spinoza, you name it. He read a lot but he had no one to discuss it with, until he grew friendly with little Clovis Rockford, Jr.

They met by accident one day at the library and after their first long talk, naturally fell into meeting there every week. They discussed a variety of subjects first in whispers, but sometimes, carried away by their enthusiasm, raising their voices, to be stopped by the disapproving stare of the librarian, giggling the way kids of eleven sometimes do.

Some afternoons, Rocky would treat Wade to hot dogs with free root beer. Then they would walk around and around the same blocks, prolonging the time they spent together. Other times they went to the park across the street from the library and sat on the grass or lay on their backs looking at the sky, or sat on the benches as it grew colder, even to freezing, their hands dug deep into their pockets, their shoulders hunched, covering their ears, talking, talking, always talking.

Wade was happy. There was something about Rocky that touched him more deeply than the sharpness of his mind. Perhaps it was his smallness, his delicacy, that made Wade feel clumsy and overgrown and at the same time protective. Sometimes in the middle of a discussion Rocky might pause and gaze earnestly into Wade's eyes, then suddenly lower his long lashes, making Wade stifle the desire to take him and crush him to his chest.

But there was also the sharpness of his mind.

From the time Rocky's eyes opened as a baby, his parents must have realized his talents and guided his life, for it seemed to Wade that Rocky knew everything and had been everywhere. He had been to all of the movies downtown. Wade had been only to the few around the neighborhood. Though Rocky had been born in Harlem, he had visited Boston, Philadelphia, Baltimore, Chicago, New Jersey. In his conversation he even talked of visiting places like Europe, where his father, who was a lawyer, had been several times. Wade, who had hardly ever been out of Harlem since he had first come, could not even start to think of what another country might look like.

One day, an unusually warm day for early fall, Rocky and Wade were sitting in Mount Morris Park talking, when suddenly Rocky silenced Wade by raising his hand. "Look, Wade," he whispered. "A blue jay." He pointed to a bird pecking at the ground not too far from them. "What do you think it is doing here at this time of the year? Do you suppose that something is wrong?" He left Wade's side and tip-toed quietly toward the bird, hoping to catch it unaware. But as the bird sensed his approach, it flew out of his way. In an instant it was soaring into the distance, becoming a dot on the horizon.

Rocky gazed after the bird sadly. "Wouldn't you like to be a bird, Wade? Wouldn't you like to be free and go wherever you want to, whenever you want to without having to pay any money?"

Wade nodded, feeling for the first time his complete inadequacy, his immobility.

After a few moments Rocky shrugged and sat back next to Wade. "But anyhow, they aren't really all that free," he said. Wade had not remembered ever hearing Rocky sound bitter before. "They are guided completely by instinct." Then as though regretting his moment of pettiness he added, "But like Mother says, their instincts are so much purer and nobler than man's reason."

For the smallest instant Wade had a vision of birds flying in the clearness of the sunlit sky, while hundreds of men in dark clothes, exchanging suspicious glances, huddled beneath them on the earth in abject misery.

They never visited each other's homes, for different reasons: Rocky was very selfish and even a little jealous. Once they became friends he did not want to share Wade, not even with his family. He disliked the way they brought their opinions into subjects that they were not fully equipped to discuss, he said, and the way they insisted on dominating a discussion because of the advantage of age.

For Wade, bringing Rocky home was entirely out of the question. Even now, Mumma had started hinting that he spent too much time in the library, that he ought to be spending some time and effort in getting a little job after school instead of wasting it on those stupid books. After all, Willie Earl had been doing a little something to help out when he was Wade's age. If it wasn't for that old fool of a professor . . . And so on.

The thought of having Rocky hear Mumma call books "stupid" embarrassed Wade to the point where some nights he woke up with his face burning. Not that he blamed Mumma. He never blamed Mumma for anything. He knew that it never did cross the line with her that there was more to people than white people and black people, good people and bad people. Her biggest worry had always been that her children should grow up to be good, decent, hard-working folks, like most all other folks, and keep out of trouble. And all of a sudden, here she was stuck with a little genius on her hands.

It hadn't worried Wade. The way he figured, Mumma had to get used to the idea one day. She might have, too, except that the line between for-better and for-worse could be so thin.

8

"Why do you think they let you out, Wade?"

Wade had been staring into his plate, hardly eating, but at the professor's words, he started shoveling forkfuls of food into his mouth, avoiding the little man's stare that suddenly felt like pinpricks. "Or have you given it a thought?"

"Faith didn't press charges."

"No, Wade," Professor Jones shook his head. "It's because they don't care."

"Don't go on any damn crusading binge over me."

"You have killed a man and you almost killed a woman with your bare hands—and they let you out. Why?"

"They got laws, you know. . . ."

"It's because they don't care. You were in the hospital?"

"Yeah."

"And you think you are really all right?"

"I'm out here, ain't I?"

"But do *you* think you are all right?" Wade thought of the hospital room, the silent moving figures of the male nurses, then he thought of the disappointment aching like a tooth way down inside.

"Wade, what *are* you going to do, now that you are out?"

The professor's insistent questions got to him. He felt the sweat coming out on the back of his neck.

"Same thing I been doing," he leered. Professor Jones pushed his face halfway across the table, forcing Wade to look into his blinking eyes, creating a silence for his words to re-echo. "Yeah, yeah, that's what I said. I'm the whiz kid, remember. The little genius. I'll be doing something. Don't you worry." He tore a piece of meat from a rib with his teeth. This nosey punk professor was sitting on borrowed time as it was. It was only a question of time before someone took a swatter to him.

"That's what I'm afraid of, Wade. That's exactly what I'm afraid of."

Wade pushed his plate back and glared into Professor Jones' eyes. "You talk like I never done nothing. You know as well as I do that when I finished school I went right into taking care of my family."

"That was years ago, and at the time, no one can deny that you tried."

"Try, hell. I did. From the time I graduated school, Faith never wanted for nothing. You *know* that. That's what pisses me off. Here I come out this morning and a bunch of studs shy away from me like I killed her or something. Everybody knows I ain't never hurt one hair of my sister's head."

"You did that time, Wade."

"I was going after Willie Earl."

"That's not the way he told it."

"Who, Willie Earl?"

"Precisely."

"You mean he's been shooting off his mouth? Did he tell you how it happened?"

"He told how it happened. He said you had been drinking when you had no business to, that you suddenly snapped." Professor Jones snapped his fingers. "Just like that. He said you took complete leave of your senses and for no apparent reason you attacked your sister. Of course that leaves quite a bit to be explained."

"Like what?"

"Well, for instance, how could he leave her without assistance, and run out into the streets for help? That certainly should be explained. You might have killed her."

Why hadn't Mumma thought about that? Seems as though she would have. "I was going up side of Faith's head and he never tried to stop me? Why?" Willie Earl was a cheap, sneaky son-of-a-bitch, but he went in more for pulling and stretching and reshaping the truth than he went in for outright lying. Why hadn't Mumma got it out of him—or Faith? Wade realized that he was bending the fork in his hand, that he had bent it almost into a circle. He threw it from him. "Honest, Professor, that ain't the way it happened. I was going after Willie Earl. Faith said so herself. I wasn't going after her."

Professor Jones dismissed that with a wave of his hand.

"But you got her, Wade. *You got her.* One month in a hospital for a beating that you got in the way of, that's quite a thing." Wade had no answers. He didn't like it worth a damn. "Yes, yes, Wade, I saw when the crime against you turned and became a crime against the whole community. Their creation is completed, Wade. You are a monster."

Wade found himself staring in amazement into Professor Jones' blinking eyes. Was this cat serious? He tried to picture how he looked to the little stud sitting there, to the shying cats on the street. He saw himself with horns sticking out of his head, and big grinning teeth. Then he thought of Uncle Dan and his watered-up old eyes. Did he look like a monster to him too? He gave a short bitter laugh.

"And just as I fought for your brilliance to be channeled into some purposeful direction is the way I'll fight to contain you. I want you to be the first to know that I am going to register my protest that you are being allowed to walk the streets of Harlem with good responsible people."

Wade let his eyes go cold and expressionless. He stared hard at Professor Jones, biting at the sneer pulling up his lip. Most people didn't take this little cat seriously; some tried to pretend that he did not exist. Not Wade, though. He could see Professor Jones now, standing on street corners, yelling himself hoarse, ringing bells and getting petitions signed at all hours of the night; just to get him off the streets. Old Professor Jones had done it *for* him. Professor Jones had signed petitions, rung bells, fought and fought and fought *for* him. He knew damn well Professor Jones would do it *against* him. . . .

Professor Jones had been on the scene when it came to choosing their high schools and he hadn't been satisfied with the list of schools that had been given them. None of the schools on that list, he said, was suited for two brilliant students who had finished their first year of high school at age eleven. Those schools were graveyards for ideas and ambitions. Oh, he carried on in such a way that Mumma finally gave her permission for him to ask that Wade be sent to a decent school.

He was told that the schools on the list were the only ones available because they were the schools for the district. Professor Jones went to the Board of Education, saying that he did not accept the zoning laws because all of the schools required travel from home and carfare— taking it, as far as he was concerned, out of the district. He hoped they could seek admittance in one of the schools *he* had listed as acceptable, schools that were not too far, and at the same time were within the same fare zone. He was turned down.

Wade had never known anyone to work so hard as the professor. From morning to night he went around ringing doorbells, getting signatures on petitions to take down to the Board of Education, organizing parents to form groups to go down to the board at regular intervals through the day to protest. He went to newspaper offices demanding coverage; all this he did by himself.

He worked hard for the small returns. From the hundreds of people willing to sign the petitions, only twelve were persuaded to go down to protest. But Professor Jones had the answer for that: he staggered them in groups of three, four times the first day, then asked them to change their hair styles and switched the groups around to four, three times the next day, saying that it was all the same to white folks, all colored people looked alike, that they would never know the difference. He was right.

Then Professor Jones took Rocky and Wade and three other boys from other schools around Harlem to the school of his choice, demanding that they be registered. He was politely refused. "Well," he said to the registrar. "You will have us on your hands until the head of this school and the head of the Board of Education come to their senses." They shrugged him off as they might have done an insane man, saying, "Have it your way, sir."

The five of them, brushed and shining in their Sunday best, "a credit to their race," began sitting in the hall outside of the registrar's office every day, until one day they came and the seats were missing. Then they stood in the hall on weary legs, over one week, while the little protest groups made their pilgrimage back and forth to the Board of Education.

But Wade had so much confidence in Professor Jones that already he imagined himself and Rocky sitting in classes, answering questions that spiteful teachers who did not want them around were firing at them, while the white children looked at them, and especially Rocky, in open-mouthed wonder.

On Wednesday of the second week an article in one of the newspapers reported that the Board of Education was considering admitting a few Negro children of exceptional ability and exceptional talent to high school. It was hoped they would be a credit to the school where they applied. That evening Professor Jones took them to an ice-cream parlor to celebrate. Wade and Rocky looked at the little man sitting at the counter, both of them caught in the wonder of his greatness. There was nothing he could not do. Wade filled up with such overwhelming happiness that he wanted to cry. Here he had two friends he never realized he needed, and life had opened up with an importance he'd never known existed. Everything had changed and all because of Uncle Dan on that barbershop pole.

(Then why hadn't it been for the better? Wade looked across at the professor and laughed bitterly into his face.)

The next day, Thursday, bright and early with their bright shining faces they were back at the school. Professor Jones had not received official notification, but he went right into the office and demanded to register. As it turned out, the office had not received word either, although it was apparent that they had read the notice. "Why don't you wait, Mr. Jones? I'm quite sure that it will come any moment now."

They all were mighty pleased by the change in tone. The registrar even made an effort to get seats, but Professor Jones, confident now, said, "Oh, never mind, we'll wait outside if it's all the same to you." Guess he wanted to relax his face with a grin, or to give the kids room to slap themselves on the back, or to jump up with joy.

But as they stepped outside, a group of about fifty people approached them. They were all grown-ups, all white, and all of them carried signs that read: "Go back to Harlem" "Stay where you belong" "Our schools aren't equipped with cages, go back to your jungle," and all of them were calling and jeering.

The crowd encircled them as they stood grounded by surprise, and Wade instinctively put his arm around Rocky's shoulders, ready to give his life to defend him if the need came. Professor Jones kept calm, making them stand in an orderly line in which he stood at the head, straight as a rod, behind his glasses.

The police came at the end of two hours to break up the line, and all that time the kids stood as though in a trance staring at the back of Professor Jones' head.

They might have made a run for the subway after the police came, but Professor Jones went right back into the school to demand that they register. Again the official notice had not come.

If Professor Jones had been frightened by the mob that surrounded them and held them prisoners for two hours, he certainly did not show it in his little pointed face and blinking eyes. All of the children, though, were weak with fear. All, that is, except Wade, who—more than frightened—was disturbed. Not because of the placards, though God knows they were bad enough, but because the people involved were grown-ups. They were grown people who shouted and called names to five little colored children, dressed up in their Sunday best.

Up until that time there existed two worlds, the grown-up world and the children's world: The children's made up of those who did the listening; and the grown-ups, of those who did the telling. Sure there was a black world and a white world, but you sort of confined yourself to hating the children your age. You poked this boy in the nose, or dreamed of giving that one a black eye. If children went out of their territory, it was the white kids they looked for. Big folks were something you respected. As, he knew if need be, he had to fight to the death for Mumma. He knew he was stronger than she was, but when she got that strap out, he just wiped his mouth dry and shut up. He might be as right as anything and she, as wrong as sin.

It disturbed the hell out of him to have a bunch of grown-ups, and peck-o-woods at that, invading his children's world, and the most respectful part of it. The first thing Big Willie had taught him in his life was that he had a name—Wade—and anybody who called him out of it was due for an ass beating; and he had learned that lesson well.

Maybe if he'd had that broad background that Rocky had, he might have dug what was happening; but he hadn't been two minutes out of the street. The things they had been shouting got all the way to the very middle of him. It was as though he were about to lose something he'd never had: It was Uncle Dan slowing down on his drinking and standing a little taller. It was Mumma staying out of church one night, so that she could go down to the Board of Education early the next morning. It was Willie Earl, standing sheepishly, rubbing the back of his head and looking at him with that new look of respect, wondering if he had done right in not taking school more seriously. It was Faith staying up half the night, studying until her brain was about to burst. It was them standing on the brink of a new kind of life. He never thought out what kind, but it was new.

All this didn't come to him then, it was just the feeling, a sense of doom, a trickle of knowledge that he was helpless, helpless as hell, to hold onto something that he wanted desperately. Years later, during the invasion of Normandy while his comrades were falling around him like stones, it became as clear as anything, making him pause with his rifle leveled at the head of a clean, baby-faced young stud, before he pulled the trigger and blew his brains to bits.

But that evening, years ago, more distressed than he had ever been in his life, he went to Mumma. "Mumma, you got to come out with us tomorrow. All of the white kids' folks, who don't want us to get into that school came out today, and Mumma, you ought to hear the things they called us."

"Look, Wade," Mumma answered, "when white folks get it in their heads that they don't want a black man to do something, ain't no use bucking them, because they do nothing but cause trouble. I know them folks. They ain't decent. They ain't God-abiding. They'll kill you as dead as you going to die, and ain't nobody gonna touch them. Ain't nobody going to touch them, you hear?

"Ain't never a white man in this country been killed for killing a black one, remember that. When that old fool of a professor come here and tell me that they went and changed the laws for you, I was bout ready to laugh right in his face. They ain't changing the laws for you or nobody that looks like you. And if they ever do, it will be if they can profit by it, and you can bet your last penny they will change it back when it suits them. It's a good thing we have the scriptures to tell us different, or else, I do declare, we'd think they was God."

"You got to come, Mumma," he insisted stubbornly. "Those white kids' folks are out there, ready to kill for them—and we—we ain't got nobody."

"Just don't go back," Mumma shouted. "Don't go following after that half-crazy fool. He ain't got the sense he was borned with. All he knows is sticking his nose in people's business. He been up North grinning in them hypocritical white folks' faces for too long. He done forgot what white folks is really like."

"I ain't letting Professor Jones down, Ma. I ain't letting him down." But it was more than that. Something had happened to him out there that was bigger than Mumma or his whole family. Even if all the things she said about white folks and the law were true, he knew he'd be out there, if he had to go all by himself, even without the professor.

Mumma looked at him and knew there was nothing she could say to change him. It was the first time in their lives, but she took it. "Well, go ahead if you want. But don't expect me to be out there with you."

"You got to go, Mumma," Faith, who had been listening to them over her homework, put in, quiet but firm. "You ain't going to let Wade go out there without *his* mother."

"What you talking about, girl? You know I'm here sick with my knees all swollen from listening to that old fool, and getting out of my bed to go down to that damn Board of Education even against my better judgment. No, I ain't going nowhere, I'm too sick."

"You'll *be* sick the rest of your life, Mumma, and staying in bed tomorrow ain't going to make the difference."

Mumma leaned up on her elbow to take a good look at Faith, and then she looked at Wade again. It was as though she saw two people she had never seen before. She lay back and stared at the ceiling. He ran out to get Uncle Dan.

They were there the next day, Mumma and Uncle Dan, and Rocky had brought his mother. Rocky's mother was pretty and young, full of the kind of life and vitality that light up a face like a lamp from inside.

Wade thought of the frightened Rocky the day before. He knew that, if the same conversation that had taken place in his house had taken place in Rocky's house, it was Rocky's mother who would have insisted that they be out here today. He felt an instant pity for Mumma and Uncle Dan—not shame or anything like that, but a sudden though short-lived awareness that Rocky's mother *was,* and Mumma and Uncle Dan *had been.*

It became even clearer when Mumma took one look at the white protectors of their children's virtue—who had grown to double the number of the day before and twice as loud—and turned her crucified gaze, a gaze that he refused to meet, upon him. Uncle Dan too, after one look at what he had allowed himself to be dragged into, got his funny, where-is-that-bottle look on his face. Oh, he was going to stick it out with Big Willie's kid all right, but it sure would be a hell of a lot easier with a couple of drinks.

Two of the other kids had dropped out, but there was one who came without his parents. At the time, Wade was too busy being disturbed to take notice; but years later, he wondered about that kid, wishing he had known his name, so he could have put it in a special place in his mind as the bravest one of them out there.

They marched into the school behind the professor, Wade keeping his eyes fixed on the back of the high proud head, right up to the registrar's office. The woman was apologetic, red-faced and stammering.

"I am sorry, Mr. Jones. It seems as though there has been some mistake. There has been no such directive released by the Board of Education. It—it might have been an error on the part of the newspaper. . . ."

"Error," Mrs. Rockford snapped. "No, there was no error. I called the paper to confirm it. What you are trying to say is that either this school or that noble body, the Board of Education, has been intimidated by those morons standing out there."

"Now, Miss—Miss . . ." The face had become redder but the apology had grown cold.

"Don't 'Miss' me. I am *Mrs.* and don't you forget it. And yes, I said 'morons' and that is exactly what I mean. They have to be imbeciles to stand out there threatening the very lives of innocent children who are only trying to get a decent education."

"Madam, I must ask you to leave. I cannot stand for this sort of conduct in this school."

"I will not leave."

"Then I will be forced to call the police."

"No, you will not call the police, at least until I have finished what I have to say." Mrs. Rockford pushed her face up to the woman's and the woman just stood there. Funny, too, because the weight of the people outside pressed like a dead weight on Wade's thinking.

"Over half of those people out there are the descendants of

jailbirds, drunks, thieves, the scum of Europe, who came here, stole the land from the Indians, and never in their lives learned what it is to live with other people. And do *you* know why?" Mrs. Rockford was sweating to the tip of her tiny pointed nose. "Because they never have been able to raise themselves up out of the scum and learn simple human decency."

"Well, you certainly said all you can . . ."

"I have only begun. . . ."

"We certainly will not allow you people to come . . ."

"*You* people," Mrs. Rockford screeched. "Look at this boy." She grabbed Wade unexpectedly and pushed him up to the woman. "This boy could not be the color he is if he did not have some of your blood in his veins. And that more than anything shows the depths of your insanity. Your sickness. You are refusing education to your children. Your own offspring. Your children's children. You deny them the right to find the humanity that you never had.

"It is your blood, forgotten and neglected, spewed over the ghettos and slums of this country that have it so diseased, so corrupted." She stalked out, Professor Jones keeping up with her, and the children, even if they had no understanding of all she said, marching right behind, caught up in her anger.

At the door Wade turned to see Mumma and Uncle Dan exchange glances, shrug hopelessly, then hesitatingly follow. It struck him sharply how much Uncle Dan and Mumma resembled each other even though to him they had always seemed so different.

What happened afterward would always be a mass of confusion to Wade. He had no sooner stepped out of the door and started down the path leading to the street than a group of parents began a dash for the school. No one ever found out why. It might have been that, when they saw Professor Jones and Mrs. Rockford marching out of the building, they believed some of the nonsense they had been carrying around on their placards, and got the bright idea that the two might have been in the school butchering their children. But whatever the reason, the surge of people blocked Mumma's and Uncle Dan's exit from the school.

For one terrified moment, Wade saw the lone boy, caught in the midst of the crush of people before Mrs. Rockford reached out and pulled him to her, holding him in one arm and Rocky in the other as she flattened herself against the railing. Then the crowd rushing past him, blocking his view, pinning him against the iron gate, away from his friends.

Frightened, Wade stood holding fast to the gate, waiting for the stampede to end, wondering if he dared chance breaking through the crowd to join his group. Suddenly he heard a woman's voice directly above him: "Why the hell don't you niggers stay where you belong?"

He looked up and saw this woman, her dark eyes blazing right into his face. A crowd locked around her, encouraging her, waiting to hear what this little black boy could possibly say, realizing that he was too scared to say anything, do anything except be a butt for their anger. "We don't want you sons-of-bitches stinking up our schools. We don't go where you are. Why the hell do you want to come around us?"

Wade's fright did a somersault and became the wildest anger in the blinking of an eye. Without even thinking, he let go a mouthful of spit right in the staring dark-brown eyes.

Surprised silence overpowered the crowd as the woman struggled to realize what had happened to her. Then she must have gone stone out of her mind, because she hit him. Full across his face she hit him.

All his anger and hurt of the past few days exploded, destroying the last bit of respect for white parenthood. For the first time in his life he reached out for a grown person. He grabbed her, knowing he had to kill her; knowing he could never rest until he'd killed her. She would never see *him* running. He was a genius, that's what he was, goddamit, and worth more than a mouthful of spit in any white woman's eye.

He had pulled her to the ground when Professor Jones fought through the crowd and grabbed him. But Wade threw aside the little man as though he were a leaf, and started for the woman again. Professor Jones jumped onto his back but couldn't stop him. He was giving the professor a free piggie-back ride when a policeman rushed up. Together they tried dragging him away but Wade broke away from them, rushing to the frightened woman. It wasn't until a second policeman ran up that they managed to get him, fighting and strug-gling, into a waiting patrol car. He remembered banging on the window of the car as it drove away, not seeing Mumma or Uncle Dan or any of the people who had been with him. He saw only the face of the woman, standing out as if she had no body, big as though blown up out of pro-portion, with his spit blurring her hate-filled eyes and running down her distorted red face.

That was his first black-out. It was his first and it was as complete as any of the other black-outs that followed. Later they told him that Mumma had been there crying for his release, that Mrs. Rockford had raised some more hell about it, and that Professor Jones had threatened them for it. But he heard nothing, knew nothing, up to the time when he found himself clutching some bars, and looking around, saw that he was in jail. It was a smaller jail than most because it was stuck all the way up in the Bronx, and they probably never used it except for an occasional drunk, but it was a jail nonetheless.

He might have been standing there silently until he came to himself, but it didn't seem likely from the soreness of his eyes, the hoarse-ness of his throat, and the stiff, almost paralyzed state of his fingers as he released the bars. His coat was torn, his socks had left the protection of his knickers and had curled around his ankles, his legs were scratched and dirty with hardened blood. He lowered himself onto the hard spring that was meant to serve as a bed, and listened to the small talk of the policemen in the next room, the ring of the telephone, the laughter, the sounds that told of the passing of time into night and the probability that he had to sleep here, miles and miles from home.

He woke early the next morning, waiting for Professor Jones. That was the one person in all the world he knew he could depend on. Mumma and Uncle Dan might come too, but there was nothing they could do for him. Life had kept them too near to nothing.

Funny how he saw so clearly that morning, when his eleven years and being Negro and alone made him feel like a speck of dust that could be flicked out of existence and forgotten. He saw it, and was happy that the professor was nosey and made a lot of noise.

He heard someone ask, "Hey, that puny guy come in yet?"

"Naw, but you can bet he'll be here. He's one of those guys always looking for trouble."

"What do you think they'll do with the kid?"

"Dunno, send him over to Juvenile, or let him go home."

"What? Let him go home? Mrs. Emerson will go out of her mind."

"But I hear she hit the kid first."

"Makes no difference, did you see the way the kid went for her? Think maybe he's a psycho or something?"

"Beats me."

They spoke in such a detached way, it was evident they were really not interested in what happened to him. Wade, listening, felt his insignificance even more deeply. He kept telling himself, "I'm Wade Williams. I'm a genius. Wait until Professor Jones comes; he'll show 'em."

Silence, coming in large slices, made his waiting unbearable. Then he could only strain his ears to catch the muttered sounds, the scraping of chairs, the ringing of the telephone. After a wait that seemed to be hours, he heard footsteps enter and someone said, "Good morning, Chief."

"Morning, Joe," the voice answered. "That kid cool down yet?"

"Yeah, quiet as a kitten this morning."

"Wonder what they feed them coons to make 'em go off like this?"

"Beats me."

"The little guy come in yet?"

"Naw. Figgered he'd show bright and early, but he ain't."

"Wish he'd hurry up so we can get the kid off our hands," the Chief said.

"Our hands? Look, we just kept the kid here so he could cool off. We got to send him over to Juvenile this morning. Or don't we?" That was the voice belonging to Joe.

"We don't. We let the kid go when the little guy comes."

"But what is Miss what's-her-name going to say when she hears about this? She'll throw a natural fit."

"She's agreed that the kid should go."

"Agreed? Why, yesterday she was foaming from the mouth."

"That was yesterday."

A voice Wade had not heard before put in, "She must realize she hasn't a leg to stand on. After all, she hit the kid first."

"He spit in her face," the chief said. "She had every reason to."

"Yeah," Joe said. "Niggers drag their kids up any old way and they have the nerve to want to get into the same schools with our kids."

Other voice: "I was on duty around the school all week and it seemed to me I wasn't exactly proud of the way some of our parents acted toward those kids."

"Lucky you don't draw your pay to think. When in your life have you heard of a child that age threatening to kill an adult? He needs to be put away and the key thrown away."

Other voice: "Yeah, but you ought to have heard some of the things those adults were saying to those kids. If they were my . . ."

"What? Are you taking up for niggers?"

Other voice: "Naw, who, me? Hell no, I got more to do then make excuses for niggers."

"But Chief," the voice that must have been Joe protested. "If you feel so strongly about it, what's all this about sending the kid home?"

"Look, Joe," the Chief said. "If it was up to me, I would not only send him over to Juvenile, but I would get a petition signed to keep the little nigger off the streets for life. But it seems as though some of those mothers got together and decided that to give this any more publicity than it already has would have a reverse effect. Maybe they're right, who knows?"

"I still don't get it," Joe said glumly.

"Well, it's like this," came the patient explanation. "Some of these parents around here feel that publicity might only stir up people's conscience and have them asking why five little smart kids cannot be admitted to one of New York City's public schools. They might start a big hullabaloo and the main issue will be lost, and before you know it there'll be a bunch of niggers flooding our schools. Then what happened yesterday will be a picnic compared to what will be happening in the future. They're thinking about their kids.

"Now do you understand? They just don't think they should give all of that publicity to something that is better killed with silence. So— there will be *no* charges. No Juvenile Court. No nothing. Understand? Just let the kid go when the little guy comes, and that's that."

And that was exactly what they did. An hour later when Professor Jones came in with a small group of parents, they let Wade go with him quietly. All he and Professor Jones won for their troubles was that he ended up being an eleven-year-old jailbird.

That, and a column in a newspaper, taking off on the rights of all citizens, including Negroes, to the benefit of the City's educational system. And that same week, a short clipping in another paper stated that the Board of Education, regretfully, had to turn down the application of a few Negro youths to a certain high school in the Bronx because the quota of that school had been filled.

Wade didn't know what to make of it. It was as if the whole city had conspired to work against him: to punish him, and he didn't know what he had done wrong. He went around for days, his hands in his pockets, his head bowed, his eyes searching the squares of the pavement. It was like writing with a black chalk on a white wall and leaving not a line; like being written out of a book when you were the leading character. He didn't understand any of it. It should have been that when a guy worked and struggled, and fought like the devil for something decent, he should win. He had believed so hard, and he had lost.

And Professor Jones had worked. If God didn't know it, the devil sure did. He had raised holy hell and never stopped raising it either. But he never won. He never won a goddamn thing. Wade wiped his mouth and looked at the professor with pity in his eyes, then he chuckled, pushing his chair back and getting to his feet. "Well, any old how, Professor, I hope you have better luck in getting me off the streets than you used to." But before he left the table he decided to cap him, just to let him know he wasn't dealing with a turkey. "But you know, you might have a bit more success in getting rid of cats like me if you added a couple of feet. The altitude might do you a lot of good."

"I agree, Wade. If I could grow by a couple of feet, the altitude might do a lot of us some good."

Wade swaggered to the cashier. He paid the bill; then, remembering, walked back to the table. If anyone knew, this nosey punk would. "Hey, Nosey," he said to the professor. "You see anything of Tony around? I been looking for him ever since I come home this morning and I ain't seen hide nor taken a whiff of him."

"You won't be seeing him any more, Wade." Professor Jones sat quietly wiping his eyeglasses. "You won't be seeing him. Tony is dead."

9

In the silence that followed, he heard himself as though from a distance, "What did you say?"

"Cut that shit out." Nat, always on the alert for trouble, grabbed his arm. The mist cleared and he realized that he was holding the professor by his tie and that he had dragged him out of his seat.

He eased his hold. "Sorry, man." He did not know whether he was apologizing to the professor or to Nat.

"It leaves you quite alone," Professor Jones said, calmly smoothing out his tie. "He was the last friend you had." It was a pronouncement, the way he said it. "Yes, they pulled him off a stoop the other night. Not really surprising. The line he was holding on life was so very precarious. Tighten it a little, or simply tug it, and it had to be the end. Yes, inevitable."

He'll be around for the funeral. Wade found himself backing away from the matter-of-factness in the professor's face, then he found himself in the streets running, running, not knowing where he was going, just getting away. . . .

"Wade. Wade." He checked his steps and looked around. "Wade, where in the world are you going?" It was Faith. He was on Mumma's street. What in the hell was he doing here? He rushed up to his sister.

"Faith, Tony is dead."

"Oh." Just a little sound to give him sympathy and a fleeting touch on his arm to show she understood. But she didn't understand. She couldn't. How could anybody understand? It wasn't Tony dying, so much, as that it fitted into place so well. Like a pattern, them herded together into one pen—a pen called "Harlem." And as if some people—the gods—a long time ago decided that it didn't make any difference whether they lived or died. Until there was nothing left to them but a bubble they called a dream—and not even their dream—then at random, they plucked that dream between two fingers, rubbing it out like ash, and as Professor Jones said, nobody cared. Nobody gave one damn.

"Is that what you were coming around the house to tell us?" Faith stood studying his twitching face. "It would have made it harder for us, you know?"

No. Nobody cared. Not even Faith, and if anybody could, she would.

"I called the house. Nobody answered. I . . ."

"This is Mumma's night to go to prayer meeting. But you can't mean that you were coming around—not in the state you're in, Wade. It's going to be hard enough this time, without you going out of your way to make it more difficult."

At her words everything flooded back into his mind and he blurted, "Faith, you know what happened to . . ." He suddenly realized that he couldn't tell her about Willie Earl without telling her of Uncle Dan—her Uncle Dan. His mouth worked but no further sound came, and the muscles in his face began their twitching again. He searched desperately through her eyes for encouragement.

"What is it, Wade?" The sound of fear, the anxiousness in her soft brown eyes, forced him to silence.

"Let's go for a walk."

"But where is Gladys?"

"In the house, where else?"

"Well, let's go there." Wade grunted and she insisted. "Yes, we must go there." And as he remained stubbornly silent. "You can't just leave her alone on your first night home."

"I got to go there to sleep, ain't I?"

"Gladys might be a little hard, Wade. But she's your friend. Every day when I was in the hospital she came to see me just to make sure I wouldn't press charges—like I would."

"Big deal. . . ."

"She's a very lonely woman, Wade."

"What do you expect with a puss like that—for her to have troubadours serenading her from the roof?"

"She's had a hard life, but then so have you."

"Not that hard."

"Stop being difficult, Wade. What I am trying to say is that you're all she has, and she is all that you . . ."

"What the hell are you talking, Faith?" His shirt began sticking to his back. "You trying to say that my life is finished, that I can't go beyond Gladys?"

"No. No, not that, Wade, I—I—all I meant was—if you'd put your mind to it, you both can make a new life together."

"What kind of crap is this?" He fought down his anger. "I got no life to make—this is it. I ain't got no time to be thinking of no simple broad who ain't got sense enough to think for herself."

"She thinks about you, Wade. And anyhow," Faith added firmly. "It wouldn't be right to leave her alone on your first night home."

"Well, say that if you want, but don't give me a lot of crap about making no new life. Life is made long before a cat reaches thirty-eight. After that, it's just a question of living it out."

They walked on in silence, Wade mad as anything at himself for sounding off the way he did. Faith had a high sense of justice that he never violated. Guess it was because she never violated *his* sense of justice. The only trouble with her, she was always busy looking at too many sides of a coin and—take it any way you wanted—a coin had just two sides.

He pulled her soft-as-a-kitten hand through his, feeling the ugliness of having hurt her and angry that the atmosphere had become too tight to tell her right off about Willie Earl and Uncle Dan. They walked in silence for a while. Then he asked, "What did Mumma say?"

"Mumma?"

"Yes, about me. She looks like she might give in?"

"Mumma wouldn't even talk to me tonight."

"She wouldn't?"

"Well, it isn't exactly a secret, Wade, that Mumma feels you should have stayed in the hospital. She's still hot like anything at me, for signing you out against the doctor's advice."

"That punk diaper changer? They ought to have paid me to stay in and give him lessons in psychiatry." He spoke with such bitterness that Faith searched his face quickly. "Faith," he pleaded. "Why didn't you tell her why it happened? Why didn't you tell her it was Willie Earl's fault?"

"Because it wouldn't make any difference, Wade." Then she did remember. She hadn't told the truth in the hospital when she said she had forgotten.

"It has to make a difference, Faith."

"The important thing is that it happened and you don't even remember." Then realizing from the pained look on his face that she had hurt him, she added lightly, "Anyway, even if I told her, what difference would it make? You know how Mumma is, hard-headed, and old-time. She's about at the end of her patience with you and she's not fixing to let you make her lose her place in heaven." Faith spoke with all her old impatience for Mumma. She had gone through life blaming Mumma for making more of her troubles than she had the right to do, and Wade had years ago stopped explaining that it was because Mumma had more than she could handle in this life.

"She'll be right out of place in heaven with all her family in the other place. Who would she have to raise hell with?" Wade teased.

"With the good Lord Jesus." They laughed and that seemed to ease some of the anxiety from Faith's face. They arrived at the stoop and stopped, facing each other, each sensing the other had to rid himself of something on his mind before going up the stairs.

"Faith, you got to tell me what I went after Willie Earl about. You got to tell me, Faith."

"I can't, Wade."

"It must be god-awful, because when I tried to find out . . ." He broke off, not knowing how to tell her. "Faith, Uncle Dan . . ." No, he didn't have the courage. He couldn't stand to lose her. He didn't want to see the worry in her face give way to hate, or fear, or disgust. Yet he couldn't keep it back forever. She had to know from him—only from him. "Faith, if you don't tell me, how am I going to square myself with Mumma? Faith, I can't stay out here in the streets like I did today. I swear to God I can't. . . ."

"Wade, if it would do any good at all, I would tell you. But it won't—not to Mumma. It won't change nothing with her."

"But if it meant so much to me that I would . . ."

"It meant so much to you. But it wouldn't mean the same to her; and my telling you or her or anybody would not change anything. I must be the judge." She searched through his eyes, waiting for the argument that would not change her note of finality; and as she kept looking at him, a shudder shook her body.

"Ha-ha," he teased, realizing that there was nothing to say that would change her mind. "Someone is walking over your grave." But she was in no laughing mood.

"Wade," she said. "What are you going to do now that you are out?"

He wanted to keep looking into her face, but couldn't. He couldn't answer her smart, the way he had answered the professor. So he searched around in his mind for an answer. He had done everything from working in laboratories to firing furnaces. And there was not one—not one job—that he could even imagine being able to fit his mind or his hands to. Not now, anyway—maybe later.

It was worse than being in a strait jacket, working in an office or lab. He knew without even trying. And the last time he fired a furnace, he had been arrested for laying a cat out with a shovel. No sense in even talking about it. There was too much he couldn't take. "I'll straighten out," he said. "The minute I can go back around Mumma and things get back to normal. I . . ."

She stopped him with a tired look. Yes, he knew she had heard it before. After Buddy, he had promised the same thing and Mumma had let him come around. But this time . . .

"And now Tony is gone. You don't even have one friend to hang out with. What will you be doing all day while I'm working? And you know how people are."

"Who gives a damn about people?"

"We always used to say that, Wade. But it isn't true. People and their attitudes mean a lot. Ever since Buddy, I've had to fight people's attitudes. It's not been easy."

No, trying to stay in his corner over the past few years hadn't been easy. "Are you telling me all this to tell me you're not going to bat for me with Mumma?"

"You know better than that, Wade. For better or for worse you belong with us. Like I keep telling Mumma, without Big Willie and the South, there would be no us in Harlem; and without us, there would be no you." She said it softly, her honesty shining out at him, her soft lips with the tiny skin stressing her avowal. His throat clogged and somehow he did not tell her about Uncle Dan.

They mounted the stairs and entered the apartment, and Gladys The Beast did not look so bad or the apartment so confining as they had earlier. They sat in the overcrowded dimly lit room, and Faith got to talking to Gladys and the place even had a touch of hominess about it.

"I sure am glad you come around, Faith. Ain't nothing I like better than some company. No sooner that brother of yours come in then, bam, right back in the streets again. Sure is good to have yer."

Faith looked at him accusingly. "Where did you go?"

"Oh, to his Uncle Dan's," Gladys put in. "Where else was he going to go?" Wade knew an instant's peeve.

"All you need is a broomstick."

"Poor Uncle Dan really got it bad," Faith put in quickly. "The doctor doesn't have much hope for him."

"Yeah, sure goofed me seeing him look so bad," Wade said.

"He overdid himself worrying about us."

"Yeah, I'll bet." He didn't mean it the way it sounded, and Faith turned her dark Uncle-Dan-looking eyes at him in surprise.

"Uncle Dan is nothing but a bunch of faults, I agree, but one of them isn't that he don't think the world of us—you especially."

He turned to hide the guilt that pushed into his eyes. "What we got to offer my sister?" he said to Gladys. "We ain't been together so long, you'd think we earned a homecoming."

"I reckon." Gladys said to Faith, "I cooked his favorite potato salad and ham hocks and greens, and I even baked him a cake and brought sodas to celebrate. But it looked to me like I had to celebrate all by myself. I sure am glad you brought him home."

He sat looking at Faith through half-closed eyes, while she talked and helped Gladys with heating the food and setting the table. She looked sweetness itself, with the light-blue jersey thing she wore, falling loosely over her undeveloped body. She was all undeveloped like a little teenager except that she had a woman's hips. He liked the contrast. The round little girl's face with round black eyes, topped by a head of curly hair that never grew longer than a short bob, the flat chest, long waistline and the woman's hips. Looking at her would have been enough for that good-to-be-home feeling to go through him, but the hardness of the bottle was like a conscience to his backsides. He half-way wished he had ditched it so he could forget Uncle Dan and Willie Earl if only for one minute, but it kept pushing at him so he only half-listened to what they said.

"Sure, Wade is uncontrollable at times, Gladys, that's the reason he needs someone around that's firm."

"I'm good to him as I know how. But your brother don't listen to nobody."

"Maybe if you demand a little more, he might give a little more."

"Stop talking fairy tales. The bitch is so punchy she don't know what to demand." He hated being discussed, and he hated that note that had been in Faith's voice, in her eyes, all evening. That anxiousness. Sounded as if she thought that, if she pushed Gladys on, she might be able to work miracles.

"Gladys, don't listen to him. He's not half as bad as he makes himself out to be."

Wade laughed. Maybe that's why he liked her so much. She liked him.

"I ain't always been like this," Gladys came to her own defense. "I used to be right pretty, once."

"I didn't know you then."

"You wouldn't a known what you was looking at."

"Too far above me?"

"Not ready for you."

"But you ready now."

"I got you now."

"Don't get used to it."

"I am already."

"That's a lot of confidence for that puss you got."

"I ain't changed none since you come. The way I figger, you ain't got many more stops to make."

"Got at least one more."

"I'll be around."

"For the funeral?"

"That way or any other way."

"You win," he sneered. "Pick up the marbles."

They were sitting around the table and Faith fixed her eyes on him, making him squirm uncomfortably. "You know, Wade, things

114   ROSA GUY

happen in life that no person is to blame for, yet we all share in the responsibility. We all share in the guilt." Wade bit down on his lip, sorry that Faith wanted to be in on the conversation.

"That's right," Gladys put in. "Like you start out in life searching for something and you get mixed up with a lot of folks all searching too, figgering they searching for the same things you searching for. And I rightly believe they are, most of the time. But somehow, when you get untangled, you find that they didn't actually know what they wanted. They leave and they all empty and they don't even know it, and they leave you weak like you been beaten to the ground. And the years done gone and you still a person, but you ain't what you used to be and you'll never be what you wanted to be."

"Amen." Wade, trying to force his collard greens and potato salad past the bar-b-q he had eaten earlier, looked up. "Like you going in for philosophy. Tell me what is this thing you and all of the rest of us were searching for?"

"Well, we try to laugh at it, but it sure is an overpowering thing that give our life reason for a long time. When you boil it all down, I reckon—it's love."

"Love?" Wade stopped in the middle of a chew and stared at Gladys, then with his mouth still full of food, burst out laughing.

She waited until he was finished; then said vindictively, "Yeah, I reckon it's a word that can trap you all right. And it done trapped a whole lot of us here searching for it on Lenox Avenue—together. You know," she leaned over as though to make her information clearer. "There were those who went over me, around me and through me but they didn't get nowhere. I seen a many of them same ones beat their heads out on the stone of this-here street. Yeah. I sit right there at the window and see it every single day."

Wade stared hard at Gladys and she returned his stare, the same mocking smile around her mouth, reaching right up to her eyes. A picture of her looking out of the window, while he bent over knocking his head against the sidewalk came to his mind, and he realized that he had always hated her, but until now he never knew how much. Nor had he realized how she hated him and how confidently she waited for his destruction. The realization intensified his hate; and like fear it gripped his stomach, twisting his intestines. Suddenly he laughed, pulling the bottle out of his pocket and placing it on the table.

"That's a real-gone one. Let's have a real celebration on that."

Faith's eyes widened on the bottle and Wade's heart did a flip-flop. His eyelids got heavy, he stared at his plate, trying to force down food.

"Wade," Faith said hesitantly, "you mean—you started—drinking already?"

"Naw, I ain't touched a drop. Bought the bottle for Gladys."

"But the bottle is opened."

"I let a fellow have a drop."

"What fellow?" Wade's mind rippled through the people who would not have anything to drink with him and settled for the truth. She had to know and now was as good a time as any for the telling.

"Uncle Dan." Even Gladys got silent as she re-entered the room and Wade, glancing at her knowing smile, thought that she looked as though it were she who had dealt the underhand card.

Faith took a deep breath. "You—gave Uncle Dan—whiskey?" He wanted to tell her the whole thing; pour it out and get it over with. But it was damn hard coming out.

"I just gave him a drop. It didn't do no harm, as a matter of fact, it did him a lot of good."

She sat quietly a few seconds, then she was on her feet, pulling on the shoes she had taken off, and searching for her bag and gloves.

"Faith, where are you going?"

"To Uncle Dan. I have to find out how he is."

"You can't leave, Faith. You can't leave me."

"But I must go, Wade, I have to know." She started through the door and he grabbed her arm, pulling her back, holding her desperately by the shoulders. She winced, and he knew he was hurting her. He let her go, wiping his damp hands on his pants.

"What's the matter with everybody, anyway?" he shouted. "You'd think I committed some crime or something. It ain't justice, I tell you. It ain't justice." He wanted to plead, to beg, to demand that she not leave him, to explain to her that if she left him now, he was finished; that she was all he had. But he heard himself shouting, "Uncle Dan's been killing himself all these years and all anybody ever did was laugh and pat him on the back, hurrying him along. Now he's about ready to put his other foot in the grave where his first one's been all these years, and right away there's a lot of talk about save him, save him. Why didn't someone save him years ago?

"When he married Aunt Julie he was already a lush, and that was before I was born. And look at you and me. We grew up on his lap and the only perfume we ever known was the whiskey from his stinking breath. Why didn't someone try to save him then—why didn't someone try to save me?"

Faith threw herself into his arms, crying, "Wade, if all is well over at Uncle Dan's, I'll be back."

"Promise me, Faith."

"Yes, I promise."

"And Faith, promise, if everything is all right you won't tell Mumma and you'll try to make Aunt Julie . . ."

"No—no," Faith wailed. "I don't have to tell Mumma anything. Mumma is going to see Uncle Dan when she comes from church tonight."

10

"What are you going to do now that you are out?" The loud voice coming through the window shattered the soundness of his sleep yet he was unable to move. Loud laughter, as though from a thousand voices crashed over his head. And the voice again, like a cry echoing and re-echoing through the eerie silence of an empty chapel, in response to the answer that he had never given, bringing the sensation of being in a dream though he knew he was no longer sleeping. He dug his fingernails deeply into his flesh trying to release himself from the horror, the numbness that held him helpless, vulnerable. He twisted his head toward the window to ward off an approaching danger, a plea in his eyes shrieking out the injustice of being trapped in this helpless state.

Sunlight streaked through the window, spilling through the branches of densely growing trees. He knew these woods well; the scene had been seared into his memory to remain until his end. His eyes searched desperately, knowing what he might find, not wanting and at the same time wanting very much to find it. But the grass, proving nature's arrogance with beauty, sprawled uninhibited, a voluptuous creation of the gods, ignoring men's memories, abusing their senti-ments, denying their worth, covering the hard necessity of the earth with the mere esthetic for the eye. Only a shadowy laughter haunting his memory insisted that *this* was the place. Even the birds hopping around, digging for worms, pecking at twigs, were oblivious of the fact that a terrible tragedy, a human drama devastating in its consequence, had been played out here.

He wanted them to know! He wanted them and the people lying around the grass, talking, laughing, loving, planning, not too far from the spot he knew, to know that there was nothing to talk about, nothing to laugh about, nothing to plan about that was more important than what had happened there long ago—long ago, yet not so very long ago.

But as he struggled with his numbness, trying to call out to tell them, he heard a shout and looking toward the window he saw figures, endless and endless figures, jumping to his window sill, stalking into the room, walking boldly down the shaft of sunlight flooding his room, marching slowly toward him; passing without ever seeing, without turning to look at the woods with its abundance of grass, with its people talking and laughing and loving, with the birds digging and pecking and hunting.

Unable to move his hands he pointed with his eyes, his chin, his manner, trying to show them the place behind them that they ought not to miss, that if they cared for him, they must not miss. "Look, look," his mind shrieked, struggling until the sweat from his body dampened the bed around him. But they came right on, talking a nothingness he could not hear, smiling an emptiness he could not bear, getting smaller and smaller as they approached his eyes, then suddenly blinking out. . . .

It came to him that he must be sleeping. Even though he was seeing these things and even though he knew that he had gone to bed, and knew himself to be lying there, he knew he had to be dreaming. He struggled in his wakefulness to get rid of a sleep he did not feel, scratching and tearing as far as his hands could move. And they never moved above his wrists, so that his legs were scratched and torn, but he did not feel it because of the terrible numbness.

"What are you going to do now that you are out?" The voice again, the same eeriness, the same unearthly quality, as though knocking from mountain to mountain over a vast void.

"Nothing, nothing, nothing," he cried. "I have no money. I have no money. I have no money." He sobbed; and he felt his sobs and his words, forcing themselves from his stomach, straining out of his throat, bulging the muscles of his neck. Yet when they left his lips they were absorbed in a cotton work of the loudest silence. "They left me with no money."

But no one heard and they kept walking up to him in all their emptiness. Then he saw Mumma. Only her face, but he wanted to call out to her face floating up to him on the shaft of light, to stop that face and point out the woods behind her. But the face, shaking from side to side, cried, "I prayed and I prayed, but it didn't do you no good and it sure God didn't do me much good. I declare I must have laid with the devil the day I begot you."

"But you joking, Mumma, you joking." She blinked out, and before he could call her back, he saw Uncle Dan stagger up to the window and stand teetering perilously on the sill.

"Uncle Dan, it's only one-half block more. Uncle Dan—please."

Still the sunlight shone hard on the woods, where people lay and talked and laughed and loved and planned. And the birds hopped about and dug and pecked and hunted and nobody cared, nobody cared. He felt lost. Like a little child who has given all but has been ignored. This was pain. Yes, this was pain.

Then there was Dr. Forest walking toward him, his green look-right-through-you eyes full of understanding. Wade fought to free his hands. He *had* to hold onto the doctor. This was his last chance. His only chance. If Doc could see the woods then he would understand. He would be able to find the bridge. He had to. Wade's hands remained enchained as Dr. Forest walked up to him, hesitated even as though wanting to be told, then he too disappeared.

Wade lay exhausted now, hopeless. No one would ever see the woods the way he had seen it, or feel what he had felt, or understand. Yes, they would know he killed Buddy, cry out because he had hurt Faith, swear him a crime against society, but they would never understand. Not in life. No one ever would.

In his despair he looked up and saw Faith. Oh God, thank God for Faith. Will she see? Will she see? Her head was turned toward the woods—but he didn't know whether she was looking—for suddenly she was stretched out naked on the shaft of light, her little-girl's legs parted, inviting him; her breath coming in short spurts showing the rise and fall of her stomach; her heart beating so he could see the thumping against the wall of her chest. He lay between the softness of her legs, feeling the undulation of her body caught close to his, squeezing and pressing her to him and into him, so that she might become an actual part of him so he might get enough of her softness. He needed so much of her softness.

But as he lay watching himself intertwined with her, he fought the feeling of her softness, desperately, in agony, in guilt, until thank God, she too disappeared, leaving one lone figure, walking toward him: A little boy. Willie Earl in his knickers, grinning mischievously, making a tight circle with one hand while he played the index finger of the other through the circle suggestively. "Mumma ain't gon' like it. Mumma ain't gon' like it."

Wade wrenched himself away from the terrible laughter with such force that he broke the bonds that held him imprisoned. His heart beat, shaking his body. He turned to the window. It was dark. He breathed a sigh of relief. Covering his face with his sheet, he let his tired body be pulled down into the deepest of sleep.

He came slowly into consciousness in the early-morning stillness but drew deeper into the darkness of his carefully shuttered eyes. The sweat of his disturbed sleep had dried and his limbs lightened from their release, yet he remained in his silence, shutting out all sounds: The ticking of the clock; the occasional car that drove by; the loud talk of straggles rising in the silence of the morning. He pulled his mind into darkness and felt peace. A fly escaping from the drabness of the street found its way into the room buzzing around his nostrils, but they didn't quiver, not even when it rested lightly on the tip of his nose. A smile formed on his lips. He was at peace. He wanted to stay here, never to venture out into the streets, not to hear, or to think; not taste, or smell; not to know. . . .

Her leg fell across him. He jumped out of bed, tangled in unreasoning anger. He turned to her. She was asleep.

He went to the window and looked out at the early-morning stragglers, some coming in from a hard night's work, others coming in from a hard night. A few making early-morning time, brisk-stepping in their importance. Charlie and his wino friends, staggering to their feet, wiping their eyes and looking around in the clearest moment they would have for the day, studying passers-by for their touch, only to sit in dismal impatience waiting for the hour when the liquor store opened.

Wade was dressed and out in the streets before his first thought was born. And when it did start moving around up there, he realized it made no difference to his reasoning. His feet had a mind of their own. They headed as straight as they could to Uncle Dan's and Aunt Julie's. Faith hadn't come back last night. Why hadn't she come back? And Mumma. What had they said to Mumma? What had Mumma said to them?

He didn't give one damn that it was only five o'clock in the morning. Uncle Dan never had known time, when it came to waking him. He rang their bell as though he didn't hear that it might wake up the dead; then he banged on the door with his fist; waited a few seconds listening for sounds and then banged again, and rang again. He heard the soft-shuffling sounds that meant Aunt Julie. He had always thought a lot of Aunt Julie, but this morning he intended to get some answers and he didn't care how. He banged again to hurry her.

The door opened and Aunt Julie faced him, solid as a rock with her oversized bosom and her stony-looking face. "What the hell do you mean banging on this door at this hour of the morning as though you ain't got good sense?"

"Aunt Julie . . ."

"Don't 'Aunt Julie' me. What the hell do you think this is? You forget who you are and who I am? You ain't coming here to bully me, boy. You try to get bad with me and I'll turn you every way but loose. Now just you turn around and let the door hit you where the dog bit you. *Your* Uncle Dan, here not long for this world and your brother in the hospital with a jaw that you done broke up and you acting as though you got some chip on *your* shoulder."

"Aunt Julie . . ."

"Your poor mother is about to have a fit. If *I* was you, I'd stay clear of her until your brother was doing better. But above all stay clear of *here* until *I* say when."

He was looking at solid door and still hadn't cracked his lips. He chuckled as he hit the street, and as he kept walking, the chuckle gave way to a little laugh. He had never been able to tackle Aunt Julie. What in the hell made him think he could start now?

Wade stuck his hands deep into his pocket, feeling like a big kid, and drifted with the mist up Lenox Avenue. He drifted slowly to Mumma's street, up her block, and stood looking up the long brownstone steps to the door. Damn shame, what was normal to most men would be a crime for him: To walk up those steps and ring the bell and have Mumma open the door and say, "Hello, Son."

Mumma would be in the big bed near the window, sleeping that easily disturbed sleep that never allowed her true restfulness. And Faith—why hadn't she come back last night—Faith would be curled up like a kitten drugged, on the couch turned bed at the other side of the room. How well he knew that scene. How often had he left Gladys to let himself in—when they trusted him with the key—and sit quietly in the darkened room looking at them until the early dawn lightened the room. Quietly, because Mumma in her almost-conscious state responded to every move he made as though looking at him through her sleep. When dawn came he would leave, going back to slip into bed and sleep the sleep of the dead. Would Mumma ever let him in again?

Walking back the way he had come, he went to sit in the island in the middle of the Avenue, watching the sky waken to life. Most of the night owls had settled in for the day. The freshly wakened, unenthusiastic workers plodded to the subways, while the sleepy-eyed night workers squinted their surprise at coming out into sunlight.

As the morning grew older, the lively step of life in the form of the painted and well dressed added its push to the swell of human fodder being consumed by the open mouth of the subway. Then it was much later and the swell reduced to a trickle. Finally even the trickle ceased and the do-nothings began spreading around to fill up space.

Wade's stomach began talking to him and he realized he was hungry. He got up, stretched his legs, deciding to go to a restaurant and get some grits and eggs. Yet when he began walking he found himself walking toward the park as though his mind were doing nothing for him today but giving him headaches.

He sat in the park, staring into space, carefully blanking his mind, because when he got to thinking, a voice kept pushing it to him: What are you going to do? What are you going to do? And because he hated like hell the silence around him, he had to answer loud, "I'll wait for evening. I'll wait for Faith." But she didn't come back last night. She didn't come back.

She had said earlier, for better or for worse—but that was before she went to see Uncle Dan. Was it for better or for worse now?

Wade pulled himself to the edge of the seat to rest his head on the back of the bench. His hat fell to the ground, but he didn't move, just sat there staring at the little spots flying around behind his closed eyelids.

She would come this evening. Even if it were to tell him that she would not see him again. Honesty and straightforwardness went with her sense of justice. But the day would be long to wait, especially without knowing. He didn't even have the pretense of looking for Tony today. No, Tony was gone the way of Buddy and that left him at zero.

Not that they had ever really been friends. In all his life he had had only one friend—Rocky.

Rocky, with his slender waist and long eyelashes. Rocky, with his great big mind. Big mind and yet he had had to give up. For that's the way it turned out to be. Even Rocky's mother with all her youth and strength and vitality had seen no point in going on. It was only Professor Jones who didn't give up; who never gave up.

A few days after Wade came out of his short detention he had met Rocky on the street. "Did you choose the school you intend to go to, or do you think maybe you'll keep on with the professor?" Wade asked him.

"No," Rocky answered. "My mother is sending me away. You know we have family in Boston, and my mother thinks it is best for me to go and finish there."

It seemed to Wade, at the time, that his heart dropped to his stomach. His defeat was complete. Rocky was the first person he had ever made a best friend. Somewhere in the back of his mind he supposed he had it figured that it was a relationship without end. As if they were twisted together, comrades in the mind, or some such joke. Now here was Rocky going a whole world away.

Some of the same feeling must have been going through Rocky's mind as he stood, hands in his pockets, outlining a square on the sidewalk with the tip of his shoe. "Why don't you get your mother to send you with me?" he suggested. They both lit up with the idea. "Oh, I'm sure my cousin will let you share my room. I don't eat much, so that will be no problem. And my mother will be sending money every week. I know they won't mind. How could they? All you have to have is your train fare." They planned and talked and the longer they planned the more plausible it seemed and by the time they parted, Wade skipped home, happy for the first time in weeks.

"Mumma," he called, rushing into the house that afternoon, flushed with excitement. "Listen, Mumma, Rocky said I could go to Boston with him and go to school there. And Mumma, you wouldn't have to worry about feeding me or giving me any money or anything, all you have to have is my fare and Uncle Dan will help you out on that."

He waited breathlessly for her answer, his gaze following her as she walked about the little kitchenette, setting the table. Finally, thinking she didn't understand, he tried again. "Mumma, you hear what I said? Mumma, Rocky said . . ."

"Sit down and eat your food and stop that stupid talking." He sat down because he did not want to antagonize her, and stuck a forkful of food into his mouth obediently. She went out of the kitchenette, then to the window where she looked out for a few minutes, then finally to her usual resting place, the rocker. He still waited for her to say something but suddenly realized she had no intention at all of answering. He ventured again, timidly. "We'd share the same room and—and—we can even share our . . ."

"Wade," Mumma turned on him abruptly. "I don't want to hear no more talk about that. You ain't going nowhere and that's that. I'm sick and tired of all this talk about how smart you are, how you can't go to a school with ordinary people. How you so far above everybody else. Almost a year now, I've been hearing all this fool talk and what did it get you? I'll tell you what. It got you in jail, that's what. Eleven years old and a jailbird already. Why, even your father waited until he was well into his teens before he saw any kind of time."

That stunned him and he sat there looking at her. All this time he had been traveling under the umbrella of pride in his family's belief in him. Now, with just a few words she had stripped him of every bit of glory except that of being a jailbird. The newspapers had written him out of history and she had condemned him for even trying. He sat there, the food turned to garbage in his mouth. He spit it back into his plate.

". . . and as for that professor, don't bring him around here no more, and I mean it. I don't want him around. We were simple folk before he started coming around with his nosey self. We were decent God-fearing people. We always been. Then here he come bringing all this trouble. It wasn't his child that went to jail, so he don't give a damn. But you tell him for me and don't you forget it, that he better stay out of my face. Talking about genius and high intelligence . . ."

She sat rocking, not looking at him, just rocking and talking, all the past weeks lost on her. He thought he was going to change their lives, but all it meant to her was that he had spent time in jail. Being in jail was bad, so he was bad and the professor—the professor was just a fool.

He stared at her, hating her more than he had ever hated anybody. He might have hurt her too, if he hadn't jumped up and run out into the cold streets without even stopping for his coat.

He walked and walked, determined to die; determined that he would not be stopped, except by the cold; frozen, never seeing anyone again. Never talking to anyone, never bothering anyone. The next they would hear of him was when some policeman found him and drove him up in some truck, rang their bell, and there he would be, one block of ice. That would show her—that would punish her—punish her—punish her. He didn't know how long he walked. It might have been hours, but one time he stopped, and looking up, found himself in front of Uncle Dan's house, and being there, decided to go up.

Uncle Dan gave him hot whiskey and put him to bed, where he developed a fever that lingered and lingered, along with his determination that he would never get well.

Rocky came there to say good-by.

Wade, seeing him in the doorway of his bedroom, turned his head to the wall to hide his anguish, his tears. Rocky seemed to understand. He entered the room and sat at the head of Wade's bed, slipping his tiny, small-boned hand, into Wade's hot fat fist, intertwining their fingers. They sat like this for well over an hour, thinking without talking. Feeling. Then Rocky bent over Wade, his warm breath fanning his face, his heavily fringed eyes dark with grief.

"I have to go now, Wade. But I'll write you. I swear I'll write." He leaned his cheek softly against Wade's for an instant, kissed him briefly on his lips, then he was gone. Gone, and Wade had lost the only friend of his life.

Laughter, like the sound of a clear bell, forced Wade's eyes open and he found himself looking at a young mother, lying not too far from him in the open field of the park, holding her baby skyward. She seemed to have picked the only spot of sunshine and in doing this had folded the brightness of the park around them. Her dress was a gay orange print, touched with green the same color as the grass, keeping her in harmony with all about her as did her dark-brown complexion and the bright-yellow suit that the baby above her, stiffened with laughter, wore. A stream of spittle ran from the baby's drooling lips reaching down to the mother, uniting their laughter even more than their bright lively look, in a happiness that pushed a surge of resentment through Wade.

Shadows darkened the sky and fluttered around like leaves. Wade lifted his gaze. Birds. He looked thoughtfully at them as they circled and circled above him, lulled by the pattern of their flight, the sound of their brushing wings. Suddenly he laughed bitterly. Not birds. Pigeons. Homing pigeons, flying around in circles, going nowhere. No goddamn where.

Wade found himself walking. Walking fast, not knowing where he was going, but moving. He realized when he crossed 125th Street, then happily 135th Street. Then he was on the bridge and looking down into the Harlem goddamn River, and he was leaving it behind him. All the way behind him. Harlem River and Harlem and Lenox goddamn Avenue.

11

He didn't know how long he walked, all lit up with the newness inside, knowing it was hot but not feeling the heat, clearheaded, mind free from thinking, uninvolved, seeing clearly the unimportance of things, of people. Looking at life as one straight sunlit road from his birth to death, knowing if he walked right down the middle, he would no longer be tangled with worry, or fear of being alone, or whose head to go up the side of, or if Mumma gave a damn. It was as if he'd lost fifty pounds off his shoulders. He wanted to skip and jump; the happy man in the steeplechase had nothing on him.

He heard laughter, saw a young couple calling to each other in Spanish from the distance of one-half block, the man in obvious flirtation with a tiny dark-haired beauty poured into a fitted red party dress a little weird for the time of day. Wade paused a moment, called foolishly, "Mi amigo, chiquita, olay, olay." The man looked Wade over in anger, then caught the gleam in his eyes. Wade laughed. The man laughed back. Wade walked on, happy.

He walked until he saw men waiting in line near a large construction area and from the look of them decided they were waiting for work. He joined them. Funny, how all of a sudden he knew what he wanted. The first time in his life! He would get a job, find a hotel for the night or maybe a few nights; then he had to start right in finding a place. Just a little place, but his own. His very own. He would begin by getting one piece of furniture at a time, a radio to come home to nights and listen to. A place to sit around and be alone, until he got used to his new-found freedom. God, he felt lucky. Lucky like anything. Throwing his head back, he laughed out loud. The man in front of him looked back as though Wade were a queer or something. Wade ignored the man.

He who had never been patient waited in the hot sun, quiet as anything while the long line inched up. Waiting to carry bricks or logs, or anything else for that matter, on his shoulders, in his hands; waiting to dig ditches or be hoisted on scaffolds—anything—anything as long as he remained free. And as he noticed how the sun beat down on the heads and the shoulders of the men, Wade prided himself on wearing a hat.

ROSA GUY

Who would care that he had gone? Not a damn soul. Nobody. Of course Gladys The Beast, but she would get over it and look around for the next one. Might not be easy, but she'd find one. Wade would just be one of the chumps who had walked through her, only he wasn't waiting around to beat his head against any stone on Lenox Avenue. She had better believe that.

Who would have thought it was so easy? Who would have thought all you had to do was throw things out of your mind and just walk away? Nobody. He chuckled, clearing his mind of all thoughts, refusing to let any new ones enter, standing first on one foot and then on the other, holding onto his feeling of light-heartedness; then, realizing how silly he might be looking, tried to stand quietly. But the moment he became quiet he had to keep moving his head this way and that, studying every little object around him, to keep something from pushing and pushing trying to be heard, something that had to be important. After minutes of pushing it back, he gave in.

"Come back, come back for the funeral, boy. Come back and stop these phoneys from shedding tears they don't mean."

That had been Uncle Dan's cry when Wade left for the Army. They had had a good drunk on and Uncle Dan had cried on Wade's shoulder because he thought he was dying. But Uncle Dan had not died and Wade had come back. Only now?

"Come back for the funeral. . . ."

Wade pulled his thoughts away to force back the thickening in his throat. He looked up at the sky. The sun had drawn a mist around itself, heating it and sending it back down like boiling water. Wade inched up on the line.

And Faith. Faith. She would be out of her mind with worry. No, maybe not after last night, not after she saw Uncle Dan. Still he was all she had. Anyhow, after he had done a few days work he would write a note and explain. She ought to be pleased. Wasn't it her idea about starting a new life? Yes, that was the way, the only way he could do it.

He studied the stooped shoulders of the man in front of him. As if the man were begging; as if he were used to begging; as if he were already up there in front of Mr. Charlie copping a plea and he expected Mr. Charlie to say no, and wanted to be in the right position. Wade took out his handkerchief and wiped his forehead and neck, then tied it around his neck to absorb the sweat running from under his hat. It would serve the bum right if Mr. Charlie did kick him the hell out. Anybody who begged that hard to work was a fool. Wade blanked his mind again, inching up.

That phoney bastard, Willie Earl, would be happy—happy as a little punk at the Y.M.C.A. Imagine him coming home from the hospital and Wade not being around to press him for answers. Just dropped out of sight. Not a goddamn soul to answer to. Wade frowned while stepping out of line to point a nasty stare at the man up in front. The son-of-a-bitch up there was really taking his goddamn time.

The Bronx—the Bronx. It rang an old familiar bell, rubbed an old, old, almost forgotten, never-to-be-healed-up wound. He didn't rightly remember which part of the Bronx. He had only been up here a few times—three, four at the most—in all the time they were together. She used to do most of the coming to see, because he never was able to keep a date so far from home. Even way back then, chicks who lived in Brooklyn or the Bronx were definitely out of the running. But Gay was different. She hadn't minded coming to see him. Even when he used to break dates she'd come, and he used to break damn near all of them.

No, he hadn't been very nice to her; but then in those days he hadn't been very nice to anybody—except Faith. But he had liked Gay. Liked her like anything. And she—she had been crazy about him. If they had got married he probably might have been living around here somewhere.

The Bronx. Yes, that was Gay. She wanted to get him out of Harlem. Worked overtime to get him out of Harlem. From the very beginning she showed she had no intention of living there, she thought that Harlem was a ghetto not fit to live in. It was alright to fall in love and screw around in, though. They would have had a mess of kids, pretty and black like Gay, coming along in age too—that was, if Gay hadn't got rid of them. He felt that strange twisting in the pit of his stomach and wrenched his thoughts away, pushing his hat back to get a bit of air circulating around his head.

That sunlit road was getting tangled up like hell, with people and things. He made an intense effort to clear it, but it was getting damn difficult. He stepped out of line to count the men before him, trying to figure how long it would take before it was his turn. It was like his salvation, for him to get to that man up there right away to start working this minute. This very minute. He had a wild urge to jump the line; to rush up front and force the man to take him on. Instead, he chewed down hard on his lip, untied the handkerchief from around his neck, wiped his hairline; then tied the handkerchief back around his neck and settled for glaring at the stooped shoulders of the man in front of him. All this to get a goddamn job. And why in the hell did he have to start looking on such a damn hot day? A job. It had been on a job he met Gay. His first job. His first and only honest-to-God nine-to-five. Old Professor had got it for him. Wade chuckled bitterly. Funny how all roads led back to the professor.

He had been nasty as hell to the little man, nasty in a way that didn't bear forgiving. Mumma had been nasty to him too, digging, and making sly remarks, and laughing at the old professor. Yet when she needed him she called for him, and he came back as though nothing had happened, as though for years Wade hadn't walked by him without talking, or walked in the other direction when he saw him coming; as though he hadn't realized that the respect Wade had had for him had long ago changed to hate, or maybe it was shame—shame at himself as much as at the professor, for putting their asses out there to be kicked; as though Wade hadn't threatened to kill him and really meant it with all his heart.

Wade had changed. He knew he had changed. From the moment when Rocky walked out of that bedroom and closed the door behind him, he had changed. It was as though the closing of that door had closed his hopes to every dream, every desire, every ambition. It seemed, with Rocky's going, there was one tear left in him to be shed, and he could not shed it; so it remained somewhere between his throat and his head, tight, hurting, a constant source of soreness until after his first year in his school—the school Professor Jones called the "mental graveyard." Then that tear had hardened into a solid rock of resistance that kept every other tear unshed.

One of the first things that got to him in his new school was when he caught a boy and girl screwing on the stairway. It wasn't that he had given up screwing, it was just that he didn't see mixing the two, schooling and screwing. They were a white couple, and they were getting it standing up, and when they looked down the stairs and saw Wade coming, they stood still, but never stopped, waiting for him to pass as though nothing a little colored boy could think could make any difference.

When he saw boys jerking off in classrooms it made him sick in his stomach, and he decided then and there to keep his own company. But what really flipped him and kept his hard going for the next few years were the teachers taking digs at children on account of their being black; and worse yet was the black children's giggling and acting the fool to keep off the teacher's hook.

He never forgot his first day in class, when the teacher, a Mr. Stone, an elderly man of medium height with very white skin and white hair—as a matter of fact he was so white there was no way to mistake him walking up and down the aisles, asking each student to call his or her name on his approach—stopped at the boy sitting directly in back of Wade.

"My name is James White," the boy said.

"What?" the teacher asked in mock amazement.

"I said my name is James White," the boy repeated.

"Well, I'll be darned," the teacher said. "Go up and stand in front of the class."

The boy walked self-consciously to the front of the room, and as he turned to face the class, everybody realized why he was target for the teacher's humor. The boy was very black. Giggles rippled through the room, but the boy stood up tall, as if he were on a block for inspection. Wade's anger stirred. He hated the boy for standing up there trying to look pleasant and a good sport. He always hated people like that, a hate that must have started with his time at the orphanage.

"This boy's name is White," the teacher drawled. "Well, anyhow, he got a pretty white shirt on. Tell me, James, do you always wear a white shirt to live up to your name?"

Another burst of giggles rippled through the room. One high giggle, bordering on hysterical, particularly pierced through Wade. He turned quickly to catch the stare of the girl. She was a Black, light brown skin, a little darker than Wade, pretty, with long hair straightened and hanging like a Veronica Lake screen on the side of her face. Wade dated her soon after, screwed her the same night, found she was a virgin, then let her drop. When she begged for the reason, he told her she was just too damn white.

Now the teacher came up to him, red up to his hair from what he considered a funny joke.

"Name?" he asked.

"Wade Black."

"What?" Mr. Stone searched his attendance sheet for the name.

"Said my name is Wade Black." He got to his feet and strode up to the front of the room, turned up for inspection, glad that his height had finally started nudging up to make his thickness more impressive.

"Yes, my name is Wade Black. I wear a white shirt every day and I want you to know before you ask that my mother starches the fucking things fit to kill." Every stare glued itself to the desk in front of it, and Wade, realizing there would be no takers, made it to his seat.

During his second year in the school, he was in the toilet, when he heard a gurgling sound in the john next to his. He couldn't get up right then, but when he finished he decided to take a look, figuring someone might need a little help. Wade didn't make out right away what was happening, but as he stood blinking, it came to him that what he was looking at was one boy, a big stud way over six feet and broad, holding another fellow's head, a much smaller guy, in the toilet bowl.

The big fellow, a dark broad-faced guy, looked up, saw Wade, let go of his victim and went after Wade. He caught him before he could get out of the door and they started a struggle that Wade knew was a life-and-death struggle. The boy was much bigger and much stronger, with a strength that must have been born of desperation and perhaps madness, but Wade had a lifetime strength that he carried in the width of his shoulders and his thick arms. For what seemed hours, but must have been only a few minutes, they struggled silently, not even allowing themselves an "ugh." But in fright, when he thought the other fellow had the upper hand, Wade broke away, then came in, head first into the boy's stomach. The stud stretched out, and Wade laid his foot, a couple of times, hard to his head for safety; then went back to his room out of breath and badly shaken.

Wade never said a word about what had happened. But later that day, the word went around that somebody had been found murdered by drowning in the toilet room. Police swarmed through the building, questioning everybody. Wade did not offer any information. A few days later the police caught the stud at his home; and the funny thing, it was because of the bruises Wade had given him. He was relieved when they caught the boy, because he knew that his life was not worth one penny so long as the stud was free. But he also knew that he would never say a word.

So he saw a lot and formed an attitude, an attitude that covered everything he did, in school and at home, and he took care of home.

Willie Earl had gone to courting and he didn't see too much of him, but he did spend a lot of time with Mumma. He did all her window washing, her shopping, all the things she was too sick or too tired to do. Even got to finding ways of pleasing her, or maybe, as Faith put it, of teasing her. He started picking up little things for her, things that she really wanted or needed, but was unable to afford, bringing them home and laying them before her.

"Where you get that?" she asked.

"In the store."

"You know I mean, how you get it?"

"I took it. I just picked it up like this, and walked away with it."

He liked to study her face, seeing how much she wanted it, and knowing the struggle she was having between God and the devil, before she said, "Well, you best take it back. I don't want nothing to cross this doorsill, if we don't come by it honest."

He laughed at this. "Aw, Ma, you know I wouldn't do no such thing like that. Uncle Dan give me the money to buy that with."

"You sure?"

"Sure, I'm sure." She never checked with Uncle Dan. That way she kept herself honest.

Sometimes money was real tight. Like when the relief check didn't come on time, and Willie Earl, instead of bringing the money home, decided to spend the night out; when Uncle Dan boozed up for days, just didn't get around to even working, and Mumma had to scrape pennies to the store to buy the little bit they had to make out on. At these times he liked to bring home a whole ham or a couple of chickens, a long bologna or salami, a big piece of cheese—things they had never been able to afford; then, laying it on the table, wait for the devil to take over.

It was so easy to look into her mind, standing before her innocently, reading her like an open book, reading that she wanted him to slip away so she did not have to question him, knowing that as long as he stood there she had no choice; praying that he had no intention of trying her, begging with her eyes, even though she made her voice casual.

"I suppose you got the money from Dan?"

"No, Mum," he answered firmly. "I stole it."

The devil took the upper hand then and, flying into a rage, she shouted, "Get out of my face with your lying self. You ain't got the sense you were borned with."

Laughing, he ran out of the house, pretending he actually had been teasing, leaving her to what she wanted to believe.

Taking care of Uncle Dan was simply taking him to one or two of his remaining drinking buddies, waiting around until he got to swimming in the stuff, then taking him home and putting him to bed. Wade himself never touched a drop. Sure, Uncle Dan pulled and coaxed him, but somewhere along the line he had turned against whiskey and it wasn't until years later that he actually started drinking. Maybe it was because Big Willie might have been a hard-gambling man but he never was a drinking man, and after all, Wade was taking over his job.

Aunt Julie used to say about Uncle Dan, "I do declare, I don't know what's keeping this fool alive. He's just too onery to die and give me peace of mind. He just scared that I will get that insurance and live without worries for a change. But, I tell you, old fellow, I'll have my day yet."

"Don't you bet on it, Aunt Julie." Wade laughed. "That liquor got Uncle Dan so pickled, he'll have many a day with us yet."

"Yeah," she laughed. "He'll be right here when I'm gone. Only trouble is, he won't know it."

They used to laugh at it in those days. But now the laughing days were over. Funny though, how long it took a man to die from what he spent his life dying of. A whole lifetime. Here Wade was thirty-eight, and Uncle Dan just ready to kick off from what he had been suffering from long before Wade was born, yet they wanted to blame him for it.

Helping Faith was the thing he had enjoyed most in those days, and the thing he felt most responsible for. They had always been close, even though he had passed her like a breeze in school. But Faith worked like the devil because following in his footsteps was a matter of pride to her. Things that were so easy for him that he hardly batted an eye caused her days of work and explaining. But she was determined, and when things finally fell into place for her, she was so happy it made him feel like God to be able to help her.

He was a few months from being fifteen when he graduated. Fifteen years old and he had seen and done about everything that a fifteen-year-old could do. He might have made it out easily the year before, but they didn't skip in high school and he had to wait it out until the end. He graduated with honors. Faith and Mumma were there, and it was the only thing that pleased him about his honors: Because Faith was there, grinning and being proud, looking up at him as if he were her big brother instead of the youngest, making him feel his weight and his size, and making him feel every bit the family man. And Mumma—Mumma took it as she took everything else. She was glad he was finished at last.

But they were not the only two who came to see him. As they were getting ready to leave, a little figure sitting in the back of the auditorium jumped up and ran to them. "Wade, Wade, I am proud of you, Son. Yes, I am very proud of you this day." Wade stood a long while just looking into Professor's eyes, not knowing what to say. He had stopped communicating with the little twerp so long ago that now the very sight of the man annoyed the hell out of him, and somehow today even more than usual. It took all of five minutes, and uncomfortable minutes at that, for Wade finally to say, "Yeah?" Then he walked away.

You didn't get rid of Old Prof that easily.

The family was having a celebration that evening. Mumma made Wade's favorite potato salad and greens. Willie Earl and Uncle Dan were lushing it up when the knock sounded at the door, and in walked Professor Jones. Prof said "yes" to a drink of whiskey, ate a little potato salad and greens, had a piece of cake; but Wade, like everybody else, knew that wasn't what he had come after. And sure enough, when everybody started warming up to the occasion, he dug in.

"Wade, have you decided what college you are going to?" Prim and proper, a blinking nuisance.

"Ain't going to none."

"And may I ask why?"

"I don't know if you may, but seeing you did, I'll explain. I ain't never been so happy to leave no place like I am to leave school. From now on, I'm walking around like a free man, my diploma in my pocket and the first person that tries to stop me from going anywhere I damn please gets a poke in the nose."

That got a few chuckles around the room but not from Prof.

"Wade, I beg you, don't waste your talents. You are much too brill . . ."

"You heard me. I said I ain't thinking of going to no college. I got a family to support. My sister here got to finish school and get this same little piece of paper that I got, and I'm the one going to help her."

"Hush, Wade, and listen to Professor Jones," Faith urged. "I never want you to make me the reason that you don't get ahead."

"It will not only be a loss to you, Wade. It will be a loss to all our people," Professor Jones insisted.

"Did you hear what I said?" Wade leered at the professor.

"Look, Wade." Professor Jones looked around the room to see if he had any supporters. "I have been making inquiries into colleges that will be interested in giving you a scholarship." He opened his portfolio and began taking out papers.

"I don't want to see nothing. I don't want to hear nothing."

"Yes—yes, now I wrote . . ." The cat kept on as if Wade hadn't cracked his lips, and something inside Wade started falling to pieces. He rushed into the kitchenette and came out with a piece of iron pipe that the plumber had left from a job, and ran up to the professor, shouting, "Now I ain't going no goddamn where, not a goddamn where. And if you don't get the hell out of here, you ain't going to be able to either." Professor Jones read the message in Wade's eyes, and without even waiting to close his portfolio, made it out of the room, papers flying everywhere.

There was a long silence after he left. Then suddenly Mumma broke out laughing. "Did you see how that old fool took off?"

She doubled up and Willie joined in. The sight of the little man making it out of the door must have been funny as hell, because they added it to their long list of lifelong jokes, like Uncle Dan on the barber-shop pole, and Big Willie not being worth spit in a white woman's eyes; but at that time it wasn't funny to Wade. Mumma and Willie Earl couldn't stop laughing. Uncle Dan too, but not so hearty. He got positively shifty-eyed and edged up to Wade, but it wasn't until a good few seconds later that Wade realized he was still clutching the iron pipe hard, looking down at Mumma sitting there all bent over with her laughter.

It hit him full-faced of a sudden, that Uncle Dan thought he was going to give it to Mumma. The shock of the thought went right through him. He turned to Faith and she wasn't laughing at all. She stood staring at him, her eyes wide and dark with fright, as if she wanted to stop him from doing something but was afraid to move. He stepped back from them in surprise, then suddenly threw the pipe from him and ran out into the street.

Inching up now in the long line, the heat suddenly blistering, the sounds of the laughter echoing and re-echoing in his ear sounded strange. Strange, because it was one of his favorite laughing pieces. But that night he had not laughed. Wade bit hard on his lips, forcing his gaze to remain on the stooped waiting shoulder in front of him, trying not to feel the pressure of the heart. He had thrown the pipe from him that night and he had run into the streets and into the park and cried.

He did not know why he had cried. It surely wasn't because he had chased Old Prof away. His great love for the little man had long gone. He had tried forgetting, along with Mumma, all the professor had done for them. Mumma had succeeded; he had not. He never forgot, but somewhere along the line it had ceased to matter. Somewhere along the line he had been forced to choose sides and of course he had chosen Mumma's. Now the little man was only a butt to their jokes: "Look at that nosey old thing; I wonder whose business he's getting into today. Sneaky runt, one day he'll sure God get his long nose in a hole he can't get it out of. . . ." And on and on, one crack after another that Wade joined in with as much glee as Mumma.

But that night he had run out of the house and cried. All that night there was nothing but confusion in his head. It had been Graduation Day; he ought to have been happy, he didn't ever have to put his little toe into another school; yet the only thing he could think about was that he had picked up a piece of pipe against Professor Jones and Mumma had laughed.

But she did not laugh too often in the six years that followed. She went in more for those long silences, the thinking inside herself, the constant complaining; searching through his eyes as if she believed God actually gave her the power to see inside his soul; the long sighs, and then every now and again a couple of tears.

Willie Earl went off and married Margie, the chick he'd been dating, and before six good months were up, he brought around a baby girl. That cut off the little money he used to give. Not that it ever was much. Willie Earl worked as a longshoreman now, and he worked long hours, but the more he worked and the longer the hours, the more he bellyached about how tough life was. He hardly came around to see them, once he had moved out. Didn't want to hear Mumma complain.

It was hard to decide who complained the most, Mumma or Willie Earl, although if it is true that people take things from their folks, it was a sure thing that Willie Earl learned a lot about complaining of how tough times were, how hard it was to hold onto a penny, how much this or that cost, how terrible it was to be alive, from Mumma.

It was hard as anything to believe Mumma, when she said after Willie Earl visited, "It sure was good to see Lil' Willie. It sure did my heart a whole lot of good for him to stop by." But then, the soap opera was Mumma's brand of happiness.

Wade and Mumma didn't see things the same way from the start. She expected him to follow in Willie Earl's footsteps: Get little jobs on trucks or sweeping out stores, or maybe going down to the garment center, dragging hand trucks through the streets. The ideas were strangers the minute they entered his ear, foreign to him as crêpe suzette. He never knew what he wanted to do, but he sure as hell knew what he didn't want to do.

The antisocial bit that caught him up in high school didn't unwind simply because he graduated. He didn't give one damn for studs talking the same garbage every day. He didn't care about baseball, hated talk about cars or clothes, and chicks were something he had his own ideas about and didn't need to share them. He was known for taking a sock at a sucker, after listening to him talk for hours without saying anything, for no other reason than that he was saying *nothing*. He figured to stop any trouble on that account, by not being around ordinary studs.

His first job was around a pool parlor. Guys around pool parlors were different, around this one on Lenox Avenue anyway. Sure, there were some who came around talking loudly and pushing a lot of nonsense, but usually the poolroom was a place where cats did a lot of things, but didn't do too much talking. Guys played and looked inside themselves and cracked jokes that were so nasty they had to be original.

Wade made good money too, with his salary and tips, and he gave Mumma every bit of it—that is, of course, except what he himself spent on the house. Telephones were coming in and a few of the big-money people around the poolroom were talking about getting them. Wade decided to surprise Mumma and had one installed without telling her.

That same week he came into the house to find the home-relief investigator giving Mumma the devil. "But Mrs. Williams, I hope you don't expect us to be feeding you and paying your bills when you can afford a telephone." She was sitting in one of the straight-backed kitchen chairs, looking at Mumma with that half-surprised stare that people reserved for nitwits and fools.

"Well, what I'm going to do, Miss O'Neil? My brother-in-law give it to me on account of I'm here with the children, and I'm not a well woman. I couldn't say no."

Wade hated hearing Mumma lie to this woman. He hated the fact that she wouldn't just say her younger son was working to help stretch that little bit of money the home relief was giving her and it wouldn't make millionaires of them, not by a long shot. It angered him that she had to sit there lying, because as far as this woman was concerned, a penny in their pockets was grand larceny against the City; and a telephone in their house put them in the same class with her, and she wasn't having any.

"Who is going to pay the bills, Mrs. Williams? It's one thing to say a telephone is a present, but the bills have to be paid every month."

"Dan will pay it. He says he'll pay it."

"That's nonsense. The telephone is in your name and we

absolutely cannot allow that. We cannot allow a telephone in your name and we absolutely cannot allow it in your rooms. That is all, Mrs. Williams. Your checks will have to be discontinued until the telephone is removed, and I really believe that your case must be reinvestigated before you can be reinstated."

"What are we going to do about food?" Mumma pleaded.

"I suggest that you ask your brother-in-law, Mrs. Williams. Certainly the money he is paying for the telephone can help you out with food." She gathered her papers together.

"Miss O'Neil," Mumma cried. "I'll see about taking that thing out of here tomorrow if you promise me you'll just not stop them checks."

"I'll do no such thing," Miss O'Neil stood up trying to add another inch to her height. "You'll take that thing out of here and . . ."

"No, she ain't," Wade said quietly. He went to the corner and grabbing the broom, snapped the stick off with his foot and advanced toward her menacingly. "She ain't going to take it out, because I'm the one that put it in here. And I say it stays.

"It's been a long time I wanted to knock hell out of you, coming in this house and telling us how we can and how we can't live; what we must do and what we mustn't. Bitch, take your goddamn checks and everything that means you and get the fuck out of here."

She had dropped her folder in the first terrified moment. Now as he stood before her, she snatched it up with shaking hands and did a Professor Jones out through the door.

He purposely let a few minutes silently slip by, then suddenly doubled up with laughter. "Did you see how that old bag took off?" he shouted. "Bet she's all the way to the relief office by now, ain't even waited for a cab." He laughed, all the while conscious of Mumma's stare trying to shame him.

"Wade, do you know what you've done?" Tears running all down her cheeks. "Wade, whatever gets in you? It must be the devil himself."

But Wade never stopped laughing. He laughed and laughed until his eyes were red and watery, yet inside he was stone serious, looking and comparing; the reasons for laughing, the reasons for crying.

"What you crying about, Mumma?" he finally asked. "You should be glad that old bag is gone and you don't have to beg no more. That little money ain't worth all them tears. Don't worry about a thing, I'll take care of you."

From then on, he really acted the part of Big Willie. He made money and he lost money. When he made money he gave it all to Mumma, keeping out just enough to buy a chick a drink before he laid her. Where men got kicks from drinking, he got kicks from laying a broad. That is, as long as it was a gone chick. He didn't mind going out with whores, or chicks who went out for kicks. What he hated was a chick who had a cherry or one who had wedding-ring ideas, or those who complained, or promised faithfulness. He hated affairs with a conscience. His conscience was all used up at home.

Still Mumma wasn't satisfied. One day Wade came home and heard her getting after Faith. "Seems to me like such a waste of time, Faith. You spending all your time over them books and nothing coming of it. You been through that class of yours a dozen times, ain't you?"

"If I go through it a dozen more times, Mumma," Faith said, stung by the exaggeration and sensitive as the devil, "I'm still going to finish."

"I'd be all for you finishing, if I thought . . . Now Faith, ain't everybody made for book learning. . . ."

"OK I'm dumb, Mumma. But I'm still going to try."

"I ain't saying you dumb, Faith. Lots of things folks ain't gifted for. Maybe you'd have done better if you taken up dressmaking or something."

"But I didn't want to be a dressmaker, Mumma. I want to be a secretary."

"You ain't doing nothing but wasting your time, child, dreaming."

"I'm willing to pay for all the time she wants to waste, Mumma," Wade put in.

"Pay for her time?" Mumma turned on him angrily. "How you going to pay for her time when you can hardly pay for yours? How do you figger we making it on that little bit of money you bring in here every week? She got to have clothes and carfare and lunch every single day. I wish some one of you would talk sense. Here she trying to be some big secretary and she can't even make it out of school."

Wade stared hard at Mumma and she returned his stare. They both knew that up to that time, Wade had brought more money into the house than Willie Earl had brought in his entire lifetime. He laughed so that his breath blew in her face, refusing to get angry. "If she never comes out of school, it's all right by me, Mumma. She can take her whole life as long as they don't put her out. And don't worry about her carfare nor her lunch or anything else as long as I'm around."

That same night Wade looked up from a game of pool and saw Archie, the big numbers banker, sporting his big diamond ring on his little finger, which glittered every time he flicked ash from his big black cigar. Wade put down his cue stick, got his hat and jacket, and walked out the door. Walking to the street where Archie lived, up the block, entering the building, Wade stood in the shadows under the steps waiting for the time when Archie would enter, not caring if he waited all night. He had nothing but patience. But as luck would have it he had to wait only an hour.

He heard the big man say "good night" to someone out on the street, enter the building and start up the stairs, grunting and groaning as he pulled his weight up step after step. Wade counted the steps until he figured that Archie might be in the middle of a flight, then silently he rushed out. He ran up the stairs two at a time and before the big man had a chance to look back, caught him in a grip that pinned his arms to his sides, threw a rabbit punch to the back of his neck, then stepped out of the way while Archie's weight dragged him down the stairs to the landing.

Wade stood over him waiting to see if he opened his eyes, waiting to see whether Archie would recognize him, knowing that if he did show any sign of consciousness, he would be forced to close his eyes for good. But he lay, dead out, a big gash on his forehead where he had hit the stairs, pouring out blood. Searching his pockets, Wade found his wallet and counted out the money—three hundred dollars. He threw the wallet back on top of Archie, then walked slowly from the building and back to Lenox Avenue.

At the corner he stood, feeling inside himself for his reaction: a touch of guilt, a bit of remorse, a hint of pity for the man he had left unconscious, soaking in his blood. He felt nothing. Nothing! Nor did he believe he would have felt anything if Archie had opened his eyes and he had been forced to close them.

He walked the two blocks to his house. Taking the three hundred dollars, he threw it into Mumma's lap, standing over her as she counted it, watching her hands shake. But if there were any questions inside her, she kept them there. She didn't even bother to look at him. It was more money than she had ever had at one time in her life, and she was afraid of where he might have got it. She must have figured it might be better all around to be able to pray for his soul in ignorance.

He settled now for hanging around the corners and pool halls, waiting until they were almost broke before going out to make another grab, then coming into the house and throwing the money into her lap, always waiting as she glanced through it, her eyebrows quivering, her hands shaking, hovering over it, finally closing determinedly around it, ignoring his grin as she forced herself slowly to her feet; hobbling over to the table, where she counted it out dollar by dollar, planning on how long it would last; then sticking it into her bosom, waiting for him to leave or go off to sleep so she might hide it even from him.

He sometimes made money gambling, but not often. He preferred to wait around a poker game, watching the way the money was going—it grew to be a science—and if the winnings were big, anywhere from a couple of hundred to a couple of thousand (for more money changed hands over a gambling table in Harlem than ever saw the light of day) leaving to follow the winner home and pulling his mug treatment.

He found real joy in giving Mumma this money. It seemed to him only right, if she had to worry and needed the cause to pray, that her needs be justified. She lived better than she had ever lived; she ate better than she had ever eaten; she bought more clothes for herself and for Faith, had more money to put in the collection box in church. Yet in the next few years, Mumma's face, which had always been the smoothest and prettiest black, started sinking here and there into permanent lines, drawing down the sides of her mouth and digging deep furrows into her forehead. Her hair, which had been slowly greying, completely whitened. She grew forgetful and her arthritis grew more bothersome, causing her limp to worsen; but her trips to the church increased to a nightly routine.

Mumma sometimes hinted to him about finding a job but he told her as long as the family didn't need a thing, why worry? He was a loner. He didn't go in for small talk; it got on his nerves, and he had been top dog in his family too long to take any orders from any little joker who wanted to say he was boss. That's the way it was. Even if he went out with a chick, she had to keep her mouth shut. They lied when they talked about love, and rent and clothes were everybody's problem. After a while Mumma stopped throwing hints.

So it really threw him higher than a kite, one day, when he walked into the house and who should be there but Professor Jones.

Mumma sat in her rocker crying, absolutely to pieces, so he figured right away that she probably had got to the professor for reasons of her own instead of the other way around. He jumped onto the defensive right away, thinking that maybe she wanted another try at the home relief. But Professor Jones didn't give him time to wait.

"See here, Wade," the professor came right to the point. "Your mother is quite concerned about you. She said you have been just hanging around the streets doing nothing and she's afraid you might get into trouble."

"He ain't never told me nothing about it," Mumma cried. That really shook him up. He had never seen her in pieces like this. It was one thing when he teased her and joked with her, trying to see how long she would hold. It was another when she broke; then his conscience took him like a wave. He sat quietly looking at her. "He stay out all kinds of hours in the night. He always got money and don't say how he got it. He don't *work*. He don't do nothing, that child. I don't know what's to become of him."

"Son," Professor Jones said, and at the sound of that word, coming from the professor, Wade laughed. It was funny as hell. Mumma had forgotten how she used to poke fun at him, now that she needed him, but with Wade, the hurt ran deeply over what he had done to the little man. "I know how hard it is for someone with your remarkable intelligence to adjust to the type of work offered. Your mother has been talking about the garment district, or trucking, and of course I know you are unsuited for that kind of work. You are a high-school graduate, you have a diploma. We have to find you something on your level."

Wade might have walked out then, only Prof hadn't mentioned about being chased out of the house, nor did he get after him for not working, or want to know where he made his money; so he sat on.

"Not saying that any job you might get will be on your intellectual level but you have to understand you do not have college training. Now, we have been fighting to get some Blacks placed on some City jobs and it is just possible that I might be able to get you on as a trainee in the Health Department."

"What, starting to fight again at my age, Prof?"

"You are only twenty."

"That's right too, ain't it?" Wade chuckled. "What do I have to do?"

"There is a test you will have to take. Then a training program."

"A test? I haven't looked at a book outside of Faith's textbooks for years."

"That's all right. You can do it if you want to. I have confidence in you."

Maybe it was Professor Jones' confidence, or maybe the fact that Prof hadn't held anything against him. Or maybe it was Mumma's tears. He didn't know. It might have been that he had already become tired; anyway, he gave in without a struggle. He took the test and got in, went through the training program, and ended with a job in a laboratory as a helper. He did not make technician because he needed two years of college. But what the hell, he was having his first experience on a payroll. He was twenty, looked like twenty-eight, and felt every bit of thirty-eight.

The job never took him to the heights that he had at first imagined. He didn't take Mumma and Faith out of the one room and kitchenette, and get a private room all to himself; but one thing that happened made a real dent in his life. He met Gay.

12

Gay was a technician. She looked up from her work and saw him when they first ushered him in, finished what she had been doing and came right over. "Hello, my name is Gay—Gay Sommers." She held out her hand and he took it, realized for the first time there was a correct way to shake a hand. "I'm very glad to see you." Her warm laughing eyes, looking into his, had told him that she was really very glad, had realized the struggle to get him in and was grateful that she no longer would be the sole Black person working here.

And he? He was grateful. Grateful because there was no strong perfume pouring out to smother his nostrils, grateful because there was no look of the flirt in her eyes, no heavy powder to cover her black skin, no lipstick. Her walk was not indolent, her manner not coquettish; everything was like her handshake and her voice—authoritative, warm, heavy, yet feminine as hell. He absorbed all of her in one quick breath and she had him. Hooked.

For the first time in his life, he spent his waking hours scheming how to get a chick. It wasn't easy. She was too straightforward. She didn't seem to know what flirting meant. And to make matters worse she was engaged to some medical student. There was only one thing he had going for him and he intended to make it work: his good looks. Not that he figured she would go for that alone. He worked overtime reading up on things he had let go for years. Read up on current events so he could discuss them with authority. Spent hours before the mirror learning how to bite down on his sneering lip. In other words, he got to developing a charm that he'd never known he possessed and by the time he got his second pay check, he was taking her out to lunch.

They were different, there was no doubt about that. Maybe that was the reason for their attraction. One never touched the other's inner world and maybe that was the reason her interest in him grew and grew. Mumma had a saying that you never stick your spoon into the middle of a boiling pot, when you can taste near the edges. Those were some wise words that Gay should have followed. But no, Gay had the idea that she could read all people the way she did the *New York Times,* analytically. He never hipped her; he knew he was better left unread.

One day over lunch she asked, "How old are you?"

"How old do you think?" He figured she would put him in the age range she wanted.

"About twenty-nine?"

"If it's important," he nodded.

"It isn't that important, it's just that there is something about you that is so strange. Well, I mean—you are young and everything—but somehow—I get the impression that you can be quite dangerous."

"Maybe it's my eyes." He smiled.

"Maybe, yes. Yes, that's it. Most people live through their eyes; you live behind yours. It's hard to know a person who lives behind his eyes. Tell me about yourself."

He wanted to tell. Break down into true confessions. Tell her that the person behind his eyes wasn't worth knowing—some of the things he had done. . . . But he knew that the mystery about him was his real drawing power and he wasn't about to give it up. Not yet, anyway.

He never tried to analyze what relationship he wanted with her. All he knew was that he wanted her. He supposed, somewhere in the back of his mind, that the moment he got into bed it would break the hold she had on his mind; set him free to decide. But it didn't happen that way.

In the first place she didn't let him seduce her. She came right out with, "Look, Wade, we have been looking at each other like two teenagers. I suppose we both know we'll end up in bed, so why don't we get it over with?"

So it happened. Only she didn't use sex like a kind of club the way some women did: as though they thought they were God's answer to all men, and the moment you screwed them you became a slave and the bargaining point for any further activity, sex or otherwise. She took it in her stride as she did everything else, even though he knew she liked him better than she had before, and after a few times with her he was hooked completely.

That somehow started a resentment toward her. It wasn't only that she did not want to use him, but he could not use her. She wasn't like other chicks, holding and pulling and begging, making him feel that his manhood was the greatest thing that women ever experienced. His resentment wasn't like hate. It was more like confusion. It was like taking a walk on a foggy day and not knowing whether the next step you took would be solid, or you might be falling over some damn precipice; or like something from out of a fog brushing against you, making you feel threatened and you go to boxing only to find you are putting up that struggle all by yourself.

That's the way it was. He got to fighting and never knew whom he was fighting, whether it was Gay or himself, and he never asked himself why. She had a party for him to meet some of her friends, in her apartment in the Bronx. He spent the whole evening refusing to make conversation, and the next day told her, "They're all squares that talk the same shit on a different level as the people on Lenox Avenue, except that the people on Lenox Avenue insist that they'll get Cadillacs with their mink coats and *your* friends will settle for squirrels with their Fords. I don't listen to them on Lenox Avenue and I won't be bugged by them in the Bronx."

She didn't get angry as he expected, so the next few times she invited him to come to see her, he didn't go. She simply stopped inviting him and settled for coming down to visit him. Looking back, he often puzzled about why she bothered; she must have realized by that time something was off key. The only reason he could see was the fatal mistake that so-called intelligent women often make: thinking they can make a man whole again, after the grinding machine of life has made chopped meat of him; a fairy-tale assumption that chicks like Gladys never got blinded by. But then, chicks like Gladys never got a chance to read fairy tales.

The family went for Gay and she liked them too although she didn't dig the closeness of their relationship. She brought Mumma flowers and candy and things like that; talked long and friendly hours with Faith; but didn't understand why he couldn't stay away from the house for more than a few hours at one sitting. He tried to explain to her how Faith had almost been done in by a stud in the house when she was little. She accepted his explanation, but he knew from the long penetrating gaze she gave him that she wasn't about to understand.

She helped him put Uncle Dan to bed a couple of times, even

held an ice bag to his head, scolding him about drinking so much; but when Wade tried to explain how much Uncle Dan needed him, she laughed, and said, "Your Uncle Dan is a big boy now."

Lenox Avenue was not her cup of tea. She walked there only because he was there, but in her walk she carried the conviction, whether she was conscious of it or not, that their relationship depended on him giving it up for her. Even guys on the block dug that. They never spoke to him when they saw them together, although afterward they usually came up and asked, "Hey, who was *that* I saw you walking with the other day?" It was significant that they never called her "chick" or "broad" or "babe," or anything like that. "She's the top of the bottle, man. She's grade A."

Somehow, that added to his confusion, and as a year passed—he had never been with a broad a week, never mind a year—his feeling for Gay grew but so did his confusion.

Faith graduated from business school that year, and he and Gay planned a surprise party. Mumma was sick, laid up in bed with a swollen knee, and Gay did all the cooking and planning, buying a cake and inviting the whole family to celebrate. They had a gay time that evening, with Uncle Dan swearing he would vomit if he touched the stuff, but making it on Coca-Cola. They were all happy, and Wade more than any. He being responsible for Faith actually finishing not only her schooling but her business course as well, and with Gay there as part of his family. There was really nothing more he wanted. Somewhere back of his mind the thought that he might be married real soon was born.

So why didn't it happen?

That night he heard Mumma say to Uncle Dan, half-jokingly, "Looks like I'm getting ready to lose me another son. You raise them, work your fingers to the bone, and when you get to the place where they can look out for you, they start getting that married look about them."

"Yeah, well I reckon, if you could turn back the clock, Evelyn, and get to looking as pretty as Gay, you'd have no worry coming," Uncle Dan answered, and they laughed.

But though Wade laughed along with them, it stung him that Mumma could even say "where they can look out for you," after all he had done for her.

Later, on their way to the subway, Gay said to him, "Wade, I have something important I want to tell you."

"What is it?" he answered, wondering if she had taken Mumma seriously about him doing nothing for her.

"I'm going to have a baby."

It was just a simple little statement but he froze, staring at her. He put his hands on her shoulders and pushed her out searching through her eyes to see the honesty there. It didn't make sense that this gone chick, this classy broad, could be having a baby for *him*. He grabbed her to him, hugging her. Then he kissed her, and then not knowing what else to do he held her hand and ran down the block, stopping before they came to the corner to grab her and kiss her again. God, he was happy. He had never been happy before in his life. He knew that now. All his confusion disappeared. He knew what he had to do. They would be married. He would move to the Bronx—that is, until he could find a house, a house like the one he remembered down South—where the children, and he knew they would have many, could run out in the back yard or the front yard and play right under the nose of their mother. Life after all was so damn simple.

Back in the house that night, he sat on a chair in the shadows, looking at Mumma, Faith and Uncle Dan talking, laughing out loud, hugging himself as though he were something precious, the most important person in the world; realizing from their sidelong glances that they were curious, they wanted him to bare his soul; but no one said a word, just left him to himself and his happiness.

Early the next morning he found himself suddenly wide awake looking at the ceiling, waves and waves of doubts like fear hitting at him. What was he getting himself into? Who in the hell did she think she was, coming in here where he had always had to struggle so hard for what he got, and simply taking over? Here she had won him away from his family and Lenox Avenue and all the other things that he had known; signed, sealed and delivered him to the Bronx, without for one minute losing her poise, her manner, her reason. Life wasn't that easy. It wasn't that goddamn easy. Was she really pregnant? Was she using that as a weapon to get him tied up there in the Bronx with her phoney friends? Did she really like his family or was she pretending? If she liked them, how could she wait until Mumma was lying in bed sick to spring that one on him? Mumma was right. He was getting ready to leave her when she really needed him.

Later that day when Gay came around to see them, he sat silently looking at her as she went around the room doing little things for Mumma: heating soup, fixing a pretty tray, and all the little things that made her special. Then for no reason that he understood, he waited until she was deeply involved in conversation with Faith to walk out of the house, staying away until he knew she had gone.

When he did come back, Faith was reproachful. "Wade, whatever happened to you? I went to Uncle Dan, and all over, looking for you. Gay got tired and went home."

"Wade, you ain't never had much sense," Mumma said. "But I'm warning you, you can't go around treating a girl like Gay just any which-a-way."

Wade chuckled contentedly, pinching Mumma's angry face. "Did she say anything before she left?" he asked, wanting to know if she had mentioned the baby.

"No. She said she would see you on the job Monday," Faith answered.

Wade grinned. This was her first reproach. It would be the first Sunday since they met that they wouldn't be spending together.

On the job Monday, he kept out of her way and she didn't push. It was as though she knew he had to make up his mind and she wanted no part of rushing him. Tuesday was the same. On Wednesday when he knew she had promised to visit Faith, he went out of the house and stayed again. Only this time when he came in she was waiting. She insisted that he walk her to the subway.

"What is it, Wade?" she asked on the way. "Is something bothering you?"

"No, why should it?"

"Is it the baby?"

"What baby?" he asked. She stopped to look at him and somehow the look of her pierced him through his heart. She reminded him of Mumma, standing there, the expression of hurt not wanting to show. Maybe that's why he turned the screw. "If you talking about that crap you mentioned the other night, I don't believe it. But if it is true, you best get rid of it. Marriage ain't in my line."

He wanted her to hit him, spit at him, even curse him out, the way a Lenox Avenue chick would do, so he could take her in his arms and laugh, kiss away the hurt expression struggling across her pretty black face. But no, her eyes became blank, and she was her sweet smiling self, that grade-A self that he had no intention of bowing to. "All right," she said. "I'll be seeing you, probably tomorrow."

She ran down the subway steps and he stood at the head of the stairs wanting more than anything to run after her, listening for the train, wishing that his big clumsy feet would carry him down after her of their own accord. He heard the train come in and pull out, and still he stood, waiting, hoping, expecting her to come back up the stairs, but she didn't. Yet somehow he did not believe she could just take that train and ride out of his life, not when he was hurting all the way to his very soul. Finally he ran down the stairs, looked around, jumped over the turnstile to make sure. Not one person on the platform. She had gone.

The next day at work, she was still calm. She spoke as though nothing had happened between them. "Hello, Wade, how is your mother?"

That forced him to say, "Oh, she's fine. Just fine." Resentful because she was showing him she was too far above him to be touched, yet she was far above him, way beyond him and he knew that all the things he had said to her, his effort to lower her, to grind her into the dust, would never make her as low as he felt, as low as he was. . . .

She kept busy that day and out of his way, and the next and the next. Even when he approached her, she smiled her warm smile, looking directly into his eyes, as though she understood every little thing about him, things he didn't even know about himself; as though she pitied him; as though she were the one in the position to pity—and this held him silent.

He let the bomb drop on his family one evening when Mumma was sitting up feeling better. Faith and Uncle Dan sat battling over a game of checkers and he lay on his back on the bed, staring up at the ceiling.

"What happened to Gay?" Mumma asked, breaking one of those long thoughtful silences. "Lord, here I thought I had me a new daughter-in-law and she ain't been to see me for weeks."

He knew she was digging and from the hush that fell between Faith and Uncle Dan, realized that they were every bit as anxious to know as Mumma, even though they would never ask. He let them wait a few minutes. Then when the silence was so loud it was about to break their eardrums, he answered casually, "She's having a baby."

"What?" Uncle Dan roared. "Well now, ain't that a bubba!" He had expected anything but for Uncle Dan to come over, pull him up out of the bed and go dancing around the room with him. "Son, I'm mighty glad to hear that. Mighty glad." Faith too, jumped up squealing and making funny noises, like oohs and aahs, and silly things girls thought they were supposed to do when they were delighted.

He heard Mumma saying with a smile in her voice, "Well now, that sure is nice. Gay is a real fine girl, though Lord knows I don't know what she sees in the likes of you."

He struggled to free himself from the center of glory, then poised the bomb. "I said Gay was having a baby. I didn't say *I* was."

"Well, it is your baby, ain't it, Son?" Uncle Dan said. "Sure it is. Gay ain't that kind of girl."

"I don't know whose baby it is and I give less than a damn. I told her to shove it."

It was the first time in his life that Faith ever drew away from him, and it caught him up in such surprise that the punch she leveled at him a few seconds later might have toppled him, if he hadn't been built so solid to the ground. "You didn't. You didn't say nothing like that to Gay. You go right to her and take it back. Take it back, do you hear? Tell her you didn't mean it, Wade. Tell her you didn't mean it."

"You fool," Uncle Dan cried. "You fool. Boy, you know what you done? You done acted the fool."

Wade tried to keep a tight smile on his face, but the muscles kept twitching and shaking and he felt more like a marionette than the fool Uncle Dan was talking about, so he turned angrily to Mumma, shouting, "Ain't you going to add your A-flat to the chorus, Mumma? It don't make sense you sitting there not saying a word."

She studied him long before she said, "I ain't never been able to make up my mind if you just mean clear through or just plumb crazy. But one thing I know, you sure ain't responsible."

"I'm responsible to you, Mumma," he shouted, madder at her than he had ever been or had any reason to be. "I'm responsible to you. What you want me to do? Go off and get married like Willie Earl and leave you here sick with nobody to look after you? How would you think Pappa would have liked that?

"Me, running to the Bronx and leaving my family. Yeah, that's what I said, the Bronx. Because if you think Gay was going to leave the Bronx and her stuck-up friends to come and shack up in a little room with you and yours, you are mistaken.

"Naw, it's me she wants. She don't want you. She wants to take *me* and change *me* over into some fucking floozy that she can call *her* man."

He walked out of the room because somehow he didn't get the feeling that his little speech moved anybody. It even sounded hollow to him. So hollow that three minutes later he found himself on a train making it to the Bronx. But though he searched he didn't find her place. He had almost never been up here by himself before. He knew the station to get off, he had brought her address, but somehow at this time of the night nothing looked familiar. He stopped every colored face he saw, asking if they knew a Miss Gay Sommers, but all the faces were the wrong ones to ask. The night was almost finished when he finally made it back home.

The next morning he was the first one on the job, waiting impatiently for her to come in. She never came. Around midday he asked the supervisor if she had heard from her and learned she had called in sick. Sick, he knew what that meant. He walked out of the job and made it to the Bronx again. This time he found the house but no one at home. He waited on the stoop, sitting there until he got tired, going to a small restaurant for a drink of coffee, coming back a short time later, trying her bell again. He waited until dark but she never came. He came back the following day and when he didn't see her decided that she must have stayed with a friend until everything was over. He *knew* that was it.

The next two weeks went by without one word, and Wade suffered. He went about doing what he supposed he always did— working, talking, fooling around with his family—but inside he suffered. Suffered in a way, strangely enough, he was used to. As though he had gone through it all his life, this bleeding inside for something, for someone lost through no fault of his own. Someone without whom he was finished.

After two weeks he heard that she was better, but had been transferred to the Board of Health. She would not be back to the lab again. The job lost meaning for him. He forced himself to work every day, hoping that something might happen and she might be sent back. Two months went by, without one word; then suddenly one day there was a big commotion. She had called up to tell some of her old friends of her coming marriage.

He lost his head and rushed out of the place. He made it to the Bronx again. She wasn't there. He waited on the stoop until she came home.

She saw him waiting and she missed a step, but when she walked up she was her same self. "Wade, what a surprise." The same warm smile, the same way of looking into your eyes as if she could read you but you could not touch her. That forced him to a calmness he was far from feeling.

"Thought I'd look you up to find out how you were doing," he said in a tone that was meant to be light but fooled nobody, least of all himself. There were groceries in her arms and he took them from her as they went upstairs.

"I'm doing well, Wade." He realized with a shaking heart that she was; that she had not been torn apart as he had been. She had been hurt, yes. Not that it showed in her face, except an agelessness that poured out of her eyes. He had seen these signs of suffering before, in Mumma's eyes. He knew instinctively it was suffering without being able to put it into words. But Gay had gone on in her same straightforward way, taking it in her stride.

"The baby?" He laid the groceries on the table.

"All that has been taken care of." Her matter-of-factness stemmed the protests his disappointment pushed to his lips but he had not come all this way or waited all this time simply to pay his respects.

"I didn't mean it, Gay. I didn't mean all those things I said."

"At the time, you did. But I don't blame you, Wade, I understand."

"Understand? Understand what? I don't even understand myself. I don't *know* what made me say those things."

"I know you don't, Wade. But I realized for a long time it would never be easy for you to leave your family. You are too close to them."

"A man has a right to be close to his family."

"Yes, but not that way. There comes a time in any animal's life, birds, beasts or fish, when he must leave the home, the nest. But it is as though your wings are clipped. You can't leave, Wade. And that's the reason you became so nasty. Unconsciously, you could not stand the idea of leaving."

"You never gave me a chance," he pleaded.

"For one whole year? I gave you nothing but chances, Wade. I gave in to you all the time because I saw you needed a chance. I pointed things out to you in a dozen different ways, because I wanted you—I wanted us to have a chance; but the more I pointed, the more you resented me."

"I—I—I never resented you, Gay."

"Yes, you did. I wasn't in this relationship by myself. We fought almost from the first, without saying a word." He was silent, hearing the truth of her words. "That's why I got pregnant."

"Because of that?"

"I called it giving you the greatest chance."

"That wasn't fair. You should have let me make up my mind without using that as a weapon."

"I know it wasn't fair. It wasn't honest. It wasn't decent. I hated myself for doing something I would condemn another woman for doing. But Wade, I *am* a woman. I am twenty-eight years old and I found myself giving up a life that I worked very hard for, being drawn into a life I did not want. I had to force a decision and you made it when you told me to get rid of the baby."

"But I didn't, Gay. I swear I didn't. I hadn't even thought it out. I just said the first thing that came to my . . ."

"It was waiting there to be said, and I think I knew it. I always knew it. I could never reach the you curled up there behind your eyes, yet you had forced me into a relationship I would never have chosen for myself. I couldn't break it. I had to pick and pick and pick in order to make you *kick* me out of your orbit, to *free* me, I think that's what I wanted. . . ."

"But I didn't, Gay. I love you."

"I know, Wade. I know, that's what makes it so frightening." She searched his eyes. "Because it's there and it's beyond my understanding, but Wade, it is also beyond *yours.*"

He hid his eyes with his hands. Everything confused him. He had gone over in his mind some of the things that she spoke of, and most of what she said came so near to the answers that it very well might mean she was speaking the truth. He just didn't know. All he knew was that here she was speaking in her simple way, with the confidence about her that she knew she spoke the truth, and he had no way of truthfully contradicting her.

"You're getting married, I hear."

"Yes, I am."

"To the medical student?"

"Yes."

"Does he know?"

She smiled at him as though he were a child.

"What is there to know? He knew that I left him because I cared for someone else. He is willing to forget, that's all."

"You don't care now?"

"It doesn't matter now."

"Not at all, Gay? It doesn't matter at all?"

She was silent for a time, then said, "I suppose it does matter. I care. I probably will always care. I care a lot about you and your mother and Faith and Uncle Dan and I think Aunt Julie is just about the strongest, most wonderful woman I have ever met. They are all good people. But it's over."

"Then you don't love him?"

"Yes, I do love him. Life with him will be simple. When you have a lot to do in life, you need a simple life—and—well, yes—I love him."

"Have you set the date yet?"

"Yes, Saturday."

That shook him up. He didn't realize it could be so soon. Yet she had set the tone and had been impersonal enough so that even when she spoke of caring there was nothing left to do but say good-by.

She walked with him to the door and held out her hand.

Suddenly the realization rushed over him that when he left that door, she was going out of his life; that the possibility of ever seeing her again was over; that is was all his fault. And it became more than he could bear. He found himself on his knees before her, his face pressed to her legs, his arms around her, crying, "Gay, Gay, I didn't mean it. I didn't mean it." Tears almost strangled him. "Gay, please, please, I didn't mean it."

"Wade, get up. Please get up." She trembled as she helped him to his feet, forcing him through the door and as she closed it against his insistence, he realized that she was crying too.

He didn't go back to the job. He couldn't. He walked around Lenox Avenue, playing cards, shooting pool and sitting around looking at Uncle Dan boozing. He didn't want to sleep because every completed day brought it so much nearer to Saturday and Saturday must never come. Only it did.

It was late Friday night when he told Uncle Dan that Gay was getting married. That must have kept poor Uncle Dan awake all night hitting the bottle, because early Saturday morning about five o'clock Uncle Dan woke him up.

"Wade!" He banged on the window and Wade got up to let him in. "You are a damn fool. You let that girl run off and marry, and you ain't never going to have a peaceful day in your life. Son, don't you be sleeping when you got things to do."

"Dan," Mumma said. "If you don't shut your drunken mouth and get out of here and go get some sleep like you got some sense, I'm going to get out of this bed and choke you."

"But ain't you heard, Evelyn?" Uncle Dan asked. "Gay is getting married today and that boy is just lying there as though ain't nothing happening."

Mumma lay silent for a while, then finally asked, "Well, what he going to do, Dan?"

Faith sat up in bed and wiped the sleep out of her eyes and suddenly the room seemed charged with excitement, as though there had been a birth or an accident or a death, or something like that.

"What he going to do? He's going to get his behind up out of this bed and go up there to that Bronx and get this girl like he got some sense."

"And just supposing she says 'yes' and comes with him, Dan. Where is he going to bring her?"

"What's that got to do with it, woman? He can bring her here, or to my house, or some damn hotel or for that matter stay in the hell on up there where she is, don't matter. Long as he stops that damn marriage."

Wade lay staring at the ceiling, tense, half-waiting for the argument that might make him get up and go charging up to the Bronx like some goddamn knight in some goddamn armor. He wondered whether, with all her sensible way of doing things, Gay might go for that.

"Don't you see, Baby?" Uncle Dan pleaded with Faith. "This thing here that gal is doing, it's a lifetime thing. If he don't stop her now, he ain't ever going to have the chance again."

"I don't know, Uncle Dan," Faith said uncertainly. "If it was me more than likely I'd say 'yes,' and maybe most of the girls I know would too. Someone like Mumma might go along with that. Poor folks, real poor folks like us, get kind of used to people doing things to us, treating us bad, stepping on us, making out like we nothing. We even get used to doing things—nasty things—to one another. We don't ever forget, but we sure do forgive easy. Forgive and make each other's lives miserable by talking about it, because we don't forget. We know that if we don't forgive, like as not we'll run into someone else that will do us the same, so we don't change our life none from one person to the next. But to a girl like Gay, why, she's been to college and everything and probably figgers there is a better way of being.

"If a man told me to take my baby and shove it, it would hurt me to my heart; but like as not if he came back truly sorry, I'd forgive him, if I loved him. With someone like Gay, it ain't a matter of just forgiving or forgetting, it's a matter of accepting one kind of life or another, and I figger that's a lot different."

Wade propped his head up on his hands, studying Faith with new respect as Gay's words came back to him: "I had to force you to throw me out of your orbit. . . ."

"But how he going to know if he don't go up there and try? He ain't losing nothing by trying," Uncle Dan insisted. "Now Wade, you get right on up out of that bed and get up there to that girl before the sun gets to shining."

Maybe that was the clue Wade was waiting for. What could he lose? He found himself pulling on his clothes so fast that he was dressed before anybody realized what was happening. Then Mumma got out of bed and started fussing.

"Listen, you two. Listen to me good. Leave that girl be, do you hear? Leave her be. She's a smart girl and she knows what she's about. Leave her be. That girl intended to have her a decent life and I don't fault her. Wade, you ain't going to give her that, cause you ain't responsible. You ain't never been responsible to us and you ain't aiming to be to her.

"You showed that when you abused her about your baby. Your Pa might have been no good down to his very socks, but he don't light a candle to you. He ain't never thrown a child of his away and he bragged about them all, them that was legal and them that was not.

"Wade had his chance, Dan, and he thrown it away. He ain't never gone up there when he had the right to. You ain't never forced him to do that. So what you sending him up there now for? To start trouble in that poor girl's life?"

"Don't you be talking to my nephew like that," Uncle Dan raged. "After all, where would you be if Big Willie didn't take pity on you and drag you out of your cotton patch?"

Wade didn't hear the rest of their argument because he was outside the door, running as hard as he could down the dark street. He didn't slow down until he reached the corner and then it was only to a fast walk. The walk slackened by the time he reached the subway, and faltered on his way down the stairs. When he came to the last step, he sat down.

"You ain't never been responsible to us and you ain't aiming to be to her." Mumma's words rang around in his head. "But I am responsible to you, Mumma. I am responsible," he cried aloud. Then sitting on the cold dark subway steps, he put his face into his hands and big sobs tore through his lips, rushed up the subway stairs, filling the street above.

"Move up, will you, feller?" a voice behind him urged, and Wade realized that there was a big space between himself and the man in front of him. He moved up to close the gap.

His throat was tight. He felt the heaviness of his clothes sticking to him; sweat poured down the sides of his face. He untied the handkerchief from around his neck, took his hat off, wiped the sweat band and put it back on, tied the handkerchief back around his neck, stepped out of line to count the men before him, got back into line again. The stooped shoulders in front of him had long been wet, but the stud stood patiently, as if it weren't the goddamn hottest day a sucker could ever stand in. Wade had the simple desire to put his knee in the small of the man's back and pull the shoulders straight, but he clenched his fists and looked up at the sun, trying to throw off the load that had settled on his own shoulders.

He searched his mind frantically for the sight of that clean sunlit road that had made his day so meaningful just a little while before. He knew it existed and it was only a matter of pulling it out and holding it with his mind to stop the tangle of thoughts and memories rising like a wall, shutting off the light. It had happened once before, he remembered, this clear-sightedness that made life simple, uncomplicated. He had felt that freedom once and he had not held onto it, but he wanted to hold it now. He *had* to. He had only to keep his mind clear of everything past and present that had ever meant something to him. Keep the road clear. Look at the future.

He fought and fought still thoughts grew like vines, a thicket entwining, cutting off the light of the road, bit by bit, until his entire mind was in shadows. Imprisoning him so he could not turn but had to stand, breathing hard while the darkened sections of his memory reeled out before his eyes.

13

"Come back for the funeral, Wade, come back." They had got stinko, he and Uncle Dan and Willie Earl, and Uncle Dan had held him in his arms and cried, because Wade was going to the Army. Willie Earl had wished him luck, all smug and contented, because he was a longshoreman and would not be called. He was happy at the thought that while Wade and a lot of suckers were risking their lives, falling dead by the hundreds, he would be making that long money putting in hours and hours of overtime.

It hadn't made any difference to Wade, though. The way he saw it, it took a war to get him off Lenox Avenue, and as long as Uncle Sam was paying the bills, he would go for the ride, sit out his time, then make it back to his family. He was no hero and he wasn't going to try to prove anything. That was why he promised Uncle Dan he would be back.

But life, even when it doesn't have a hell of a lot of meaning, is never that simple. He had been given a gun and forced to kill people he never knew, for reasons that he gave less than a damn about. But for the first time in his life he made friends outside his family and laughed and joked with guys he would never had thought of laughing and joking with before. They were a special brand of guys, though. They had to be special. They had to be special to form a special kind of joke, that wasn't so funny as it was tough, to hide the hurt and relief that got to you when, after walking and laughing with a guy one minute, you saw his guts blown open the next.

There were other kinds: There were the guys who got scared and tried to dig holes to hide in, as though the holes would last the duration; and there were those who just got stoned and could not move; there were those who pissed and messed all over themselves; and there were those who did all those things and still came up with jokes. Then there were the special few, mean and evil—some said even half-crazy. Maybe they had lived too long curled up behind their eyes; they laughed and joked all the while. Some called them ignorant but there were many times he had seen them leading the leaders.

It was out there, lying in one of those fox holes after the invasion of Normandy, that he looked upward and saw the sky and realized that in all his years in Harlem, he had not ever really seen a star. He got to looking up at the sky every chance he got, studying the stars and the moon and thinking of his life back in Harlem. He got to thinking in some vague way that he might not go back after this bit, that maybe he might start looking for new horizons, shake out his mind and see what he might be able to do with it. It might be that he was still brilliant, still the whiz kid.

But even with all this going around in his mind he looked out for home and Mumma. Faith had at last landed a job, not as secretary, but with the shortage of workers they had begun to hire Blacks in department stores as salesladies, and with the allotment and all the extra money he didn't need while he was in combat, he figured she must be doing better than she ever had done in her life. He played crap and blackjack and sent home all his winnings, asking Mumma to save him a part of it, telling her he had plans, big plans, a lot he wanted to do in the future. Even after he met Michele he kept sending Mumma money and making sure that things at home were always under control.

He didn't as a rule go for ofays, even the broads, but there wasn't much else you could do over there, except if you wanted a WAC, and the way he looked at it, anything American had to wait until he could do no better. They went to bed with a guy and thought they had a club, always pulling more out of him than he was willing to give.

That was something that he made up his mind one day to investigate: What did they think they had between their legs that inspired dreams? Even the lowest whores he ever went with had the strange idea that all they had to do was spread out one time and they had themselves a fish, hook, line and sinker. Yet a lot of studs went for it, laying their leave around as though they were in some screwing paradise, leaving all their money behind to go back behind the lines to finish their dreaming.

Michele wasn't like that. She was colorless all the way through to her soul. It wasn't that she was bad-looking, she just had a face that had seen a hell of a lot and couldn't be impressed any more. Before he got her into his bed, she said, "L'argent." And he had to pay up. Then she lay there not moving until he had finished. That got him mad as hell. Her eyes were not friendly, not unfriendly, just empty.

When she started out the door, he got in her way and she said,

"L'argent" again, and he paid her and this time it was the same. By then he was boiling. The next time he stepped into her way and she said "l'argent" he shook his head. She made to pass around him but he stood solidly still. She looked into his eyes and realized that it was useless. She shrugged and went to sit on the bed.

He didn't let her up for a week. At first her stony silence, her hostility, got to him and he met her scorn with scorn. He pulled her hair, slapped her face, pushed her around with his feet. She never changed expression, just looked at him from eyes that said she was used to it. After the third day of bread, cheese and wine, which he had a hustling kid bring to the door, and Michele, he became as gentle as a lamb.

He tried like hell to get one word out of her, one expression of softness, of warmth. By the end of the week, he was blubbering like a nine-month baby starting to be weaned. He got up one morning and she was gone.

He began to feel the bottomless depths of his loneliness. It was not new to him. Being in this strange country far away from his family had only released the familiar sensation that he had known so long ago. Maybe since the time Big Willie died, maybe when he and Faith had been put away, he couldn't exactly remember but it had seemed like always. He lay looking out at a shaft of sunlight playing on a line of clothes across the cluttered court from his room, wondering what he would do with the rest of his leave. The idea of another chick left him unmoved.

He heard a slight sound at the door and looking around saw her entering the room, her arms full of groceries. She went about fixing a long-overdue meal while he stood in the middle of the floor, turning around stupidly, following her movements around the room. He wanted to cry more than anything, but when she stood before him all he could do was take her in his arms.

They lived together for the rest of his leave, and all the week ends while he was stationed in France, and they might have been happy except that happiness is one of those words that have meaning only in a dictionary.

It had been one of those evenings when a whole day had gone by without a blemish and they were at the very top of their spirits. Maybe they were a little drunk, but he knew that Michele had started looking downright pretty to him. They had reached the point in their relationship when their eyes gave out messages. He didn't know whether he was in love. It wasn't the same feeling he had for Gay. It was more comfortable. Somewhere along the line, he had stopped trying to prove anything.

Being in France was just about the best of it. Sure, they had been the liberators and so everyone looked up to them, but it was much more than that. It was as though a weight had dropped off your shoulders, this being away from home. You got aboard the metro and sat down and the feeling of intruding didn't dig into you, making you tense and belligerent. You walked on the streets jostling people or being jostled by them without your hair standing up at the back of your neck. Being able to argue with a cab driver over a sou and get cussed out with you returning the compliment, and it was only that sou you argued about. It was slow getting used to—that you were a man and not a special kind of man.

It was funny as hell, the light feeling that came over you when you fully realized that at home a whole country had been standing solidly on your shoulders, looking at you upside down, and you had been trying to move and get around, acting like a normal man, with that weight on your shoulders. You went around pretending, and telling yourself and shouting out loud to anyone who would listen that you were like all other men. But it wasn't true! How could it be true with all that weight upon you? You had to be different. Wade started thinking of the reasons studs back home talked so loud especially in white areas. It was to try to convince the white man that he wasn't really on your shoulder, even when *he* knew it was a lie. The reason why, when he came out of the subway in Harlem, he could push out his chest and make his back a little straighter, wishing he could hide forever in the flowing tide of pure people.

Being away from the scene made you feel as a bird must feel when he could just spread his wings and soar. And when he thought of making it permanent, he didn't think of bringing Michele home and sealing her in his prison. He was finished with prisons. After all this crap was over he would go home and settle Mumma, get the money she was holding for him and make it back to Paris. He knew it wasn't so easy as he was thinking, but then life was never easy.

ROSA GUY

So they were almost happy when they stepped into the café, because they had been reading all kinds of things and meanings in each other's faces and they were, as the French say, d'accord. He had heard a loud singing before they entered but the tune had not penetrated their togetherness. As he and Michele sat at their table, he heard the song dying out and a loud silence rose to hit him and he knew that they had stumbled into and were about to be drowned by the atmosphere of good old USA That was when the notes of the song started echoing and re-echoing deep down inside him: *I wish I was in the land of cotton.* "Dixie."

When he saw the group of white officers his first impulse was to quit the scene. They must have begun early because they obviously had pushed everyone else out of the joint by their loudness. It was funny how much louder they were in France than were their black brothers. Wade wanted just to be gone and forget that he had trespassed into U.S. territory, but not backing down from the bastards had become a way of life with him.

They had run Big Willie over the Mason and Dixon Line; they had got his own backsides torn up by Mumma when he stepped out of his boundaries; they had been responsible for making him a jailbird at age eleven; had succeeded in keeping him in his own private world in Harlem, USA But Paris, France was everybody's playground, and he wasn't about to start running here. They had better believe that.

Wade called the waiter with a nonchalance he was far from feeling, looking around at the same time to size up what he might have to put up with. His heart almost paused in its beating as he saw a big, red-faced captain, the hate stinking out through every pore in his body and oozing out of his eyes through the glassy drunken stare that he slobbered over them. Some of his buddies tried to pull him back into what they probably thought was a balling time, and Wade hoped they'd succeed, but the fool wasn't having any.

Michele sipped her drink without realizing anything was wrong, but the waiters had that quiet look on their faces, and they got busy with a hundred little things, trying to get the cat's intention wiped off his face. Wade, too, calm as anything, tried to level a stare of warning to the cat, letting him know he was no turkey, that there were limits he never went beyond, that he had no gods, hoping the cat was sober enough to read it. But he wasn't.

"Well, look at what we got here, an African monkey all dressed up like an honest-to-goodness u.s. soldier," he shouted across the room.

There was relief in the knowledge that Michele did not speak English, yet it didn't make him feel like a whole human being, worth a damn. He was exposed for what he was. An American. A black American.

"Boy, do you know what we would do to you if we had you back home?"

Wade looked over to their table because he had the feeling that the captain had stood up and he wondered what was keeping him from approaching their table. It was a chick. She was trying to persuade him to sit back down. Cute as hell, too. The kind of chick who would make an army of mouths pucker, but that thing in the captain was a hell of a lot bigger than her charms. Even when she managed to drag him back down, Wade knew it was only a matter of time before he would be up again.

Wade drank up and ordered another, wishing that his good intentions toward Michele would make him get up and take her out of there, but this thing between him and the captain seemed bigger than all the chicks in the joint.

Michele realized that something was going on by this time, and she sipped her drink, waiting for her cue. This chick had lived! She didn't fear a thing. He smiled across at her, thinking how wonderful it was having her with him, because he realized, sitting across from her, that the abuse she had lived through as a woman made her his equal.

The men with the captain started leaving. It seemed that he had killed the hell out of their party. A few stayed on because they were too stoned to move, sitting with their heads on the table, their bodies wavering, undecided whether they should fall off their seats. The captain's chick sat on, a puzzled frown pleating her brow as though she were trying to figure what more she could add to her charms. But the next time Wade's gaze traveled the room, she must have come to the amazing revelation: nothing. She had gone and there the captain was, still sitting staring at them.

Wade poured all of his attention into his drink, and into that quiet waiting look in Michele's eyes, but every pore in his body stood at attention, and when the captain finally rose and staggered toward them, it was as though every pore got to marching, doing a military drill right down his back. But he never moved his gaze from Michele's, sat smiling quietly, reassuringly, at her.

Then the captain was swaying over their table, holding onto the edge of support, leering down at Michele, drunkenly. "Where I come from," he said, "ladies don't drink with niggers, so you must be a whore."

Michele must have recognized the word "whore," because her face went suddenly blank. Wade could have kicked himself for not taking her out of there sooner as he saw the weeks of pleasure, the days of happiness emptying out of her eyes. Yet he never let the smile leave his face, or his eyelashes give a blink, as he called the waiter and paid him. Then he was ready.

Rising slowly to his feet, Wade gave Michele enough time to take a few significant steps toward the door. Then passing in front of the captain, he said in a hard whisper loud enough only to penetrate the captain's drunkenness, making sure that no one else heard, "Where you come from, Captain, your mothers have to fuck our fathers to know what a prick is. You don't call that prostitution, you call that destitution."

Leading Michele through the door, he hurriedly pressed some money into her hand, telling her to get a cab. Then leaving her standing near the curb, he walked slowly down the street.

There was no guesswork about it. The captain *had* to follow Wade just as steel has to follow a magnet. It was there, bigger than the two of them, that American thing that tied them together, like a sickness that neither one could do anything about. Wade knew instinctively just when the captain staggered out of the café. He stopped to make sure the captain saw him. From then on it was a matter of timing. He walked slowly enough for the drunk to think he was catching him and every time Wade thought the captain might be ready to lunge, quickened his steps, leading him directly down the street that he and Michele had traveled earlier, laughing and being happy, on their stroll through the Bois.

It had turned chilly, with a damp raw sharp wind cutting through even the thickness of the heavy Army coat; but that didn't stop the captain. It probably only cleared his head, for his steps became steady and Wade didn't have to keep stopping so often in order to lead his quarry deeper and deeper into the Bois.

A hazy moon lit their way into the woods, and Wade hoped that for a little while longer the blond-haired, blue-eyed captain would not get the idea that he was being taken. But the whiskey plus that fact that he was a good three inches taller than Wade was enough to keep him brave.

Wade walked on, and finding a cluster of trees that caused deep shadows he ducked into them, waiting silently, holding his breath, not daring to look out but praying that the turkey wouldn't miss him and walk back the other way. But he came on, passing the spot where Wade stood, peering through the darkness, puzzle and disappointment showing over him as though he had really lost a good thing.

Wade stepped out of the shadow behind him. "Captain, you looking for me?"

The captain spun around, breathing heavily. Then seeing Wade, he sneered, "Yeah, I'm looking for big-mouth black Sambo. That's you, ain't it?"

"At your service, Captain."

"I just want you to repeat one more time what you said back there in that café. Just one more time."

"I said, Captain, that your mother fucked my father so she could know the feel of a man. And that's why you are here, Captain, you want to feel a hot rod up your ass, too. You are just like your goddamn mother."

The captain started pulling off his coat, and that was a damn-fool thing to do. Wade let him have it just like that. He didn't believe in fooling around with a stud he knew he had to beat. He had no intention of getting hurt for nothing. The captain did not get to his feet again until he had rid himself of his coat, a point that was not lost on Wade—that the cat sobered easily or maybe he was not so drunk as he had made out. When he jumped to his feet again, he bore no resemblance to the staggering fool who had wavered before Wade a minute before. But Wade, his coat thrown aside too, was waiting.

This time Wade clasped his hands and brought them down, first on one side of the captain's neck, staggering him, then on the other side of his neck, then with his fists full in his face. The captain fell back against a tree and Wade kept at him with both hands to his face and head until he slid to the ground dazed. But the captain wasn't ready to give up, and made his unsteady way to his feet, holding onto the tree for support. Before he could get fully onto his feet or lift his head, Wade clasped his hands again and let him have one with all his strength at the back of his neck.

By this time the captain must have realized that he wasn't being taken by a push-over, and maybe the idea was coming to him that he didn't have a chance. But he was a game stud. He had fallen on his stomach. Now he crawled around on his hands and knees until he found Wade's feet, then pulled himself slowly upward. Wade waited to hear whether he wanted to say something, but obviously the captain didn't, because he went right into balling his hands into fists again. This time Wade wasted him.

Months afterward, Wade tried to think back to what was in his mind at the time; but try as he would, nothing came. Maybe it was that other him curled up behind his eyes, coming out alive, violently alive, determined, determined as hell to even some score, there in the Bois in France, in that little shaft of light allowed by the moon. Later he thought of getting into trouble, possibly of getting caught, but at the time nothing was on his mind but beating the hell out of the stud.

He heard a little movement not too far away and looking up, saw Michele. There she was just standing, saying nothing, as though this scene were routine in her life. A rush of love that he had never felt before overcame him because of her calm, her way of looking at punishment and seeing it because she was part of the whole ugly stinking scene. She wasn't going to make any more of it than that. She had passed from player to spectator and all she wanted was a chance to live a little, to breathe, without paying any more dues. That was what he wanted too.

He realized suddenly that he was twenty-two years old and had lived and become old without ever having been young, without ever being able to breathe, never feeling free or light of heart, or being what other people called "happy." Now suddenly he wanted to be young, to breathe, to live.

"Now," he said, out of breath, panting, pulling the limp form of the captain up by the collar of his jacket. "Now, mother-fucker, say 'I'm sorry.' Apologize, you low-down Mississippi cracker, for all of those things you said and all of those things you meant to say, if you only had the chance."

The captain looked up into Wade's eyes, his thickened face turning up into a sickly smile, his blue eyes cleared of the drunken haze, blazing clearly in that tiny shaft of moonlight. Fear for his very life glistened there but it did not hide or erase the hatred that poured out of him. "You still," the captain gasped painfully through his bloody lips, "ain't nothing but a goddamn nigger."

Wade's anger rose like some terrible thing, hardly a part of him, bigger and mightier than he, pushing the man to the ground. Then using his foot he kicked his face, stomping where he knew the head should be, feeling the crushing of bones beneath his shoe, then bearing down on his heels, grinding and grinding until he felt nothing but a mass of pulp under the heel of his boot. Anger spent, Wade leaned weakly against the tree wiping his face, trying to get his mind together; but somehow he wasn't able to function. Dazed, he kept looking down, and if it hadn't been for Michele pulling on him, insisting, "Cheri, we must go. We must go," he might have stood against the tree the rest of the night.

But as he pulled himself up to follow her, he realized that he didn't want to leave the body out here just like that and it was more, much more, than the fear of having the body traced to him: He had been shaken to his very soul by the intensity of the man's hatred of him; but he had also been shaken by his own hatred of the man, of his reaction brought on by this hatred. It was *madness,* this thing that had tied them together out here in this senseless battle, but it was *their* madness and should not be aired to the world. It was a sickness that was a part of both their lives from the time they were on their mother's milk, but it was a private sickness, something that ought not to be shown.

He found himself suddenly understanding the colored cats who lied and bragged about how important they were back home and how real gone things were for them back in the States. He knew now that they had to prove they were like all the world's peoples. That the quotation, "From dust you came and to dust you will return" had to have the same meaning for them as for all. That there was nothing written up in the Bible or any other goddamn book that said, "From dust you come, you will live like dust, and dust you will forever be." A man had to feel that in all this crap there had to be something working for him—a soul— and home was like having a soul. You were fighting and working like hell for it, saying in effect that you were willing to give your life for it, and where did you stand? What were you, if it were all a lie?

They began a frantic searching around the neighborhood near the Bois, and it was strange they were not seen, they were so busy trying to keep out of the way of gendarmes and the military police. But finally, they found a shovel. Wade forced Michele to leave him, making her promise she would wait in the room for him—something she consented reluctantly to do.

He insisted, not because it would not have been easier with another hand to break through the earth, nor did the thought of having her implicated entered his mind. Strangely enough he simply wanted to be alone with his fellow American there under the Paris sky, where they had played out their battle of hatred.

He dug a damned decent grave, and dragged the cat into it, putting his coat and hat over him, bowed his head—he didn't know why, he didn't pray—then covered the body with the earth. When he had finished, he stood a while trying to think, but found nothing to think about. He had killed men, since the war, for whom he had felt much more: a little savagery if the cat had a mean, set face; a little awe if he had a poetic face; a little regret if he had a young face; and relief when it was a close call. But here, at first, he felt nothing. He listened to the insects, the brush of branches hitting against branches; smelled the brownness, the sweetness of the freshly turned earth; but felt nothing.

Then suddenly it came: The sense of being unshackled, the lightness of heart that he must have read about somewhere. He moved his feet as though they had really been in chains, then he threw back his head and laughed.

He almost skipped out of the woods, shovel in hand. Skipping and feeling what it meant to be gay and happy and really free for the first time in his entire life. He took the shovel home and gave it to Michele as a souvenir. Then he asked her to marry him. He was sure that he would never live in the States. He had got the man off his back and he wanted to keep him off.

Funny thing, he and Michele never discussed the shovel or that night. It was as though it never happened, only it had, and it had changed the hell out of him. They spoke of the day he had to leave and when he intended to come back, the house they intended to build right outside Paris, and the babies they intended to have. And when she spoke, Michele got to laughing and it surprised him how young she looked. He even began looking at himself in the mirror, and funny thing, he looked young too.

It might have happened that way, too—if it hadn't been for Mumma. He came home a stranger, feeling like a stranger, wanting to remain a stranger, not wanting to be sucked in by the life and the doings around Harlem, not wanting to sleep in that, or any of the other kitchenettes that had all, all of his life, deprived him of privacy. He wanted to break out of the bonds of 110th Street and walk downtown and be a part of that big life that was New York, and the USA and America. In one quick minute out there in the woods in France he had seen himself in relation to *his* country. He had seen how chained he was, how limited, inside and out, and he meant to change everything. He intended to take one good swing at changing and be gone.

But there was no money.

"Money? What money?" Mumma said after all the excitement of his home-coming had died down. "I ain't got no money." The sound of her words made it seem as though someone had taken a drill and was boring right through the top of his head. "You talking about that lil' bit of money you sent me? That's all gone."

He didn't know how he sat so calmly trying to explain. "I'm not talking about your allotment, Mumma. I'm talking about the money I sent you to save for me."

"Wade, I just don't have it." She said it as though it was the most natural thing in the world. "I started to save some of it, but then I took sick. I was so sick from this here arthritis that I had to spend months in the hospital. I told Faith to write you, but she didn't want to worry you none."

"But, Faith," he turned to his sister, his voice hoarse in his effort to control it. He had never asked his family for one penny since he was big enough to hustle or steal. Yet here he was asking for his own money and they were acting as though he had taken leave of his senses. "*You* were working."

"I know, Wade," Faith answered. "But it seemed when Mumma got sick, the money just went. And it wasn't as though we were throwing it away, or living better. But it all went."

It was true they were not living better. They had a new spread on the bed, new curtains at the window, a couple of new pots and pans, and that was it.

"But Willie Earl could have helped out."

"Wade, you know how tight Willie Earl is with his money. The war ain't changed him none, except to make him tighter."

"Willie Earl got his family, what you expect him to do?" Mumma sat rocking in her chair, looking down at her hands, as though her words, clear and decisive, made the end of the matter. But the deep threatening silence her words caused finally forced her to turn to look at him. She jumped as though he had struck her. "What you looking at me like that for?" He didn't know how he had been looking at her. "What was I supposed to do if I was sick?"

At that moment he didn't really know. At that moment he was too numb to think. All he could do was sit there and look at her, realizing in a vague sort of way that the crackers had forced her to her knees and his whole life had been spent paying for it. He was still paying.

Faith, seeing the expression on his face, rushed to him and caught his head to her chest. "Wade, you need that money real bad for something, don't you?" Just hearing her say it, with her hands so motherly, rubbing his head, caused the tears to start and he cried as hard as he had the day Gay walked out of his life, only louder. The sound of his sobs, harsh and broken as with people unaccustomed to tears, filled the little room and he could not stop.

"Oh, God. Oh, God," Faith sobbed too. "We ruined your life, didn't we? We ruined your life. There, there now, you're home and I'm still working. We'll get the money together in no time. You can have every penny I make until we pay you back."

He nodded, feeling tired as though he had spent his life.

Sure, he would get a job and work and save and in a few months—a few months . . . He wrote Michele, sending her part of his mustering-out pay and explaining to her that he had to go to work, but only for a short time.

Yet even as he wrote, trying to believe, he knew that the war was over. It had been but a pause, an interruption to the flow of his life but it had changed nothing. Even before he realized there were no jobs for the returning soldiers, that the government was smearing their eyes with the grease of fifty-two weeks of unemployment insurance to ease the soreness of guys who had risked their necks overseas, coming back to pull the dirt load without any help to pull it with, he knew that the war was over.

He had paid his dues all right. He had been responsible. He had done everything he could—for Mumma. He had given up school and gone to make a living. He had given up his child and Gay; and his dreams, every one of them. Then that money—all that money. All to make a better life for them. But their lives had remained the same. They never had more than a one-room kitchenette. One goddamn room.

The heat from Wade's body seemed to blend with the hot crushing heat of the sun, and he stood burning from its onslaught and his thoughts. One goddamn room that he couldn't go to. But Willie Earl could go! Willie Earl with his talking on both sides of his face could go. Willie Earl, who'd got married; who didn't let anything stop him from having his baby. Willie Earl could come and go as he damn well pleased. And big-hearted Wade Williams had left them to it. One big happy family minus him who had given his entire life for it. He had just walked out and left them to it.

"OK, OK. Step up, step up." Wade looked down for a puzzled moment into the faded blue eyes of the heat-flushed man sitting at the hiring table. "What can I do for you?"

"What . . ." Wade fumbled for his thoughts.

"Come on, will ya—I asked what can I . . ."

"Not a thing," Wade snapped into the red overheated face. "Not a fucking thing."

14

It was hotter than hell on an overcrowded Saturday when he walked back into his section of Lenox Avenue, with the sun pulling the rest of the earth's moisture to join the already hazy air, making the heavy grey mist hang like a curtain between earth and sky, pressing the atmosphere down on Wade's head as though trying to get to the base of his skull through the top of his hat.

He made it right to Mumma because he wanted some answers. He wanted some kind of justice, and he damned sure didn't feel like waiting. Waiting for what? She had crossed him off. Why was it that she always saw Willie Earl's side of everything? Willie Earl or any other goddamn body's except his? Why was he locked out? How could he be locked out of his own mother's house, when he had spent years footing the bill, keeping her backsides out of the gutter?

He rang the bell five times. That was supposed to be her ring. He waited. No one came. He rang five more times and then five more. What the hell was this? No one home? Or was she there, and knowing it was he had decided not to come down? He rang two long and a short. That ought to bring her neighbor. No one came. He rang again. Everybody couldn't be out in the whole damn house? He raised his foot to kick the door in but a voice stopped him from behind.

"If she out, she out. What the hell you ringing all the bells for?" He turned to face the angry stare of the West Indian woman who owned the building. She was another one who never had any use for him. He ran down the steps to face her. "Get out of here, before I call the police, you hear?"

He stood before her, working his fingers and his mouth; but before he could decide what move to make, a policeman walked up and stood a short distance away, eyeing him and swinging a billy. Wade turned and walked away.

He was home and under the shower before he realized that he didn't remember how he had got there. He didn't remember seeing a car or hearing a horn blow, or for that matter, seeing any one person. Yet here he was with the full force of the cold water dragging him into a consciousness that he had not known he'd lost.

He remained in the shower for more than an hour, turning this way and that, letting the cold force fall upon his head, the back of his neck, his shoulders. The water seeped through his pores and the layers of his skin, refreshing him; and he damned sure never wanted to be so hot again. Going to Mumma like a bat out of hell would have made no kind of sense. Sure he had to have his answers but he might as well be calm about it. No sense getting her scratching mad.

"Where's my breakfast, woman?" he asked Gladys. Refreshed, he could joke now, and anyhow the poor woman deserved a joke. But she didn't laugh worth a damn. Just sat in her chair and studied him as though she were looking into his very soul. Figured she had probably been sitting right there when he came in all hot and bothered, and didn't know what had come over him, that's why she looked as though she might have been taking one long last look.

"What the hell you think you got on your mind?" he chided. "Well, you ain't."

She still didn't laugh. Simply sighed and got up to start preparing his breakfast. That was about the nicest thing she had ever done for him, because it was damned near dinner time.

When he got to eating he dragged a silence about him so he could plan on his approach to Mumma. He wanted to get there and get everything settled before Faith came home. He would surprise the hell out of her. Just imagine how silly she would look when she walked in and saw him talking to Mumma just as chummy as anything.

But he had to let Mumma know that he wasn't for being an outdoor child. He had done too much for her, for her to let him hang around the streets biting his teeth over some crazy punk's attitude. Sure he had done wrong, and he expected some punishment, but he had had it. Hell, he ought to cut off his arms to the shoulders for even touching Faith—and Willie Earl—well, he had it coming to him, but Mumma had to make Willie tell why, if she wanted justice. And why had he spent his entire life for them if they wouldn't give him justice?

He dressed carefully so that she would be pleased with his appearance. Mumma went for good appearance. He looked in the mirror a couple of times, which was more than he usually did, fixing the collar of his sport shirt over his jacket, adjusting the brim of his hat, all the while feeling

Gladys's gaze heavy on him. He glanced at the clock: six o'clock; home thirty-one hours and it seemed like thirty years, and hard years at that.

He went to stand over Gladys at the window. She gave him a long searching look, then turned her attention back to the street, with a thin bitter laugh. As if she were saying good-by without tears, and was now waiting to see him finishing himself off when he hit the streets.

He stood studying her longer than he had ever studied her before, feeling free of her for the first time since he had known her. And as her bulky figure blended in with the dimness he called, "Don't cry at the funeral." He walked slowly down the long hall, let himself out, slammed the door hard to give her a feeling of finality.

The graying curtain of mist had become heavy hanging drapes of darkness, with flashes of lightning darting through and a deep throaty rumble rolling over, clearing the streets of people.

"Hey, Wade, how about a drink, huh? How about a drink?"

"Sure, Charlie, go help yourself." He took a quarter out of his pocket and flipped it to the drunk.

Then he was walking up the stairs to Mumma's, his heart beating like anything. Funny how much like a little boy he felt, even though he was going to her like a man. He knew when he spoke to her face to face and showed her the truth she'd have to listen to reason. She couldn't turn him out again.

Luck was with him. A girl came out of the door as he approached. He didn't have to ring the bell. He ran up the stairs and right to her room and knocked, then stood listening to the soft gentle scuffle of her slippers as she approached the door. It sounded like music, only drums, because it mixed in with the pounding in his chest and at his temples, which was so loud that he almost didn't hear her when she called.

"Who's there?" Was a time when she would have just opened the door, but it seemed she was getting careful in her old age. He didn't answer but knocked again, lightly so that she might imagine a small hand and think it a neighbor, or maybe Faith coming home early. He waited in a silence loud enough to burst his eardrums, then finally the knob turned as though she still hesitated. Then he was looking at her through the slightly opened door with his tongue heavy and the thoughts he had planned so carefully all burned out. He swallowed hard trying to force out words, even a smile, but everything stammered on his face. "Mumma . . ."

"What you want here?" Her sharp voice pierced him in the middle of his chest, forcing his eyes to widen in the sorrowful stare he always used for her.

"Mumma, please—let me in—Mumma, Mumma . . ." he whispered.

"Get away. Get away from here, do you hear me? Get away from me."

Mumma—Mumma, listen—please listen." He pushed the door against her weight and squeezed himself into the room, forcing her backward so that he might close the door against the neighbors' curiosity.

"Ain't nothing to say, you done tried to kill my child!"

She was talking the talk that confused him. He wanted to say that Willie Earl was no child. He was a man. A goddamn big man. That Willie Earl had it coming to him. He wanted to say so many things, yet all he said was, "Mumma, listen . . ."

"You're just like him. Just like your Pa. Dirty and ugly and mean clear through to your soul. Lord knows why He didn't take you the day you was born."

"Mumma, Willie had it coming . . ."

"Like Faith had it coming to her? Like that poor boy you done killed?" That kept him silent. "What you want to do, kill us all?"

"No, Mumma, listen." He tried desperately to catch her gaze so that she might read from his eyes some of the begging things he wanted to pull from the farthest corner of his heart: He missed her; he was lonely out there on the streets; he hadn't meant to hurt Willie Earl; he'd rather die than hurt any member of his family. He struggled with his heavy, heavy tongue, but not a word came. He reached out and took both her hands to place over his heart so that she might feel the pounding.

"Don't touch me." She snatched her hands away and their gaze met.

The plea died confusedly on his lips and a roar in his head muddled his thinking. He found himself outside the door, running down the stairs and out into the streets. His footsteps guided him to the park even though he vaguely realized that large drops of rain spattered his arms and shoulders and hit the straw of his hat with a force that suggested a real downpour.

He sat there forcing thoughts back to his mind by rubbing his hands together, listening to the trees over him hit themselves together in a sort of desperate whisper. It had been too hot for many days and the sun had sucked them dry. Now they moved restless, opening themselves up like oversexed bitches to the moisture in the gushes of hot wind that promised them relief. He wondered what he was doing there listening to the trees when he had important things to think about, goddamn important things. Yet somehow his mind remained blank, as though it suffered the silence of the coming storm that forced the emptiness of the park and the streets. He kept looking around nervous, as though some object might start his mind moving, as when sometimes a roll of film got stuck and all it needed was a little pushing. But the silence became more oppressive and he had no thoughts at all. He found himself murmuring over and over, "Mumma, Mumma, Mumma—sure is mad as hell. Sure is mad as hell."

The drops fell harder and he wondered why he didn't get the hell on up and go the hell on home. Did he need a whole park to think in? Funny how Aunt Julie had been so hot about Uncle Dan that she hardly paid any attention to what happened to Willie Earl, and how Mumma was so mad on account of Willie Earl she hadn't bothered to give a thought to Uncle Dan. That was the way with them—his family. He was the only one who cared about all of them.

A streak of lightning flashed across the sky followed by one still more blinding. Why hadn't he stayed with Mumma and made her listen? Why? He had known what to expect. He had known it wouldn't be easy. So why had he run out of the house like a fool?

A sudden clap of thunder made him start, and in that instant he gazed again into his mother's eyes and what he saw there made his stomach and his heart squeeze together into one painful knot. His breath caught in his chest and became a sob that ripped through his throat, like the cry of an animal blending into the sounds of the wind.

Mumma was scared of him! Mumma was scared of him!

He was on his feet and out of the park, running down Lenox Avenue, his feet not feeling the ground, the wind, like passion gone wild, smothering his mouth and nostrils, brushing savagely against his ear, responding to emotions deeply hidden in confusion, emotions now being ripped into shreds, then into smaller pieces adding to the confusion, like confetti thrown into the wind on a snowy day. He knew he had to stop, gather the pieces, fit them together, examine them, put sense into them, figure out a pattern where he knew a pattern should be; but his feet were in flight against reason.

He heard the scream of fire sirens, the roar of the engines racing down the Avenue, and he was suddenly filled with one concern: That they should not overtake him. His life depended on it. And with this thought, his feet became winged. He ran neck to neck, breast to breast, keeping the giant red flashes at the corner of his eye, never losing sight, never letting them get beyond him, knowing that in this race that meant life or death both he and the fire trucks were caught up in a desperate flight from destiny.

Then suddenly he tripped.

He saw the sidewalk rising to meet him, he heard the engines roar past his head leaving him behind, he raised his eyes in anguish to the tense backs of the firemen, their rubber coats flapping in the wind, their urgency written across their backs as they turned the corner and disappeared from his sight. He looked around dazed as though he had been in a terrible fight and had lost the decision because of a knockout. He struggled to his feet, swayed, held his head, waiting for balance. Then he looked up, his gaze climbing, climbing, searching the building in front of which he had fallen, his head moving backward as though pulled by a string. And then he saw her.

The Beast. Gladys. Framed as much by the light behind her as by the sudden streak of lightning that lit up the window, grinning down at him with that insipid grin, her gold teeth glittering, mocking him, her beady eyes laughing as though she had won some untold victory. Wade backed away. The frame detached itself from the building and came whirling down at him.

He turned, found himself running, running down Lenox Avenue again. He ran and ran until there were no sidewalks on which to run, just the giant crossing of streets that led in all directions, then the park, Central Park, loomed dark and mysterious before him. The end of Lenox Avenue. Dead end.

He stood staring at the Park, wiping his face with his hands. No farther to go. And as he stood undecided what to do, the drops of rain turned into a downpour. It sure got him together. He looked around, wondering what it was all about; looked up the way he had come and the way he had to go. The only place he knew. The place he could not run from.

The Avenue lay before him, dim and deserted, being cleaned by the bucketfuls of tears that came pouring down, it was as if the Man up there had decided He was tired of seeing a whole bunch of shining, sweaty people, breathing in and out, talking a lot of trash, turning a whole world of good intentions into a playground for the devil. Wade didn't know how He was making it, but one thing was sure, He had done him a big favor: Washed Lenox Avenue clean of people. Not one man in the whole world but himself and that was the way he wanted it.

The rain beat on him, sticking his clothes to him like skin, hammering the brim of his hat flat to his forehead so that water flowed in streams down his face. He walked slowly, his face grim, every step definite, as though his feet had grown used to not needing his head to do their thinking. He found himself plodding ankle deep through puddles of water, bracing himself against the rain that beat down on his shoulders like overdue punishment; not knowing exactly where he was going, hardly caring, just wanting to move—a solitary figure in a desperate world, not thinking, never thinking. Yet with the roar of the thunder, the giant flashes of lightning, the heavy downpour, one thought kept pushing, pushing: Mumma is afraid of me? Mumma is afraid of me?

No, it wasn't that way. He'd misread the message. She hadn't given it out right. How could Mumma be afraid of him? He had withstood her anger, suffered her faults, understood her mistakes—her lifetime of mistakes—all at his expense, and she was afraid of him?

Why? The *Why* hung suspended about him untouched by the rain. How could she be afraid of the one person who had fought her battles, protected her from the time he knew about putting one foot before the other, done for her what no one else would do—what few sons had ever done for their mothers? Why should she be afraid unless—unless—unless she had reason?

He stopped, stood drawn up into himself, waiting for the sharp pain of anxiety and apprehension to loosen its hold. Had she reason?

Like Willie Earl? Breathing hard now, trying to force his mind to function where previously he had prevented it, welcoming the coldness of the rain on his hot hot body, searching again for those answers that remained locked in the blank passages of his memory, he pushed himself on with long determined steps.

In front of Sam's barbershop, closed for the day, he halted for one brief moment, his eyes narrowed by the force of the rain as they followed the lazy spiraling of the stripes on the pole. He pushed himself on.

Across the street he lingered for one more moment looking down past the Father Devine shoe-shine parlor, past the building where Mabel used to live with her whore of a mother, down toward the house where Big Willie had fallen over dead—the house where he had spent his tender years, his poverty-stricken tender years with Faith. He wanted to stand awhile, mix more deeply with the memories, the soft childhood memories that had sustained his love, his faith in his family through all the years. He pushed himself on.

He walked past the street and the building that he had last called home, never looking for his window, never looking for Gladys because somehow she seemed to have slipped into a never-to-be-relived past. He walked past the spot where he had held, for one brief moment, the breakable neck of a child in his hand; the bar where he had suffered the meaninglessness of talk, then up to the street where he had visited a hundred times in his mind, a few times in reality since yesterday; not having planned to be there, not surprised that he was, not planning now, or knowing what he intended to do; but gratified to be there because there was really nowhere else for him to go.

Wade walked slowly up the block feeling the heaviness of his rain-soaked clothes, the singular strangeness as the water invaded the straw of his hat and dripped monotonously down onto his head, like a finger tapping out a code. He moved slowly, determined, but as he drew near the center of the block he suddenly stopped. A lone figure sat on a stoop a few houses from the one to which his feet had been guiding him.

A fool who hadn't sense enough to get out of the wet. Wade chuckled grimly. It did not seem funny to him but an affront: The world was his and this turkey had no right to squeeze himself into it. He moved toward the figure, giving the fellow a chance to look up and see him coming, a chance to get away.

Yet the stud just sat.

He sat on the stone slab that separated the basement from the street, his shoulder leaning against the stoop, the collar of his coat pulled around his face as though to protect him from the onslaught of the rain. He never looked up as Wade stood over him, watching the water pour down on his head, slide off his knuckles and run into streams to his wrists, bounding off his already overflowing sleeves and falling to his knees like a waterfall.

Wade stood a long time looking down at the stud, not thinking, simply looking, waiting for him to look up; but since he never did, Wade reached for him. He had no thought of what he really intended to do, but the moment he touched him, Wade knew something was wrong, for the cat kept rolling forward and Wade had to step back to make room for him to hit the ground. Stone dead.

Wade stood peering down at the stud, thinking suddenly of Tony. But this boy was of a much younger school. He had fought no wars, not even the one of life, and here he had copped out before he'd even had the entrance exam. Life was no picnic out here in this big jungle of a city, it was true, with dreams running wild and no way to make even one become real. A guy had to take something to blind himself to his confusion, when he realized that though he was a man like all men ever written about, he didn't know how to go about making dreams come true. He and Willie Earl and the rest of them around their time had cut their teeth on grog, using that for blinders; but today, the chap that had cut Tony down, and this young punk, was easier to get than a hot dog and it made pretending easier.

But at least they had given Tony some years to play with his bubble, some years to come to terms with the idea that his life was a waste, that he was expendable, that the space he took up could be more profitably used to make waste of younger people's lives, that though he might not have been ready to go, he knew that the dream he carried in that bubble was all used up. It had been blown up and deflated too many times. It was a damned tired dream. But this young stud—his bubble was in its first blow, big and tight with promises that he had the world to gain. But they had not allowed him that. Not even that big lie.

And who would care? Who would care that one black boy's dream was snuffed out on a stormy night in the bowels of Harlem? Nobody. There would be two more to take his place and it would go on and on until the disease that the gods created became the disease that consumed them all.

Wade sat on the stoop that the boy's body had vacated, gazing down at the young dark face made eerie by the falling rain. The boy still clutched the collar of his jacket and the rain formed streams from his closed eyelids and hammered on his partly opened mouth.

Why hadn't he gone home after he had had that last shot, when he had become sleepy and fallen to nodding and halfway knew what was happening? Why hadn't he died at home? It wasn't right that a stud should die out in weather like this, alone. Just as it wasn't right that a stud should die in a strange land looking square up at a foreign sky, sick with a disease that he didn't know he had and would never know he had.

And how did it profit the gods? How did it profit them, this waste of minds and lives and bodies? Where was the gain? True, there were those who made it in money, like the ones that got the stuff to this kid. But then they unleashed an army of zombies, stretching out like giant spiders' arms, spreading destruction and death across the nation that in turn *had* to come home to them. Just like the disease of hate that made a waste of the minds and twisted the souls of cats and had them dying overseas not *for* their country but *because* of their country.

But this young stud had not even joined in that battle, he had nothing to do but sit on this stoop and die. Yet looking down at the too-young face, Wade knew this was a lie. Somewhere in that wasted young life, there had to be a pin point of reason that had led him to this jinxed-up stoop to die in this pouring rain. He who had never laid eyes on him—where were their lives hooked up, so that unseen force pushing his footsteps along had directed him here to find this body?

Wade turned to look at the window in front of which he sat, the shades drawn so securely against the storm that not even the sense of death had penetrated to make them open up to see what was happening on their very doorstep. He wanted to run down the three short steps to the window and break it in with his fists, shake up their indifference, because it was their indifference that had this boy dying, that had *him* out here. They were so damned indifferent that they became victims of their indifference. Yes. The gods had good agents to work for them.

And this little young mother's child, why hadn't he made it home? Was he too scared to go home? Or more likely he didn't have a home to go to. His mother probably got scared of him and put him out. Told him not to come around any more. That was the way they did, these mothers. They bore you, brought you and sealed you into this crap, set your limits to make sure that you didn't go beyond it, rubbed your nose in it all your lives and when you became a solid part of it they got scared, put you out.

Wade wanted to get up and walk away, but as he looked around the deserted street, the flooded gutters, the rain-shrouded houses, he just couldn't get up. Somehow he was unable to shake the feeling that maybe he had been appointed guardian of some terrible truth encompassed in that young, too-young body, lying out here on this bitch of a night, meaning nothing to a living soul except that he was a junky. No, there was more to it, this finding him here, there had to be. A body didn't lose its meaning simply because it had no life. Somewhere within it, stilled, perhaps just under the closed lids, the full meaning of his particular life lay, or else what was the use?

In a few hours after the rain had stopped, his body would be found and taken home to his mother. Then she would come rushing down, probably from some top floor to the street, crying as if she were about ready to flip her lid, about her boy—her boy, forgetting that she had put him out, that she had been afraid of him. Oh, she would raise much hell, crying and moaning so that people would plaster her with pity; and she would grab that pity like a cloak to hide her shame, never admitting for the rest of her life that she had spent half of his life holding him in a trap while she spent the other half punishing him for being caught in it.

Wade jumped from the stoop, startled, as a flash of lightning slashed the darkness too near to his face. And as he stood dazed, a roar of thunder that seemed to shake the very foundation of the houses with its violence forced him to bow his head. When he raised it again to look at the sky, every part of the puzzle had fallen into place: He knew now why he had gone after Willie Earl that night.

It had happened just as he remembered. He had not been drinking that much. Faith had been keeping an eye on him. She'd made it her life's work to keep her eye on him. Yet she had gone along with that one drink celebrating Willie Earl's spurt of generosity for buying a bottle.

Yes, Willie Earl had been crying, not so much because his wife had put him out and didn't want anything more to do with him, as because she had taken him to court and they had decided that Willie Earl had to pay money through them instead of to his wife directly.

"Oh, you don't mind being put out," Faith teased. "You just don't want to get up off that money. You want to keep sitting on it like you hatching."

"And he don't want to go to jail," Wade laughed. "Damn, Willie Earl, that sure is a hard decision for you. No wonder you need a drink."

Willie Earl needed more than that. He kept pouring the whiskey down as though it were water and after a while both Wade and Faith got the idea that it was more than him being put out.

"You can talk to your bro, Willie." Wade made a dig at him. "Some cat cutting in on your time? Old Margie must have herself another Joe D."

"What are you talking about? That woman don't even want to look at another body but me. She's just salty with me because I don't let her go through my money like Epsom salts."

"Well, she's going through it now."

"Who says?"

"The court says."

"Oh, the court says, the court says. For all you know I might even be getting off cheaper, staying with Uncle Dan and Aunt Julie."

"If you have anything to do with it, you are," Faith said sarcastically.

"He still got to pay two rents," Wade pointed out.

"What two rents?" Willie was fast reaching the bragging stage. All he needed was one more drink. "I ain't paying no rent staying with my uncle."

"All of a sudden it's 'my uncle,'" Faith mimicked.

"That's what I said, '*my* uncle.'" Willie Earl gave Faith a sly grin. "All they expect me to do is buy a little food and I don't have to pay but half the rent at home."

"Then what you bellyaching about?"

"Well, I ain't never paid but half the rent since Margie been working, but now I got to shell out for that extra booty. I tell you these chicks out here is harder than some nails."

"I'm sure glad Margie got to her senses," Faith said. "Imagine having a big man like you around, and not having him even pay the rent."

"But I was around to give her the loving she needed."

"That loving didn't seem to satisfy her none," Wade chuckled. "She must have got hard up."

"For some money." Faith laughed. "If you ask me, you should have been put out years ago. Just like Mumma will put your butt out when she comes in here and finds out you bought a bottle."

"Mumma ain't going to put me out nowhere," Willie Earl bragged. "She would put anyone and their mother out before she would put me." He said it jokingly enough but the truth of it stung the hell out of Wade, and he decided to turn the screw on Willie.

"Tell me, Lil' Willie, what in the hell do you do with all your money?"

"One thing, I don't play nobody's fool with it. Not nobody."

Willie Earl's tongue was getting heavy and knowing that he would rather talk about his mother than his money, Wade kept pushing the whiskey at him, pouring it into his glass without letting anyone know. When he thought Willie had his full load, he eased up on the pouring and began fishing.

"You know," Wade said to Faith, "this here Willie Earl was always the shrewdest stud I know. He ain't never in all his life missed one trick. Did I ever tell you about that time we went out shining shoes?" He had picked this topic because it was his lifetime joke on Willie Earl.

"You know how Mumma used to wear us out, if we ever left out from our part of town." Wade waited for Faith's nod. "Well, I ain't had no more sense than to follow this fool all the way down to wop-town, he talking about we going to make a whole lots of money.

"We had no sooner got to shining shoes real good, when I looks up and there is this bunch of real bad studs surrounding us. I tell you, Faith, I could feel those studs' breath on my neck, and I just knew we were as good as dead. I don't know how Willie Earl managed to get out of that one, but the next thing I know, I'm flying through the air. Willie Earl just dragging me. He got out of that one with me, his shoe-shine box and all of his money, every cent."

Willie Earl went to laughing so hard that he doubled up and even Faith let go of her annoyance long enough to smile. "And to top it all, here we are coming home, all beaten up and stuff and I'm so scared at what Mumma will say that the piss start running out of me. And you know what this turkey here is doing?"

"What?" Faith asked, as though it were the first time she'd heard the story. Willie Earl laughed until he rolled off the couch.

"He's counting out his money. One for Mumma, two for me. One for Mumma, three for me. One for Mumma, four . . ." Willie Earl was on his knees beating the floor with his hands. "I declare, even when Mumma got hold of him and went to beating the hell out of him, he ain't never turned one penny loose. That cat and his money is really one for the books."

Wade waited for the laughter to let up, then put in on a more serious note, "Yeah, it don't make no damn sense to start off so smart in life and end up without even so much as a damn roof of your own over your head—not one damn thing to show for it."

"To hell you say." Willie Earl laughed.

"That's right, Willie Earl. Thought you had so much going for you when you were a young stud, but here you end up without a goddamn thing. Like the old folks say, not a pot to piss in, nary a window to throw it out of." Wade's voice grew nasty with scorn.

"That's what you think," Willie cried angrily. "You were supposed to be the smart one, remember? The kid genius. While I was the hard hustler, the stupid worker. Well, let me tell you one thing. I always keep me some money. I ain't never going to be without. Let that wife of mine keep that apartment and everything she got in it. Let her turn me out. She'll never drain *me* dry.

"See here." Willie reached inside his shirt and pulled from a hidden pocket, a pocket that must have been sewn in purposely, some kind of book. A bank book. He flipped it under Wade's nose. "That's what's worrying her. She won't be satisfied until she sucks me dry. She got one look at it one day when I got careless, and now she's ready to die unless she gets her paws on it. She thinks that I'm so broken up about leaving home that I'll give her everything. Well, let her see. Them women are the agents of poverty, but they'll make no beggar out of me. I ain't nobody's fool."

Wade snatched the book away from Willie Earl before he could get it back into his pocket. He flipped the pages, letting his eyes travel quickly over them. It was an old book, a goddamn history book. He reached the final figures and it rocked his head. Willie Earl had over ten thousand dollars in the bank.

"Willie Earl, what you doing with all that money?" Wade realized it was a stupid question to ask but he couldn't help it.

Willie Earl snatched the book out of Wade's hand and stuck it back into his inner pocket and Wade found himself wondering whether he sewed pockets into all of his shirts to hide the book—maybe even into his sleeping clothes.

"What do you mean, what I'm doing with that money? That's my money. I worked damn hard for it, that's what I'm doing with it. I got the first dollar I ever made, you can believe that."

"And Mumma?"

"What about Mumma? Mumma got her religion and I got my back. I work for what I want and she pray for hers. That's what divides the meek from the mighty."

"You mean all the time she was in the hospital, you ain't never helped her out and you had all that money?"

"What hospital? What time?" Willie Earl blinked his eyes as though Wade were out of his mind. "What in the hell you talking about?"

"What hospital? You mean you don't remember Mumma being in the hospital?"

"Naw, I don't remem . . ."

"You remember, Willie Earl," Faith put in. "During the war . . ."

"Oh, way back then. Yeah, during the war. Well, what about it?"

It was funny to Wade that for Willie Earl it had been such a long time ago it might not have happened, and yet to him it seemed only yesterday.

"Yeah." Wade's throat was suddenly dry. His voice came out muffled, stuck somewhere in his throat. "During the war. You were making all of that long money then, and you let her spend all of mine?"

"She ain't never need mine as long as she had yours," Willie Earl leered. "Ain't you the little genius in the family? Ain't you the little family man?"

That was when Wade reached for him. That was when he blacked out.

Wade shivered violently and the wetness of his clothes became suddenly unbearably cold against the heat of his body. He felt as though he had become enclosed by four walls of glass heated by some terrible light that penetrated to his very bones yet never touched his clothes. Looking down at the body of the boy gutted by the rain, he cried, "How long has this night been sealed in your past?"

Lifting his gaze he looked toward his mother's stoop, then let it fall again to the boy. "Yeah, they are the pin boys that set us up, then give us the blame when the bowl comes down. They pin-point our doom, then put us out into the streets to rot in the gutters. Then they cry so that they can be washed in pity, prayed over by a fucking preacher, hoping like hell that their two faces can pass through the gates of heaven as one. And we let them do it. We love them for it. That's why they become scared when they see their handiwork: They know they don't deserve that love."

This came to him like a revelation, staggering him with its impact. He caught his face in his hands, wanting to blot out his past, the present, the touch of the rain, the sound of the thunder, the look of the boy being beaten by the rain. "No, no," his mind shrieked.

His life had been a waste. A terrible waste. But in this one thing he was pure. He was a family man. A family man. He wanted to move away but stood there cowed, burdened by the chains that previously had been only a silent weight. Now he heard the rattle as he moved, sensed the feel of them as they pulled him down, down toward the ground; and heard the clatter they made as the ground opened up inviting him, blowing the warm smell of earth and green and growing things into his nostrils.

He heard Mumma's voice laughing. "Willie Earl, I swear I lay with the devil. . . ." Then Willie Earl laughing—just laughing. He heard Faith's sigh, almost like the sound of the wind—and suddenly—Uncle Dan's voice: "Careful, boy—careful . . ."

Wade lowered his hands and looked around the deserted street. He moved his arms and they were free. He bowed his head over the still body and said, "If my prayers would do, I'd say one for you. But I am damned too. If I could cry, I'd shed a bucketful, right along with the Man up there, for you—for me—for us." He turned and walked down the lonely street a little guilty, a little sad. He hated leaving the little stud to the bastards who had made garbage of his life.

15

Wade walked the few steps that brought him to Mumma's house and running up the steps two at a time, tried the door. As he expected, it was locked. He pressed his shoulders hard against it; it shook but did not give. Stepping back a little he came again full force. The door crashed open and he was inside running up the stairs to her room. His breath came hard, the sound of her laughter filling his ears. Oh, how she must have laughed! Maybe *that* was her lifetime joke on him. She had probably laughed the way she laughed over Professor Jones running out of the house, or the hundred other little things that meant robbing him of his life. She had probably sewed the little pockets into Lil' Willie's shirts to add a little zest to the great big joke.

He stood before her door a brief moment, then put his foot against it and pushed. The door swung open like the door of a doll's house and he stepped into the room.

A sudden rush of warm air embraced his wetness, calming him for an instant. This was the room where he longed to be, looking at the gay curtains that Mumma used to lighten her sunless kitchenette. Familiar sights pushed out to greet him. Sights like the picture of Pappa on the mantel, with Wade on his lap and Faith at his side staring country-fashion, awed, into the eye of the camera; the smell that rushed over and through him like memories. Every place had its own particular smell, every home, that rushed to meet you and greeted you more profoundly than its owner. It was your smell, the smell that meant Mumma and Pappa and sister and brother.

The room was quiet, as though it were empty except for him, with his hard breathing and the pounding of his heart that was filling the room. Only he *knew* it was not empty. Not only because the light was on, but from all the other telltale signs. He took his time reading them: The table in the little kitchenette, set for one. That meant Faith had not come home. Probably held up somewhere by the storm. It would stay that way until breakfast on the chance she might not spend the night with a friend. Half a ham stood in the middle of the table, butchered into thick slices by the little paring knife that lay on the platter. They had either had cabbage or greens with corn bread for dinner, possibly baked sweet potatoes to fill out the menu. He glanced at the little two-burner stove, and sure enough there stood the big pot that meant greens and the flat frying pan covered with a plate: corn bread. Two small sweet potatoes on top of the plate. Habits that never changed. Never could. Nothing new to add.

The small area set aside for the living room, in order, as if nobody lived there. The old never-was-new couch sitting like an old never-was-loved maid, the cushions stuffed into cheap satin cases, souvenirs from Atlantic City, a place where none of them had ever been. Doilies crocheted and starched, standing out like petticoats, hiding the back of the couch and the one stuffed chair and hugging the bottom of the bowl of artificial flowers on the beaten-up coffee table.

His gaze rested on the old rocking chair at the foot of the bed, which had followed them from kitchenette to kitchenette, and remained there. He wanted her to keep on feeling that he did not know she was there, staring at him as she might stare at a scythe—fascinated, knowing in its descent it would level her, hoping by some miracle that he might miss her, or that she might disappear before his glance turned full on her, ripping her open, exposing her innermost soul for all the world to see.

His gaze never moved from the chair even when the side of his face prickled from the heat of her stare, and the room crackled with the fragility of her silence. Then his whole face quivered as though he had lost control of his muscles, and he had to bite hard on his bottom lip to keep it from falling to pieces. He forced his head to turn slowly, up the length of the bed, tuning himself to the quiver of fear shaking her body, her tightly held breath, the tenseness of her body.

Then his gaze mixed with hers and she lay as though she wanted to persuade him, by the expressionless cast of her face, the blankness of her eyes, her stillness, that she did not exist. He wanted to laugh, to show her rather than tell her that he knew that behind the blank wall of her face lay the fear that had opened up to him earlier, that had sent him running out in confusion only to lead him right back to her, now that the confusion had cleared.

He moved slowly toward the bed, trying to force her fear back into the open by letting her read in his face his accusation, his knowledge of what she had done to him. But the blankness did not shift, nor did a quiver of muscle or the blink of an eye mar the stillness of her face. She lay there, waiting, waiting for him to say what he chose, do what he wanted, as if she had already given up.

He stood over her now, looking down into her face, trying to get words together. No words came and he realized it was because of her stillness. He could not accuse a lump of flesh lying inert without any pretense of defense. Maybe that was what she counted on.

"Get up." His voice sounded strange, muffled, as though coming from a long distance. Maybe it was because they were the first words he had spoken since he'd left her earlier, when he had begged her to listen to him, begged her to love him. Well, there would be no more begging. "Get up, I said." She lay, unmoving. "Do you hear me, Mumma? Get the hell up out of the fucking bed."

He had never cursed at her in his life. None of her children, no matter how much hell they raised outside, had ever had the nerve to curse Mumma. Maybe that was why she lowered her eyelashes now, and why her breathing grew hard, moving the covers up and down, and why something that resembled life came back into her body. She lay another few moments as though making up her mind, then slowly she raised herself, leaving the bed on the side farthest from him, and made her unsteady way to the rocking chair.

Lowering herself into the chair, she sat, rocking slightly, never looking up, folding her hands in her habitual way, making him want to scream out against the familiarity of the picture she made on this night that was anything but familiar, this night that had nothing to do with the ordinary. He wanted to grab her, throw her out of the chair, crush her with his hands, stamp her with his feet. But more, he wanted to engulf her with the feeling of her own doom.

He stood for a long time letting his silence get to her, but she never raised her eyes to look at him or even gave a sign that she knew he was there. She simply rocked and looked down at her hands, waiting.

The silence had blown up to the size of the room when he decided to break it. "Ain't you gonna say nothing to me? Here is your baby boy come back home. Ain't you gonna say something nice to greet me?"

She kept rubbing her hands together, and the silence grew again, grew and grew, cracking the eardrums, until she suddenly gave him a quick look from under her lids and said, "What you standing there dripping all over my things like a fool for? You going to ruin everything I got."

That shook him up a little, it was so ordinary, like the sitting and rocking in her chair, something she said every day in the week, every week in the year. Maybe it was just habit, or maybe she was smart. Smarter than he had thought. She might have said it to get him off his guard. He used to laugh and tease her when she said something like that, making a joke of it, running to escape a backhand slap or ducking from something she might throw.

"Everything you got?" Wade said finally. "But, Mumma, you ain't got nothing. You ain't never had nothing. So you see if I was to drip over everything and even flood over everything in this room so that it got washed out of the window, you wouldn't be losing anything—but your life. And how much is *that* worth, Mumma?" She went to rocking again. "So you see Mumma, you ain't never had anything but me."

She quieted the chair a moment, made as though she wanted to answer, thought better of it and got the chair moving again.

"But maybe you don't count me. Maybe like you said, you begot me by laying with the devil. But then maybe you liked laying around with the devil, because you sure to God laid up with the devil when you begot Willie Earl, too." She stopped her rocking then.

"You remember what Pappa used to say, don't you? Pappa said that if you laid with the devil your children are all misbegotten. Then I suppose Faith is the only one beholden to him, huh, Mumma? Faith is something like a freak you never rightly appreciated. The beholden among the misbegotten. All Big Willie's breed conceived through you, misbegotten. Ain't you ashamed, Mumma?"

He heard the sharp intake of her breath and knew that he had hit her where it hurt most, right in the middle of her Biblical cord. He waited now for her to break. He knew she had to break.

"What you want from me, Wade? What you want?" She burst out as though her heart had filled to the brim. "Ain't you done enough to me? Ain't you hurt me enough?" The anguish in her voice got to him. How dared she sit pretending it was *he* who had done the hurting?

"What I ever done to you, Mumma? You tell me."

"What ain't you done?"

"I never let you go begging. You never starved."

"It ain't your fault I ain't starved. And it ain't your fault that I ain't dead these many years from worry."

"I ain't taken care of you, Mumma?"

"How you taken care of me, boy? By running around and getting into trouble all your life?"

"It ain't always been this way, Mumma."

"It ain't ever been much different where you was concerned. You been evil clear through since the day you was born. You ain't never been able to pray and ain't nothing you ever did in all your days that wasn't pointed out for you by the finger of the devil."

"If I wasn't taking care of you, who was, Mumma?"

"The good God above, that was Who. If He hadn't answered my prayers, I don't know what would have become of us."

"Mumma," Wade said, "from the time that Pappa told you to get off your knees, I think your God forsook you. Maybe it was because you swore out that Big Willie was on the side of the devil and you still kept eating his bread. That was it, Mumma. Maybe that's how the devil got in your bed. Maybe that's how your children are misbegotten, because you sure wasn't blessed, Mumma." His head was hot and his body burned, making his clothes cling to him icily. He had the urge to pull them off and stand naked but dry, indicting her.

She had become a stranger, an old shell that he looked through. In his amazement at her interpretation of her life, which was so far from his reality, he saw clearly that the hurt she had cried from was not really hurt but hypocrisy. The need to be hurt where habit and custom dictated: Not from the heart, from the head. Not from the bowels, from the belly. Mr. Charlie had forced her to her knees a long time ago and she had made *them* pay with her prayers.

That must have been why, from the first, the God she prayed to was the God he mocked, adding to her need for self-deceit. Every five or ten or one-hundred dollars he had laid in her lap—thrown there carelessly, laughing, to show his love, his affection, or perhaps his contempt—had forced her to look inward and had scraped another layer of honesty from her. Every time her poor and greedy fingers had closed over any amount of money she had become more a shell and less a person. He had helped scrape the mother's milk from her tits and forced her to substitute holy water.

But it should not have happened. She was the mother. What was there in the setup of things that allowed her guilt, her deceit, to make her into less of a person and the agent of this poverty she had trapped them into; that had allowed her—no, forced her—to use God as a shield between herself and truth?

"I did my best for you, Mumma. I tried to make sure there was nothing you would want that a woman blessed didn't have." He chose his words carefully to wring from her the whole distortion that had become part of her life and to use it as a whip to drive her to her end. "And I did it, Mumma, nobody else."

"It was the good Lord that took care of me, Wade. You would have it different but it was the good Lord. If I didn't have Him I would sure be in my grave today, with all the sins you done pulled down on my head.

"Lord, when I heard how you killed that poor boy, Buddy, I thought it was my end. I, who had tried to live in this world so righteous, had raised up a killer."

"*That,* Mumma, is another one of your lies. When I came home in my Army uniform the first time, you couldn't shut your mouth from grinning, you were so proud. What you think they pulled me in there for, to make babies?"

But she might never have heard him. "I swear I walked into every funeral parlor around the Avenue, until I come to the one where he was in. Yes, Lord, there he was, out just as stiff and cold, dead as he was ever going to die."

"I killed many that would make Buddy look like a grandfather."

"And it was my son that did it. *My* son, that *I* brought into this world, that had put that poor boy out so stiff and as dead as he was ever going to die."

"And you responsible."

Mumma jumped at that. "How come you want to blame me for your sins?"

"It was because of your lying and cheating and deceiving."

"How come you talk to me that way? After all I done for you?"

"What you ever done for me, Mumma? Bring me into the world?"

"You ask that? When your father left me a poor, sick woman with three children, helpless to care for? If I ain't never done nothing for you, how you come up? You think you was born grown?"

He studied her in amazement, this woman who had become wrinkled and gray from sickness and the cares that she thought she had.

"I ain't forgotten a thing, Mumma. Matter of fact, after tonight, there ain't nothing I can ever forget. I ain't forgotten me and Faith being locked away like we ain't even had a mother, while you kept Willie Earl . . ."

"What you talking about, boy? Wasn't it better that you went where you could eat than stay home and starve to death? And the minute I see my way clear, ain't you come out?"

"And school, I guess you did a hell of a lot for me to see me go through school?"

"I ain't saying I didn't make some mistakes, Wade. I reckon I should have done a lot more to keep you in school. I realize too late, and don't think it did my heart any good to see you bumming around the streets. But them ain't the things that made you a killer."

"Mistakes? That's what you call it?"

"Ain't a person going through life entitled to some?"

Wade didn't believe what he was hearing. "You ain't even seeing that the only reason you call it a mistake now is because of the trouble you say I cause *you*. If I had got some job pulling carts around in the garment district, it wouldn't have been no mistake. If I had gotten a job on the docks, or on the streets shoveling coal, it wouldn't have been no mistake."

"All I wanted in this life was to see my children grow up decent law-abiding citizens, get married and have a family. Under the eyes of law and God ain't nothing wrong with that. What can poor folks do? What more can poor folks expect?"

"Honesty." She threw her hands up, not wanting to listen. "Yeah, Mumma, Honesty. You ain't honest, Mumma. And Willie Earl ain't honest. You sitting there talking and talking, but you scared, Mumma. You scared and you ain't honest enough to show it. And you know why you scared, Mumma? You scared because you figger I'm going to kill you because you ain't ever been honest in your life. You scared because you know, when you pray to God, you keep your eyes closed tight so you won't see that you doing the devil's bidding.

"You never admitted in your life that we were so heavy around your neck that your tits were dragging the ground while it was your head up in the clouds, where you figgered your soul should be. You couldn't get rid of the load fast enough. That's why Willie Earl ain't gone through school and if it wasn't for me, Faith would never have made it either. Why, you ain't even known if Lil' Willie was smart or dumb in school, you rushed him out so fast. He was the oldest, so you got to him first."

"Willie Earl was always a right smart child and . . ."

"You mean he was always a dishonest bastard. He took one look into your eyes and got lessons about tricking your butt. But you understood him. It was the kind of smartness you understood. Faith and I were something else. You couldn't dig us. If all three of us had gotten penny-ante jobs and thrown a few cents your way, while we stuffed the rest in our back pockets, you would have been telling yourself and the rest of the world the lie that you raised us successful. But no, I made it a different kind of way and poured it out to you like my soul, and you had to close your eyes because suddenly you found my life to be your conscience.

"But all you had to do was to be honest, Mumma. You let Willie Earl leave school because of those few pennies he threw your way, and you kept me out so I could make your life better, yet all the while you knelt on your stiff sick knees, with your eyes closed, covering your mind with prayers. But everything boomeranged, because I was honest and you never had no use for honesty, so you said I was no good and that gave you the best reason to rob me of my life."

"Rob you of your life? I gave you life, boy. And you, you ain't done nothing but make me suffer."

"But Willie Earl made you happy?"

"We ain't never lived in a big house, but it was a clean one. You ain't never left it hungry, nor have you been anything but clean and proper. And many is the day the pennies that your brother brought home did fill your stomach."

"I ain't seen it that way, Mumma."

"Ain't nothing in my life that I ain't done for you children. I ain't never had a word, a thought, a prayer in my life that wasn't for you all. I ain't never had no happiness . . ."

"You was too poor to have happiness."

"Maybe too poor, but I had dreams."

"You ain't never had a dream, Mumma. You only had a thought. To have a dream, Mumma, you have to have an image, and the only image you ever had was of a man pinned to the cross. And you would have pinned us all there for *your* salvation. That's where you sinned, Mumma."

"If I have sinned, I sure to God have paid for it through you. Lord, I ain't never going to forget when I walked in that funeral parlor to look at that poor boy whose head you had done bashed in. You don't think I suffered . . ."

Wade thought suddenly of the boy in the streets and with the thought the sound of the rain, still falling steadily, came into the room. He had not meant to do all this talking. He had meant only to come in, say his say, strip her of the cloak of honesty, and leave.

Mumma, too, had found relief in her talking and he could not bear this thought. "Anyway," he said. "After today you don't have to worry about suffering."

She sat silent, as though she did not want to push his meaning, but the inner fear was too great.

"How you mean?" she cried.

"I mean, Mumma, that you and your misbegotten children will quit the scene, before the rain stops falling. There'll only be one—the beholden—to see the morning, to justify Big Willie's life." He had not known what he intended to do until now, but suddenly he saw clearly the one reason he had come to her; and seeing, felt at peace with himself and with her.

"You talking like you ain't got good sense."

"Oh, I got good sense, Mumma. That rain I walked through tonight cleared my brain of a lot of things that was clouding it, and I swear to you, I never had better sense.

"When the sun comes up in the morning, Mumma, it's going to shine on a little more honest world, because Big Willie's misbegotten breed will be dead."

"You done gone clean out of your mind."

"It's you and me and Willie Earl, Mumma." He spoke calmly

because he wanted her to understand as clearly as he understood. "First you; then I'm going to whatever hospital Lil' Willie is in—then after—me." He chuckled suddenly. "Ain't nobody going to be left for the funeral."

She made a move to get out of the chair and he sobered expectantly. But after a quick search of his face, she lowered herself, fighting for her calm. He was sorry. It wasn't easy to go after somebody sitting quietly, to finish her off. Especially Mumma. If she were running past him or away from him—yet he knew from the tension of her body that she wanted to make a try. He moved to get out of line with the door, hoping that she might feel free. But she seemed to be reading his mind. She simply sat, waiting.

Even if she should cry out, beg, talk about her helplessness, her sickness, that same old unhappiness bit, it would give him a chance to go at her, silence her. He looked around the room for something that would pull the fear out of her: Not a pillow, for he had to see her face, her begging eyes, pleading when she finally realized, at the very end, the things she had done.

His gaze leaped to the table in the kitchenette, to the knife supporting the piece of ham. He turned his back to her, deliberately moved toward the kitchenette, gauging with his senses the moment when she might make a dash, timing his steps so that he might know how to quicken them, grab the knife, make his turn in time to meet her, head on, as she made it toward the door.

She never moved. He picked up the knife and waited near the table, playing with the blade to hurry her terror, pretending to be relaxed even while he waited for the bolt to take her to the door. But no, she sat grasping the arm of the chair, tension holding her body rigid.

Suddenly, impatience rushed through him; he no longer wanted to wait. He wanted to see the tension go out of that body. He wanted to know that he was the one to cut the string of that life which had been so tortured for no reason other than that it had lived. He moved quickly toward her and she put out her hand to ward him off. Her mouth opened but no sound came.

"Wade," he heard movement behind him at the same time he heard the voice. "Wade, what in the world are you doing?" He turned to Faith, who was standing in the doorway. There must have been something about him that terrified her because she cried out again, "My God, Wade, what are you doing?"

Then whatever was holding Mumma together snapped loose because she found her voice and started crying. "Faith, Faith, talk to your brother. He done gone clean out of his head. Talk to him."

Faith moved into the room like a breath of air and rain from the outside. "Wade, you know you don't have no business being here, and soaking wet at that. Look at the puddles you got all over the place." He knew from her voice that she was going to ignore what she saw him doing, and that she would try to work him into acting silly so they could laugh together, and maybe that way disarm him. He had no intention of letting her do so.

"Faith, I know. I know, Faith."

"What's got into you, Wade? Breaking down doors and everything. I know it must have been you that broke down the door downstairs."

"Yes, but it's because I found out, Faith. You wouldn't tell me, but I found out how Willie Earl and Mumma screwed us up." His words stumbled out in his anxiety to explain to her. "Yeah, Faith, I know, I know."

"He been talking like this since he been in here. I tell you he done gone clean out of his mind."

"No, no, Faith. I found out why I went after Willie Earl that night."

"What are you talking about, Wade? What has Mumma got to do with that?"

"She was in it with him."

"No, I swear, Wade. Mumma never knew anything about it."

"Yes, she did, Faith."

"I never told her either, Wade. I swear I didn't."

"But she knew."

"No, Wade. You know how Willie Earl is, always tight and close to the chest."

"She's the one that caused it, Faith. She was the one that caused him to be dishonest. She robbed me of my life. You knew it, that's why you never liked her."

"What are you talking about, Wade? I love Mumma. I never worshiped her like you did. I always accepted her faults but I love her."

"But she did me in, Faith. You remember how they took my money when I was in the Army? She and Will . . ."

"No, Wade." Faith pleaded. "It was me. I am the one who never sent to tell you that Mumma was sick, so you could know where your money was going. I didn't send to tell you because I knew you would worry no end about her. Of all her children, I know you love her best."

That caught him in his heart and he tried to smile, but only a sadness descended on him. Of course she knew. She was the only one who knew. The only one who knew the depths of his love, the depths of his sorrow; his loss.

His eyes searched deeply through Faith's but his senses were still tuned to Mumma and he knew when she gathered herself for the dash out of the room. Her fear charged through him and Faith must have felt the current because she held tightly to the arm with the knife, trying to urge him toward the couch.

He did not move, and for the first time in his life allowed her to feel the terrible strength in his arm, the iron that refused to yield. She had always known he was strong, but there had never been the time when she had not been able to take his arm and move it at her will. The feel of it caused her to look again into his face and what she saw there made her shrink away from him. Yet some unholy courage forced her to keep holding his arm in her effort to protect Mumma.

"Wade," she spoke hurriedly. "What are you blaming her for? What are you blaming us for?"

"I ain't blaming you for nothing, Faith. You are the best part of us. The one who must survive. You know I wouldn't hurt you?" His tongue was heavy, fumbling for the words to stop that shrinking that he sensed deep inside her. "It's them, she and Willie Earl, that robbed me. It's them that got no business living on account of they ain't honest."

"They honest enough, Wade. But they poor. God knows, you got no right condemning people because they poor and sick and miserable."

"Who *you* going to blame? God?"

"If you must blame somebody, blame Him. He's the one that decides where you going to be born, how you going to live . . ."

"Then He got to take the blame for how they must die."

"Wade, listen to me." Faith pulled desperately on his arm. "All people make mistakes. I don't care how rich or how great they are. Ain't it natural that living the way we were forced to, we had to make a few? Poor people don't have a chance because in doing what they think is right, they have sometimes to go against instinct to save themselves— their children."

"Is it saving them when you make them into nothing? Litter for the garbage collectors, bulk for the city prisons, killers for a kick? Ain't you going to give them blame for that?"

"They *got* the blame, Wade. Their whole life is one big blame. They got the blame for where they were born and they suffer from where they have to work. They have off-limit signs hung on them for the clothes they have to wear, never mind the color of their skins. They do penance in their ugly houses, in their ugly streets. They pay every day the penalty for having to live there without ever seeing the part they play in their crime.

"Wade, you never expected any soap sculpture of yours to turn to gold. So why would you expect us to be so much better than the things that made us, that shaped us, that formed our thinking? Why must we be supermen? Super-people? Giants? Yes, you must blame the gods, Wade. There are no innocent gods."

"They don't go free, Faith. They don't go free—I . . ."

"Listen to me, Wade. There's a lot of folks that don't remember how smart you used to be. I—I remember. What ever so little I did with my life I owe to you. There were a lot of things you wanted to be, probably could have been too—but you never had the chance. But all that don't have to be dead, Wade. You're not old.

"Why, there is a kid working with me, her old man is over forty and he just went back to college. All you have to do is stop drinking and get yourself together, brush up on some studies and you can start again. I know you can, Wade. I'll help you. I swear to God, I'll help you if it takes every single day of my life."

He listened to her trying to push back the clock: A dead rusty weight refusing to budge. He almost heard the squeaky denial to her exhausted panting. A side of his face shook up into a grotesque smile. "I did what I wanted to do, Faith—once in my life. And I know it's that feeling that makes life worth living."

"How is that, Wade?" She coaxed him, trying to keep his attention away from Mumma who, he knew, was easing to the door. Saddened by this betrayal, he still held her glance trying to pour under-standing into her.

"It's doing what you have to do and feeling free with the world around and in you. It's when you don't go against instinct. It's when you can feel free—like a bird—when you can sort of spread your wings and take off . . ."

"I reckon that's a strange feeling, huh, Wade? Because we are beasts, we ain't birds."

He lost the sense of Faith's words as Mumma made her dash for the door. Shaking off Faith's hand he jumped quickly in front of Mumma, grabbed her arm as she reached the door, thrusting the knife downward into her chest. But her body did not move. He found himself looking down into Faith's eyes, saw her startled gaze changed into meaningless-ness, her mouth open, gasping for air. He pulled the knife out. Too late. He stared up at Mumma, searching for the sorrow, the sympathy she must feel for his mistake. But the hypocritical mouth above him opened up. Screams tore through it as though all her insides were gushing out through the opening. He reached for her . . .

It was coming back from a long stretch, of blackness, where even the sun had been denied him and though a mist covered his eyes it was not the red mist that he knew, but a black mist, as though indeed he were blind. It was a darkness that the sun did not penetrate, for it had to do with dirt and earth and closeness, so he knew the end had come. Cold. Never had he been so cold. Yet there would be no arms to hold him, no shoulders to lean against, no bed to support him, not even a blanket to ease the chill of his bones. He was alone. He would forever be alone.

"Wade, Wade, what's the matter, boy? You been sitting out here all night. What's the matter, you don't feel good?"

The mist slipped from his eyes and Wade looked into Charlie's lined, begging face. He was sitting on the island in the middle of Lenox Avenue next to Charlie. He closed his eyes and wiped the sweat dripping from his brow. He looked down at his hands: Blood. At his shoes: Blood, caked, hardened. At his shirt . . .

He squinted up at the sky, at the clouds moving quickly away at the demand of the sun. Yes, he had been out here a long time, no wonder he was cold. Cold, yet dripping with sweat. He looked all around him, looked up at the sign on the street where he was: Mumma's street. The street that he wanted to be on more than any other street in the world.

"Wade, Wade, come on, give a guy two bits to buy a drink, huh? Come on, be a good buddy," Charlie pleaded.

Wade stuck his hand into his pocket searching for change.

COFFEE HOUSE PRESS

Black Arts Movement Series

THE POSTWAR 1920S was the decade of the "New Negro" and the Jazz Age "Harlem Renaissance," or first Black Renaissance of literary, visual, and performing arts. In the 1960s and 70s Vietnam War era a self-proclaimed "New Breed" generation of black artists and intellectuals orchestrated what they called the Black Arts Movement.

This energetic and highly self-conscious movement accompanied an explosion of urban black popular culture. The Coffee House Press Black Arts Movement Series is devoted to reprinting unavailable works of this period. We have tried to choose work that is masterful, that deserves another chance and other audiences, and that will help us keep the windows to the future open.

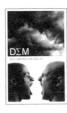 

dem, WILLIAM MELVIN KELLEY
Upper middle-class Manhattanite Mitchell Pierce is convinced he has it made. With advancement at work, an attractive wife, and a comfortable apartment, he has achieved the sixties version of the white man's American dream. Slowly but surely that dream becomes a nightmare, and Mitchell can't seem to wake up.
1-56689-102-7 • 5.5 X 8.5 • 224 PAGES • $14.95 • PAPER

Captain Blackman, JOHN A. WILLIAMS
"Mr. Williams has written a provocative book in which fantasy and history merge and flow. His well-researched retelling of history is valuable, his novel fascinating reading and his message compelling."   —*The Baltimore Sun*
1-56689-096-0 • 288 PAGES • 5.5 X 8.5 • $15.95 • PAPER

Good books are brewing at coffeehousepress.org

27 North 4th Street, Suite 400, Minneapolis, Minnesota 55401 (612) 338-0125